OUT
OF
SIGHT

SECRETS OF BROOKHAVEN

BOOK ONE

CHAPTER
ONE

It hurt to move. Hurt to breathe. Hurt to do anything other than lie there curled up on the cool travertine tile of the kitchen floor.

The door clicked closed, and Ainsley flinched at the sound. Knowing he'd left wasn't a relief. It just meant he would be back, expecting the mess to be cleaned up, a smile on her face as she welcomed him home.

She heard his car start, then pull out of the garage. The rumble of the engine grew fainter as he turned out of the driveway and headed down the street, until finally the sound faded altogether.

Grimacing against the pain, she unfolded from the protective position she'd curled into when he'd attacked her. Tears burned the backs of her eyes as she pressed her palms to the cold floor and attempted to sit up. Agony ripped through her torso, and a sob caught in her throat. It felt like a vise had closed around her lungs as she gasped for breath, pain lancing through her ribs.

She knelt there on the ground for what felt like forever,

trying to calm her racing heart and gather the strength to stand. A flash of red caught her attention, and her gaze was drawn upward to the large, fragrant bouquet of red roses on the counter. They hadn't yet begun to wilt, but they would undoubtedly be replaced by a large collection of fresh blooms tonight when he got home.

It was their routine; they would fight, Joel would lash out and hurt her. Later, once he realized what he'd done, he would bring home a huge bouquet of roses and apologize, professing his undying love for her.

The blooms swam in front of her as tears clouded her eyes. How many times could she do this? How long until she finally pushed him over the edge? One day, she knew, he would go too far. One day, she wouldn't survive.

As she stared at the roses, a startling clarity settled over her. She had to leave. Today.

Gritting her molars together and shoving the pain away, she cautiously levered to her feet, then stood. Glass littered the floor around her from the mug she'd dropped when he'd lashed out at her, and she stepped carefully around it to avoid being cut. The broken cup was an added infraction, and today's beating had been one of the worst yet.

Every cell of her body still aching, she retrieved the broom and dustpan from the closet, then began to clean. Once the kitchen sparkled, she headed to the bathroom to take care of herself. While she waited for the shower to heat up, she stripped off her shirt. Every muscle protested as she lifted her arms over her head, and tears burned over the bridge of her nose.

Dark bruises were already forming around her ribs

where he'd landed several brutal kicks, and she winced as she gently touched a spot. More than likely they were broken, but there was nothing she could do about that right now.

The shower helped to relieve some of the ache, and afterward she bound them as tightly as she could. She hung the towel neatly on the rack, then made her way to the bedroom and dressed. Just that little effort had exhausted her, but she couldn't afford to rest. She had too much to do.

Moving into the home office, Ainsley fired up the computer and logged into her email. Sending up a silent prayer, she typed out a quick message to her friend, Tess. They hadn't spoken in years thanks to Joel, and she hoped her old college friend would respond. She briefly explained that she needed help and asked Tess to contact an Uber for her under Tess's name.

While she waited for her friend's reply, she retreated to the closet and searched for a bag. She didn't want to take anything noticeable; she didn't want him to know she'd left until long after she was gone. She finally found a drawstring backpack that had been gifted to Joel as some part of a promotional package. It wouldn't hold much, but it would have to do.

Inside she stuffed several pairs of socks, then selected underwear she knew he wouldn't miss. She carefully chose one pair of jeans and three shirts, then rolled them together and added them to the bag. She took none of her favorite items; he would look for those first.

She carried the bag to the bathroom and stared at the vanity. She couldn't take her normal products. Rifling through the drawers, she managed to find travel-sized deodorant, toothbrush and toothpaste. She added those to the bag, then pulled the strings closed.

Moving back to the bedroom she carefully made the bed, then tucked the bag underneath—just in case. She didn't expect Joel to be home for several hours, but she couldn't take any chances. Her life depended on it.

Retreating to the office, she mentally crossed her fingers as she opened her email. She felt faint at the sight of the unread message in her inbox, and her fingers trembled as she clicked the link to open it. The message was short and succinct. An Uber would arrive one block over at 11:00 to collect her and bring her to Tess's house.

Relief poured through her and tears glazed her eyes. She managed to tap out a quick thank you, then told Tess not to respond. She carefully deleted the email, making sure it wouldn't be found, then shut down the computer.

Ainsley made her way to the kitchen and pulled out the Crock Pot, then added ingredients for Joel's favorite dish. She cleaned up the kitchen, making sure everything was in its proper place. She would have to leave her purse behind, so she selected a lesser used bag from her closet to use instead.

A glance at the clock told her she had less than half an hour before she had to leave to meet the Uber. Everything was almost ready. Now she just needed money.

Checking the driveway once more and finding it blessedly empty, she grabbed the step stool and climbed the stairs. She stepped into one of the spare bedrooms and placed the stool beneath the smoke detector. Her ribs ached as she lifted her hands high over her head to remove the cover, but she fought down the debilitating pain.

The cover popped off easily, and she retrieved the small pouch inside before replacing the cover. She tucked the pouch of bills in her back pocket, then folded the step-stool and used her foot to smooth out the indentations it had left in the carpet.

Back downstairs she put everything away, then retrieved the bag from under the bed. She glanced around to make sure everything was perfect. She didn't want him to suspect anything was wrong until she was far, far away.

Leaving the lights on, she slipped out the back door and locked it behind her. Everyone was at work at this hour, so she wasn't worried about slipping through the neighbors' yards. She hit the cross street then started walking toward the meeting point.

Her heart accelerated when she saw the blue sedan pull to a stop at the side of the road. She lifted a hand in greeting, her pulse thrumming rapidly in her veins. She climbed inside, tossing a quick look around to make sure she hadn't been spotted. Nothing seemed out of place, and she let out a heavy breath.

The driver glanced at her in the rearview mirror. "Ready, miss?"

For the first time in months, she smiled. "Let's go."

CHAPTER
TWO

He'd given her *everything*. How dare she run from him?

Joel seethed inwardly as his thoughts turned once more to Ainsley. When he got her back home, where she belonged, she would never be allowed to leave again.

He'd been absolutely furious the night he'd found out that she was gone. At first, he wasn't even sure what had happened. Surgery had run late, and he'd gotten home from the hospital about nine o'clock. The lights were on in the kitchen and living room, and the savory scent of roasting meat and vegetables filled the air.

He'd set the roses on the counter next to the others, then went in search of Ainsley. But she wasn't there.

He'd torn the house apart looking for her, searching every room. But instead of waiting up for him, as he expected of her, she was just... gone.

Her purse hung on the hook next to the door as it always did, and her car was parked in the garage next to his. He'd spent a restless night in bed, tossing and turning, running different scenarios through his head. A few days later he'd run into a neighbor standing by his mailbox. Joel had decided to do some fishing.

As it turned out, the guy's kid had been sick the day before, so Dave had been home all day. According to the nosy neighbor, an Uber had pulled up near his house late that morning and a woman matching Ainsley's description had climbed in with only a small bag.

Joel had immediately gone home and searched through her things again. That's when he found it. Ainsley wasn't good with technology and though she'd tried to delete the email, he'd been able to retrieve it easily enough.

Joel grimaced as he shifted, wishing he could stretch his legs. For the past several hours he'd been nearly frozen in place, waiting.

He'd sneaked into the house early this morning when the woman left for work. She'd pulled out of the garage and turned onto the street, completely oblivious to the fact that the garage door hadn't closed behind her.

Joel had spent the day exploring the house, looking for any sign of Ainsley. There was nothing. It was obvious she wasn't staying here, so where was she? It seemed only Tess knew the answer to that—but he was damn well going to find out.

He'd listened to the sounds of the TV, of the woman moving around the small house as she made dinner, then got ready for bed. Finally, everything was silent and still. He waited another hour before venturing out of his spot in the closet of the spare bedroom.

On silent feet he crept to the kitchen and removed a knife from the block. He'd taken the time to sharpen it earlier before replacing it, leaving no room for error.

Curling his fingers around the hilt of the knife, he made his way down the hall to her room. The door stood open, and he watched her a moment before stepping silently up to the side of her bed.

She lay curled on her side facing away from him, and he stroked a finger down the length of her arm. She shivered at the feather-light touch and rolled toward him, her lashes flickering several times before opening. He could see the wheels turning as she gradually came awake and his presence registered. "Hello, Tess."

Her lips parted on a silent scream but he covered her mouth and nose with a gloved hand, one knee pressing into the soft cavity of her stomach. She thrashed beneath him, eyes rolling in terror, and he climbed atop her, using his weight to pin her to the mattress. Incoherent sounds came from low in her throat as she tried to scream, call for help, plead for her life.

Pulling a roll of duct tape from the pocket of his sweatshirt, he glared down at her. "I'm going to move my hand now. Scream and I'll kill you. Nod if you understand."

Her head moved briskly up and down, and he lifted his hand. Her words came out on a whisper. "Who are you?"

Ignoring her question, he tore a strip of tape from the roll. "Lift your hands."

She did as he asked, and he looped the strip around her hands. "Please, I have money, I can—"

He shook his head. "I don't need money, Tess. I need answers."

Confusion clouded her eyes for a moment before recognition dawned across her pretty features. "You."

"Yes, Tess." A cold smile curled his lips. "It's me."

"You'll never find her." Her voice shook, and he pressed his lips into a firm line as he wove the tape in a figure eight around her wrists. "She doesn't want to be with you."

He made a tsk-tsk sound low in his throat. "All you have to do is tell me where she is."

"Never."

Her gaze was hateful, and exhilaration zinged through him. He was going to enjoy knocking her down a peg. Grabbing her bound hands, he yanked them high over her head. Tess bucked wildly beneath him, trying to throw him off, but his weight kept her pinned in place.

He grinned down at her. "You sure you don't have anything to tell me?"

She remained stubbornly mute, and Joel looped the tape around a slat in the headboard. She yanked and pulled against him, and he dug his thumb into her pressure point, causing her to cry out. Once her hands were secured, he glared down at her. "Ready to talk?"

"Fuck you."

A harsh ripping sound filled the air as he tore another strip of tape from the roll and held it up. "Mouthy bitch."

He leaned forward, putting more pressure on her torso. "Last chance, Tess. Just tell me where she is."

She shook her head, eyes hard as she stared up at him. "No. Don't you get it? She hates you," she spit out. "You're an abusive prick, and she—"

He slapped her hard, snapping her head to the side and halting the flow of of ugly words. She had no idea what she was talking about. Ainsley meant *everything* to him. "Shut the fuck up."

She tossed her head in an effort to get away, but he fisted one hand in her hair, trapping her in place. Tess let out a soft shriek at the sharp bolt of pain, and Joel slapped the tape over her mouth. "I warned you."

Reaching into his black boot, he retrieved the knife and held it up, the long blade glinting in the moonlight. Her eyes rolled with terror as she writhed against him. The blade slashed against her forearm and blood trickled from the wound as a thin red line appeared.

She recoiled, her voice muffled as she tried to scream, hampered by the tape.

"You should have listened," Joel warned, digging the blade into the fleshy part of her upper arm before slicing into the soft skin.

"You had to know this would happen. Did you think I would let you live after what you've done?" Her eyes widened as he lifted the knife and dug the blade into the space between her ribs. "You took her away, poisoned her against me."

She screamed as the tip dug deeper, cutting into her flesh. "I'm going to find her. I'm going to bring her back home—where she belongs. And I'll kill anyone who stands in my way."

The knife sank deep, and she arched violently, her scream penetrating the tape over her mouth. Her face twisted in pain, and his pulse accelerated.

He pulled the blade free, blood arcing through the air and spattering on the wall and headboard before he plunged it deep once more. Over and over he drove the knife into her torso until her body was limp, her flesh and nightdress a shredded, mangled mess. Blood saturated the bed, seeping into the dark clothes he wore.

For a moment he sat there, chest heaving with exertion. He'd held people's lives in his hands before. But never like this. It was... exhilarating.

But he'd spent too much time here already. Every minute he spent here increased his chances of being caught. Reaching over, he picked up the woman's phone sitting on the nightstand and used her lifeless hand to bring up the main screen.

He scrolled through her contacts first but found nothing. Next he went through her emails. That was how Ainsley had contacted her the first time; perhaps they'd stayed in touch, though she obviously wasn't using the same email address. He'd been watching it periodically, but there had been no activity since the day she'd disappeared.

He scowled when her email history turned up nothing of value. There had to be something, damn it!

Next he sorted through the call log. There were dozens of unlisted numbers, probably sales calls or offices calling to confirm appointments. Finally, he hit pay dirt in her messages.

Tucked between conversations with other friends and family members, he found a short chat from an unknown number. The person on the other end recited that they were okay and had picked up hours working at a bar.

His pulse kicked up. Was this Ainsley? It had to be.

He scrolled the rest of the message. The mention of the bar's owner, Marv, had red creeping into the edges of his vision. Ainsley was *his*. If the man was trying to make a move...

He shook his head. One thing at a time. The important thing was, he had a lead. She was working at a bar with a man named Marv. Couldn't be too hard to find him.

Joel crawled from the bed and glanced down at the woman. Her eyes were open and vacant as she stared at the ceiling.

She deserved this. She'd taken Ainsley away from him, turned her against him. But he would find her. He would bring her home where she belonged.

And no one would come between them ever again.

CHAPTER
THREE

Ainsley paused on the brick walkway leading to her parents' house and glanced around. For the past two weeks she'd constantly had one eye over her shoulder, watching her surroundings for any sign of Joel. So far everything had been clear. Still, she refused to let down her guard.

The moment the Uber had dropped her off in Tess's driveway, it was as if a tidal wave of relief washed over her. Tess didn't ask questions, didn't offer advice. She just pulled Ainsley inside with a smile that put her at ease.

All evening they'd reminisced on the past, intent on catching up. Not once did they speak of Joel or the past few years in which Ainsley had virtually disappeared. For the first time in years, Ainsley felt like she could finally relax.

She spent the first night at Tess's house and though she was grateful for Tess's help, Ainsley couldn't stay there and risk her friend. She had to move on to keep them both safe.

Tess's mother had passed away several months prior, and Tess had graciously offered the use of her car. Though

Ainsley had tried to decline, Tess insisted. It was still in good condition, and Ainsley would need a vehicle at her disposal—just in case.

Ainsley briefly explained that she wanted to move closer to her parents and sisters. Of course, she couldn't move back to Brookhaven; it was undoubtedly the first place Joel would look. Instead, Tess had suggested a small town about two hours' drive northeast. It was close enough to visit, but far enough away to be safe.

Ainsley glanced over at the small Honda parked by the curb. It had been so long since she'd seen everyone. She hoped it was safe enough to visit. Just for today.

Since he hadn't spotted her in Brookhaven, Joel would most likely assume she'd moved far away. Maybe he'd given up looking for her. A shiver rolled down her spine. He wouldn't stop looking; she knew that with absolute certainty. Her only option was to lie low until he eventually—hopefully—moved on.

The air was thick with the pungent aroma of roses, and Ainsley closed her eyes, swallowing down the bile that had risen in her throat. If she never saw a red rose again, it would be too soon.

Before her hand even touched the knob, the front door swung open and her dad appeared, a broad smile on his face. He tugged her inside and pulled her into a big bear hug. "It's good to see you."

Her ribs still ached, and Ainsley held back a wince as she wrapped her arms around his waist and leaned into him. "Hey. It's good to be home."

Guilt pricked at Ainsley. She hadn't been home to visit

in almost two years, blaming her absence on work. In reality, that was the furthest thing from the truth.

She felt like a disappointment and she could only imagine her family's reaction if she ever told them the truth. She couldn't bear to see the pity in their eyes.

Garrett Layne pulled back and stared intently at Ainsley, not saying a word. She started to squirm under the scrutiny and finally gave in. "What?"

Her dad studied her for another moment, concern emanating from blue eyes identical to hers. "I just worry about you," he replied.

She shrugged nonchalantly and pasted on a fake smile. "Just busy. You know how it is."

A raised eyebrow told her he wasn't convinced, but he let it drop. "Your mom's in the kitchen. She can't wait to see you."

He wrapped an arm around her shoulder as they made their way to the back of the house, and she was grateful for the temporary reprieve. Her mom would grill her, too, though her line of questioning would more than likely refer to Ainsley's love life. Or, currently, lack thereof.

"Sweetheart! You're here!" Charlene called happily as Ainsley and Garrett walked into the kitchen. She wiped her hands on a dish towel and came around the large kitchen island, holding her arms wide for a hug. "Oh, honey. It's so good to see you."

"Hi, Mom," Ainsley replied, melting into her mother's embrace. Tears pricked her eyes and she blinked them away before pulling away. "Where are Kinley and Brynlee?"

"Kinley's on her way," her dad replied, sliding into a

seat at the island. "I hung up with her right before you got here, and Bryn should be here soon."

"How have you been, honey?" Charlene studied her, a frown tugging at the space between her brows. "I feel like we never see you anymore, with you living so far away."

Ainsley forced a small smile. "You know how it is. Work keeps me pretty busy."

Her mother huffed out a breath. "Honestly. You haven't been back home for nearly two years. You're going to work yourself to death."

Work was the least of her problems. She felt terrible for lying to her mother, but the truth was so much more complicated. And so much uglier.

Years ago, she'd loved Joel, and she thought he loved her. She hadn't even noticed how deftly he'd isolated her from her friends and family, so she would have to rely solely on him. It made her sick to think how easily she'd fallen for the ruse.

She and Joel had met her junior year of college when they'd bumped into one another at a coffee shop. Handsome and worldly, he'd swept her off her feet almost immediately. Within just a few months, things had turned serious, and she'd invited him home to visit her parents.

Unsurprisingly, Joel had won them over with ease. He was charming and charismatic, and the fact that he was hardworking and successful only added to his appeal. Though his career as a cosmetic surgeon was incredibly demanding, he always made time for Ainsley. She'd never felt more in love than she did in those early days.

Six months into their relationship, he'd come to her with news: he'd been offered a more lucrative position in

Minneapolis. Not wanting to be apart from her, he begged her to come with him.

Ainsley had just one year left until graduation, but it seemed like forever. Heartbroken at the thought of him living so far away, she'd decided to make the jump. Joel was thrilled, and he'd told her not to worry—if she moved in with him, she could take her time finishing her schooling and finding a job. He would take care of her.

Everything had seemed so perfect. Until it wasn't.

She remembered the first time he'd hit her during an argument. The slap was so unexpected that it had shocked her into silence. Joel seemed horrified by what he'd done and had apologized profusely, telling her he was just stressed. But instead of curbing his abuse, his desire to control her had only grown. Over time the abuse had gotten worse, his cruelty coming more and more frequently.

For the past two years Joel hadn't allowed her to leave the house except to run errands. Though she'd begged to come home for a visit last Christmas, he'd refused. It was a day Ainsley didn't like to remember. She still carried the scars of that particular argument. After that, she'd stopped asking to do anything.

Instead, she'd begun to formulate a plan for escape. She slowly sold off designer items Joel had purchased for her and hid the money away where he would never find it.

It still didn't feel quite real. She was certain one of these times she would look over her shoulder and he would be standing there, just waiting for her.

The front door opened, and she jumped at the sound.

Her heart was still pounding a minute later when Kinley rounded the corner. "Hey, everyone."

Her cerulean eyes lit on Ainsley and flared wide. "Ains! You're here!"

Kinley rushed forward and pulled Ainsley into a tight hug that took her breath away. Still, it felt so damn good she couldn't make himself let go. Finally, Kinley eased away and stared at her. "God, it feels like forever since you've been home."

"I know." For the first time in forever, Ainsley smiled. "I promise it won't be so long next time."

She wasn't sure how often she could make it home, but Joel no longer had control over her. This was her life, and she was finally taking control.

Her sister plopped into a chair. "How's Joel?"

Ainsley had been waiting for the question, but it still managed to catch her off guard. "We, um... We're not together anymore."

For a moment, it was so silent she could have heard a pin drop. Thankfully, Kinley recovered quickly. "Well, I'm glad you were able to come today. Are you thinking of moving back?"

Ainsley studiously avoided her gaze. "I'm not sure yet."

Charlene cleared her throat as she pulled the roast from the oven. "Set the table, will you, girls?"

Ainsley pulled silverware from a drawer to her right while Kinley grabbed plates and they made their way to the large table just off the kitchen.

"How's work going?" she asked Kinley.

She let out a haggard sigh. "Same shit, different day."

"Language," Charlene admonished loudly from the kitchen.

Ainsley and Kinley shared a smile. Despite the fact that they were in their mid-twenties, their mother was a stickler for manners. There was a time and place for swearing, and the dinner table was off limits. Not that they hadn't heard their mother cuss up a blue streak before—Charlene could swear with the best of them, especially when her competitive streak kicked in.

Ainsley deftly changed topics. "I'm sure you did just fine. Are you doing anything fun this summer?"

"Doubtful. With working on the house, I won't have the time or money to do anything else."

Kinley had just bought her first house, a little fixer-upper a few streets over, and she was currently pouring everything she had into it. "What about you? What's been going on with you?"

Ainsley shrugged as she continued around the table. "Just working."

Kinley glanced over at the kitchen, then back to Ainsley. Her voice dropped several octaves. "Where are you living now?"

"Some little town no one's ever heard of." She flicked a look at her sister and smiled, but she knew it fell flat when Kinley continued to stare at her.

"Have you ever thought of coming back home?" Kinley asked softly. "You're more than welcome to move in with me"—she grinned—"if you don't mind the mess."

Tears pricked Ainsley's eyes, and she dropped her gaze to the table. The thought of moving home, being near her family, sounded so damn good. But she couldn't come back. Not yet. "I'll think about it."

Kinley smiled as she placed plates around the table. "So, where are you working now?"

"A bar." She didn't dare offer more than that. If someone mistakenly mentioned Woody's to the wrong person, it could lead Joel straight to her. She hated lying to her family, but no one could know her hell of the last few years—she didn't need to drag anyone else down with her.

"Hey, everyone!" Brynlee called as the front door opened again.

She let out a little squeal when she saw Ainsley and practically threw herself into her sister's arms. "Oh, my gosh! You're here!"

Ainsley's heart twisted in her chest. She'd missed this— the camaraderie, the closeness... She and her sisters were each only a year apart, and they'd been thick as thieves growing up. They'd had their squabbles, of course, but they were the best of friends, and it had killed Ainsley to be separated from them for so long.

Brynlee pulled back and studied Ainsley intently. "You seem tense."

Ainsley gave a tight smile. "Maybe a little."

Brynlee twirled her finger, silently ordering her to turn around, and Ainsley reluctantly spun around. Brynlee's hands slipped over her shoulders and gently dug into the knots at the base of her neck. Ainsley dropped her head back with a soft groan as exquisite relief rushed through her. "God, Bryn. That feels amazing."

"How long are you in town? You should come by the salon, let me pamper you a bit."

"As much as I would love that..." Ainsley let out another moan as Brynlee worked a particularly tense spot. "I have to head back tonight."

"Next time, then."

Ainsley threw a grin over her shoulder at her sister. "Can't wait."

The next couple of hours passed by quickly and for the first time in a long while, Ainsley enjoyed herself immensely. She sat back and watched her parents and her sisters interact, joking and laughing with one another. Maybe she should come back to visit more often.

After they'd finished dinner and sat making small talk, Charlene turned to Ainsley. "I'm sure you'll want to get on the road soon. Would you mind running an errand for me?"

Ainsley smiled indulgently. "Whatever you need."

"The sheriff lives just outside of town. Would you mind dropping off some apple pie for him? It's his favorite."

Ainsley's brows drew together. "I thought he lived over by the school?"

"Oh, no." Charlene made a face. "Aggie passed away a few years back, you know."

Brynlee and Kinley traded glances and Garrett opened his mouth as if to speak, but Charlene steamrolled right over him. "Anyway, he lives over on Echoglen, right next to the lake. I promised I would send some along next time I made it. I'd hate to disappoint him."

"All right," Ainsley finally relented, holding her hands up in mock surrender. "I would hate to disappoint him."

Her mom gave her a sunny smile. "Perfect."

She spooned a generous portion into a Tupperware container, along with some leftover roast and potatoes from supper. Ainsley cocked an eyebrow at her mother as Charlene thrust the containers into her arms. "What? It's the neighborly thing to do."

Ainsley shook her head. Charlene was like the proverbial mother hen, always trying to nurture everyone around her. How in the world the sheriff had ended up in her sphere was beyond Ainsley, but if her mother thought he needed help, who was she to say no?

With a wave to her father and sisters, she headed toward the front door. Checking to make sure her family was absorbed in discussion, Ainsley cracked the door and peered outside. Nothing appeared to be out of place, and she sailed down the sidewalk and climbed into the car.

So far, so good. She smiled as she pulled away from the curb, her spirits high. Maybe Joel had given up on her after all.

CHAPTER
FOUR

Dare tossed the phone on the desk and scrubbed a hand over his face. The paperwork never stopped.

With a groan of frustration, he threw himself into the chair behind the desk and massaged his thigh. It had been almost two years since the incident and even after months of physical therapy, he still wasn't back to normal. He worked out every day to keep the muscle supple, but the gunshot wound had altered his leg almost beyond repair.

It had taken him off the streets and out of duty for nearly six months, and he was still salty over it. He shouldn't complain; his job as sheriff was a good gig. It kept him involved and Brookhaven was a nice town. But it was boring as hell.

The citizens apparently had faith in him, because they'd encouraged him to run for sheriff last year and, maybe stupidly on his part, he'd decided what the hell—why not run for office? He was a damn good cop, stern when he needed to be, but also fair. In a small town like this, balancing the two was imperative. It was a constant battle of politics.

He leaned his head back and his gaze came to rest on a crack in the ceiling. He rolled his eyes. One more thing to add to his list. He'd inherited the large house from his grandfather after he'd passed away, and it was too damn big. He really should just sell it and take the profit, go live somewhere more manageable. But he liked the view of the lake, and it had a lot of space for Sarge to run.

The sound of gravel crunching in the driveway drew his attention, and he swiveled in his chair to glance out the window overlooking the front lawn. An older Honda sedan pulled around the circular drive and came to rest directly in front of the wide steps leading up to the wraparound porch.

The driver unfolded from the front seat, and his eyebrows lifted as he took in the unmistakable female curves. Her blonde hair glinted like gold in the bright afternoon sun, but her face was hidden behind a pair of large sunglasses.

Apprehension coupled with anticipation snaked through him as he continued to watch her. The woman walked around the car, and his groin tightened in appreciation. Her loose blue shirt clung to her body in the slight breeze, and her tight-fitting jeans stopped just above her ankles. He didn't recognize her right off, which kind of surprised him. He knew most everyone in town, at least by sight—especially the women as beautiful as this one.

Who the hell was she?

Dare pushed out of the chair and headed downstairs. His hand tightened around the knob just as the doorbell rang. He yanked open the door and she jumped, her eyes flying wide. "Oh!"

Dare catalogued her features in less than a second. She'd pushed her sunglasses to the top of her head, revealing a pair of steely blue eyes. A slight blush tinged her peaches and cream complexion, matching the hue of her rosy, full lips. She was slender and petite, but his original assessment had been spot on—she was gorgeous.

He continued to peruse her body, stunned into silence. Whatever blood had been in his brain had fled much farther south ten seconds ago when he'd opened the door to find her on his front porch.

"I hope you don't mind me showing up like this." She shifted uncomfortably, her hands tightening around the containers she held. "I'm Ainsley Layne, Charlene and Garrett's daughter—"

Her words stalled, cut off by Sarge's sharp bark as he tore around the corner of the house. Her eyes went wide and she screamed at the sight of the large German Shepherd. The plastic containers hit the porch, and she threw herself toward the open doorway.

"Halt!"

The dog abruptly skidded to a stop at Dare's command, and he turned his attention to the woman standing just inside his foyer. She shook like a leaf, looking like she would faint any second.

"Sorry about that," Dare apologized. "That's Sarge. Don't worry, his bark is worse than his bite."

His joke fell flat when her expression didn't change one iota. Her obvious fear made him feel like a complete dick for teasing her. Dare scooped up the containers, then closed the door.

That seemed to jolt her out of her trance, because she gestured wildly as she moved forward. "Oh, my God, I'm so sorry!"

"No problem." He waved her off as he held the containers out to her.

A blush crept up her neck and stained her cheeks as she retracted her hands and crossed her arms over her chest. "They're actually for you. I think." She glanced around the house before meeting his gaze again. "You are the sheriff, right?"

Dare couldn't help but laugh. "Yeah. You're at the right place."

"Oh, good. I was worried for a second." She swallowed hard, her gaze flitting around the room, looking everywhere but at him. It made the hairs on the back of his neck stand up. Something wasn't right.

It was possible that she was still caught up in the fog of fear that had enveloped her the moment she'd seen the dog, but he sensed there was more to the story. She kept her arms wrapped tightly around her waist, her face a tightly controlled mask. She shifted anxiously, like she would run right back out the front door and away from him if it weren't for the dog.

He could call Sarge off and let her leave since she was obviously uncomfortable. For some reason, something told him not to let her go—not yet. It might be wrong of him, but he needed to know more about her. "Come on in. Let's take this stuff to the kitchen."

She threw a quick glance at the door and took an

immediate step backward, away from him, when he gestured toward the kitchen at the back of the house. She preceded him, back stiff as a board, making sure to keep plenty of space between them.

Interesting. Everything about her intrigued him—and not necessarily in a good way. He'd met Mr. and Mrs. Layne several times. Both were warm and cordial, the epitome of small town hospitality. Ainsley, however, was almost standoffish. The tiny looks she tossed over her shoulder told him she was waiting for a dagger in the back.

What had put her on guard? He knew she didn't live in Brookhaven, but he couldn't remember if the Laynes had told him where she currently resided. Most people who lived in the city were extraordinarily cautious of their surroundings, especially women. Maybe she was just a single woman on guard trapped in a small space with a man she didn't know.

It was possible, but again... Something about it just didn't feel right. Maybe she didn't want to be here. Or maybe she just didn't like him.

He shook his head. Sometimes he wished he wasn't so damn suspicious of everyone and their motives. It wasn't any of his business why she acted so uptight.

He set the food down on the butcher's block island and motioned to a stool. Ainsley glanced around as she slid into the seat. He made sure to keep his distance, standing on the opposite side of the island. Her gaze moved past him and out the large picture window over the sink that highlighted a perfect view of the lake.

"It's beautiful here," she said, her tone reverent.

While she stared at the lake, he studied her. The

tightness around her eyes and mouth had eased a tiny bit, making her look younger and more beautiful. Her features were soft and symmetrical, but it was her eyes that drew his attention. They were the eyes of a person who'd seen far too much in their short life, shadowed with wariness.

He knew what it was like to feel despair. First responders saw some of the worst of humanity—gruesome images that stayed with you, no matter how hard you tried to wash them away. It was the same look he saw in her eyes. What had this woman seen that had affected her so deeply?

She was not his responsibility. He clenched his jaw and willed himself to think about something else. Ainsley glanced over at him. He could only imagine the look on his face, because she flushed bright red and fidgeted in her chair. "Are you sure I'm not keeping you from anything?"

He shook his head. "Nope."

"Okay."

Dare had found that he could usually learn more by staying silent and not asking questions. Most people couldn't stand the silence and would start talking out of nervousness just to fill the void. Not so with Ainsley, apparently.

Definitely more to the story, he thought.

"I thought maybe you were here about the rental."

Her brows dipped together. "Rental?"

"The suite." He pointed toward the patio. "Part of the house was converted to a mother-in-law suite several years ago, so I decided to rent it out."

"Oh."

She nodded but didn't say anything else, and Dare floundered for a moment. Ainsley was most definitely not a talker. He'd never met another woman like her, and it threw him off kilter. He didn't like things he didn't understand, and as he stood there studying her, the questions in his mind only multiplied.

Curiosity finally got the best of him. "What all did your mom tell you?"

Ainsley looked over at him and lifted one shoulder. "Not much, really. She just asked me to stop over and drop off some food."

He thought about what he'd told Charlene the last time they'd spoken. He'd posted fliers around town about a week ago, advertising the suite for rent. Charlene had run into him outside the supermarket and asked about it. He'd assumed the youngest daughter, Brynlee, was looking for a place of her own. He wasn't in the least disappointed to find out he was wrong. Finding Ainsley on his porch was infinitely better.

But that presented a bigger problem: did he really want this woman around all the time? Ainsley clearly had shit going on in her life. The question was, what.

Dare studied her. "What brought you to town?"

"Dinner with my family." She darted a quick glance up at him before returning her gaze out the window at the lake. "They get together every Sunday. I haven't had much of a chance to see them recently, so…"

She trailed off, and the wistful look in her eyes sent alarm bells ringing in the back of his mind. "Do you live far away?"

She paused for a moment, almost as if contemplating whether to tell him the truth. He could find out easily enough, but he wanted to hear it from her. For some reason, it seemed important that she open up to him of her own accord.

She didn't meet his gaze when she spoke. "Sandstone."

Dare knew of it. The small town was about a half hour away, just over the border into Wisconsin. "Sounds like you exchanged one small town for another."

"True." She glanced over her shoulder and smiled, but it didn't reach her eyes.

"You don't want to be in Brookhaven?" he pressed.

"I thought about it," she replied noncommittally. "I do miss my family."

The quiet admission was the first truly genuine thing she'd said all day. He wanted her to confide in him, tell him what was weighing so heavily on her mind. He shouldn't even care. What he *should* do was show her to the door and let her figure out life on her own. Instead, he surprised them both when he said, "If you do decide to move back, the suite is all yours."

"Really?" Surprise lit her eyes as she snapped her head his way. "Don't you have other people interested?"

None who mattered. "I've shown it to a half dozen people already. Haven't gotten a single bite." He smiled wryly. "Most of them are ready to leave the second they realize the sheriff would be their landlord."

Ainsley smiled at that. "Well, I'm not a partier, and I keep to myself. I can promise you I wouldn't be any trouble at all."

Oh, she would be trouble, all right. She just didn't know it. Dare tipped his head her way. "Let me give you my number so you've got it."

He scrawled his number on a piece of paper, then passed it her way. "Call me."

Ainsley's cheeks flushed bright pink again, but she reached for the slip of paper. Their fingers brushed for barely a millisecond, and Ainsley practically jerked her hand away.

His stomach clenched with apprehension as her body language changed rapidly, going rigid as stone. She was never completely at ease, but as they'd spoken, she had begun to relax. With that one tiny touch, Ainsley had retreated almost completely.

His first instinct was correct—something was wrong. And as much as he didn't need the trouble, he knew she needed this offer of a safe haven. "Take a few days to think it over," he said quietly. "I'm not in a hurry to rent it out."

She stared at the scrap of paper clutched in her fingers. "If you're sure you don't mind..."

"I would expect nothing less."

Ainsley tucked the paper in her back pocket and offered a little smile. "I'm sure you're busy. I should probably get out of your hair."

He nodded. "I'll walk you out. If you decide it's what you want, we can work out the details later."

She smiled gratefully and made her way to the front door. Just as she had before, she walked in front of him and slightly off to one side so she could keep him in her peripheral vision. A horrible suspicion occurred to him, but he bit his tongue. Better to let things play out and see what happened.

At the door, she turned to him. "I really just wanted to say thank you again for the offer. It's really nice of you."

He opened the front door for her. "You'd be helping me out. Take your time, just let me know what you decide."

Sarge lay in the front yard, his dark fur dripping wet from an apparent dip in the lake. He held up a hand signaling the dog to stay and Ainsley watched anxiously as she cautiously skirted both Dare and the dog, then slid inside her car.

She tossed a small wave his way as she pulled away. Dare lifted a hand in farewell as he watched the car disappear down the driveway, past the blossoming Magnolia trees, until it was finally out of sight.

Would she call about the suite, or would she ghost him? Had he scared her off for good?

He whistled for Sarge, then closed the door and leaned against it, thoughts of Ainsley parading through his mind. He let out a low growl. It was going to be a long damn night.

CHAPTER
FIVE

Ainsley pulled into the parking lot of the bar shortly before nightfall and drove around back, parking next to the stairs that led up to her apartment. She sat in her car for a moment and stared at the dilapidated old building. The bar was a staple in the small town, first opened by Marv's grandparents after Prohibition. The red brick building was crumbling in places, but the bar and Marv had been a Godsend when she'd first left Minneapolis.

Over the first few days she'd constantly been watching over her shoulder, expecting Joel to appear at any moment, but he never had. Ainsley was surprised and a little wary. It was unlike him to let go of something so easily, but she wasn't going to take the reprieve for granted.

She climbed out of the car and slowly made her way up the stairs to her apartment. A chill snaked down her spine, and she paused in front of her door. Something felt off. She turned in a slow circle and glanced around, but everything remained quiet. She listened harder and examined her surroundings once again but still couldn't find anything out of place in the dim light.

Shaking off the eerie feeling, she let herself into the apartment and locked the door behind her. Ainsley let out a shaky breath and touched her hand to her forehead. She had to get her imagination under control. Joel wasn't here.

She moved around the small apartment, taking it all in, thinking what she would need to pack when she left. It was amazing what her life had been reduced to. She had so few belongings, bringing only what she absolutely needed when she'd fled Minneapolis.

Moving from the small kitchen into the living room, Ainsley curled into the corner of the couch and picked up a book one of the bartenders had loaned her.

Though she tried to focus, her attention continued to drift away from the story. As she stared sightlessly at the pages, her thoughts turned almost inevitably to Dare. She'd almost passed out on the porch when the door opened and she found those intense hazel eyes boring into hers.

Ainsley had expected the sheriff to be older—and not nearly as intimidating. Dare towered over her by almost a foot, and his shoulders had filled the doorway. He was big and broad, and her heart had nearly stopped at the sight of him. She didn't trust men—especially not men who looked like him. He might be the sheriff, but that didn't mean he was a good man.

She still wasn't entirely sure that renting his suite was a good idea. It put her far too close to him. And as much as she would love to be close to her family, she needed to be certain she would be safe. She'd just escaped one man; she wouldn't put herself in that situation ever again.

She'd dated a few guys when she was younger, but Joel had been her first serious relationship. She thought she'd loved him and it hadn't been all bad—at least, not in the beginning. Joel had been charming and sweet, and she had admired his ambition. He was determined to make a name for himself. She hadn't realized at the time how swiftly he'd alienated her from her family and friends.

He had kept her busy, first with school, then by moving her into his home. While she had thought it romantic and the logical next step in their future together, Joel's motivations were purely selfish. He'd wanted her under his control at all times and what better way to do that than keep her close to him? Joel had been all-encompassing, and Ainsley had decided she was better off alone. She might be lonely, but it was better than feeling powerless and subservient.

Ainsley did a walk-through of the small apartment, checking the locks on both windows and the door, then climbed into bed. Her body was exhausted but her mind whirled with anxiety.

It seemed like her heart hadn't slowed down for a single second ever since she'd left Joel. She was terrified she'd look over her shoulder one day and find him watching her, waiting to draw her back into his web.

Ainsley blew out a long, shaky breath and strove for reason. Even if he did show up, there was nothing he could do to make her come back. Marv would support her. And if she moved into Dare's suite... Well, Joel was no match for the sheriff.

She couldn't keep running. She needed to be strong, needed to put Joel where he belonged—in the past.

"Last call."

Ainsley bit back a yawn as she cleared the sticky, empty glasses from the table, then wiped it down before heading back to the bar. Dunking the glassware into the tub of sudsy water, she threw a look down the bar to the handful of men still seated on the stools.

From his spot in front of the tap, Marv glanced over his shoulder at me. "Can you get the trash together?"

"Sure. If you want, you can finish up and I'll take it out."

One grizzled brow arched toward his hairline. "You sure?"

She nodded, deeply appreciative of his concern. He knew how much she hated being alone outside in the dark. "I'll be fine."

"All right."

Marv had welcomed her in with open arms, watching over her like a surrogate grandfather. He'd offered her a job as waitress and allowed her use of the small apartment situated above the bar.

She stayed mostly behind the bar, away from the patrons, where she could avoid the flirtatious remarks occasionally flung in her direction. If anyone ever came on too strong, Marv stepped in. He had deemed himself her protector, and she appreciated it immensely. She owed him so much for helping her to get back on her feet.

She finished drying the glasses, then wiped her hands on the stained apron before untying it and setting it aside to toss in the laundry later. Making her way through the bar and kitchen areas, she collected the bags of trash, then glanced at the clock. Marv had yelled last call fifteen minutes ago, and now only two men lingered at the bar. As she twisted up the bags, the men downed their drinks then pushed the empty glasses toward Marv, who collected them and dumped them into the soapy water.

Once she'd gathered all the trash bags together, she pushed out the back door into the alley. A security light to the left illuminated the dumpster, and she used a brick to prop the door open before carrying the bags over and tossing them in, one by one. The lid shut with a bang, and she dusted her hands on her jeans before drawing in a deep breath of the muggy early summer air.

A soft scuffle behind her made the hairs on the back of her neck stand on end, and she whirled around, already looking for him. Her eyes scanned the dark alley but found nothing. It had sounded almost like... a footstep. She slowly edged her way toward the door, scanning her surroundings.

Suddenly, a steel trashcan from the insurance agency next door tipped over, landing with a crash. A scream caught in her throat, and she slapped one hand over her heart as an opossum waddled out of the wreckage. His beady eyes met hers for a moment before he turned and headed in the opposite direction. Breathing heavily, she collapsed against the jagged brick wall and blinked back the tears that had sprung to her eyes.

He wasn't here. She was safe.

Shaking off her wayward thoughts, she strode back into the bar then closed up, making sure that the door was securely locked. By the time she made it back to the bar,

Marv had already washed the remaining dishes and set them aside to dry.

Ainsley quickly spoke up. "If you have a minute, I'd like to run something by you."

Marv's sharp eyes landed on her, quickly assessing her words. An excellent judge of character, the older man could read people like a book. "You leavin'?"

She bit her lip and fidgeted with the hem of her shirt for a moment before speaking. "Maybe. I wanted to talk to you about that."

Marv raised his eyebrows. "Did something happen?" He let his arms drop to his sides and ambled over to a stool at the bar, gesturing for her to join him.

"No. Not exactly." She wound her way around the bar and sat with a sigh. "Every once in a while, I feel like someone's watching me, but there's never anyone there. Maybe I'm just being paranoid."

"You think he found you?"

Ainsley lifted one hand in question. "I honestly don't know."

Marv pondered her statement for a moment. "Maybe you need a fresh start. Find a place to clear your head."

Ainsley drummed her fingers on the bar top. "Actually, that's kind of what I wanted to talk to you about. I was visiting my parents yesterday and noticed an apartment for rent."

Marv studied her for a moment. "Is it safe?"

"I hope so," she said slowly. "The sheriff would be my landlord."

Marv nodded appreciatively. "I think I like this guy already. Just make sure you leave me his address, so I can track him down if you don't return my calls."

Ainsley smiled. Although Marv's tone was teasing, she knew he was deadly serious. "Deal. We should probably get to bed. It's been a long day."

He slid from the stool. "You and me both, missy."

"I feel bad leaving you short a waitress," Ainsley said as she followed suit and climbed to her feet.

"Don't you worry about that. I've been takin' care of this bar more years than you've been alive." He threw a grin her way. "You just take care of yourself."

Her heart warmed at his support. "Thanks."

Marv reached over and flipped a switch that turned off the neon lights in the windows displaying the names of various brands of beer, then held the door for her. "Any idea when you'd be moving?"

"I'm not entirely sure. I'll need to get a job lined up first." She stepped onto the sidewalk and glanced up at the stars dotting the dark sky. It was just after three in the morning, and within a few hours the velvety black night would fade away into the dawn.

She was excited for tomorrow; she planned to start looking for a job—something close to Brookhaven, but far enough away that Joel wouldn't immediately be able to track her down.

"Well, let me know if you need anything. Have a good night."

"You, too." Ainsley paused near the base of the stairs and waved as he climbed into his car.

The now familiar feeling of being watched crept over her and she scanned the area. She turned in a circle, examining every car, person, and object she could see, but nothing stood out.

Damn it. This was driving her crazy.

She remained there for several moments, until Marv's car disappeared down the street, then blew out a hard breath and sprinted up the stairs to the apartment.

Ainsley unlocked the door and stepped inside, simultaneously reaching over to flip the light switch. The fluorescent fixture overhead flashed twice, then flickered to life. Her heart stalled in her chest as the bright light fell over the kitchen counter and a huge bouquet of red roses.

He'd found her.

CHAPTER
SIX

No.

No, no, no.

Panic assailed her and she stumbled backwards, catching herself on the doorframe. Her vision clouded as black crept into her peripherals and her lungs constricted tightly in her chest. She took a breath, forcing oxygen into her burning lungs, and slammed the door.

Ainsley turned and fled back down the stairs, unlocking her car with the key fob. She jumped inside, hitting the lock button with her left hand and shoving the key into the ignition with her right. The engine turned over and she threw it into reverse, quickly backing out of the spot and heading out of the parking lot. She fished her phone out of her pocket and called Marv.

He picked up on the second ring. "Ainsley? Is everything—"

"He's here. He was in the apartment. I went upstairs and they were right there." She knew she was rambling hysterically, but the words just kept pouring out as she sped out of town, driving blindly. "I didn't see him, but he must still be there somewhere."

"Okay, just take a deep breath." Marv's voice filtered over the line. "I'll go over and take a look."

"No! Please, Marv, don't. I don't know what he might do. Oh, God, why is he here? Why now?"

"Hey, everything'll be okay. You're safe, that's all that matters. We'll figure something out. Where are you now?"

She relaxed her grip on the steering wheel, stretching her fingers for a moment, and she looked around her. "I'm near the interstate."

"Okay. I'll keep an eye out over here, make sure no one follows you. Do you have somewhere you can go for a while?" he asked.

Ainsley debated for half a second before flipping on her blinker and merging into the right lane. "Yeah. I'm going to Dare's. I'll call you when I get there."

She headed east for about a half hour before making a large circle and heading south, paranoia prompting her to check the rearview mirror every few seconds. She didn't see anything out of the ordinary, but that was half the problem. She really had no idea what she was looking for.

A WalMart sign towered over the buildings up ahead and, making a split second decision, she exited the highway. At this time of night the parking lot was relatively empty, and she pulled into a spot under a lamp post as close to the store as she could. For several long moments she searched the dark parking lot, examining her surroundings before turning off the engine. She grabbed her purse and climbed out of the car, double checking to make sure it locked behind her.

Inside, Ainsley pulled a cart free and made her way toward the women's section. Into the cart she tossed shorts and jeans, then haphazardly pulled several tops from the racks and threw those on top. She saw some cheap flip flops hanging from an end cap and tossed a pair of those in the cart as well. Steering her cart toward the toiletries, she quickly tossed in shower necessities.

That would at least hold her over for a few days, until she could get back to the bar to retrieve her things. Just the thought of him being in her apartment made her blood run cold. How close had he come to catching her?

Ainsley checked out and carried her purchases to the car, keeping a vigilant eye on her surroundings. She tossed the bags in the back seat and climbed into the car, then headed back to the highway.

A glance at the clock on the dash revealed that it was just after five-thirty. Brookhaven was only a half hour away, and she nervously drummed her fingers on the steering wheel. She couldn't show up at Dare's at the crack of dawn, and she couldn't risk going to her parents' or Kinley's house.

If Joel had tracked her to Woody's, he'd more than likely suspect she'd go straight to her family. She couldn't put them at risk. It was probably stupid of her to go to Dare's, but surely Joel wouldn't find her there.

If she laid low for a while, maybe he'd eventually give up looking for her and move on. Besides, Dare was the sheriff; she would be safe there, tucked away in his house by the lake, out of sight.

She would, however, need to find a job. Preferably something she could do online where she wouldn't have to be out in public, watching her back every second of the day. She'd been on edge working at the bar, but Joel had stolen the last remaining shred of security when he'd shown up at her apartment.

A sign next to the highway declared there was a McDonald's off the next exit, so she followed the large yellow arches to the restaurant drive through where she ordered a cup of coffee. Unable to sleep after leaving Dare's house two nights before, she'd been up for nearly twenty-four hours. She was exhausted, both mentally and physically, and she desperately needed the jolt of caffeine.

Sipping her coffee, she drove around for nearly an hour, all the while keeping one eye on her rearview mirror. From time to time, a car would fall in behind her, and her pulse thundered wildly until it finally turned off. Though she watched for any car to show up more than once, it never did. Just to be on the safe side, she took several extra turns to get back to the highway.

Calmed slightly and feeling relatively safe, she headed toward Dare's house. The lake came into sight, and Ainsley sighed. So much for her plan. She'd just blown over a hundred and fifty bucks at WalMart on clothes for the next few days since she couldn't go back to her apartment to get her own. On top of that, she'd have to spend a good chunk of her money on rent. She mentally crossed her fingers, hoping she'd be able to find a job right away.

Her pulse accelerated once more as she turned down the long driveway leading to Dare's house. The Magnolia trees lining the drive were in full bloom, making it look like something out of a fairy tale. The early morning sunlight streaming through the blossoms lent them a sense of peacefulness, and hope suffused her chest.

She reached the house where the driveway circled around and parked in front of the steps leading up to the porch. A sense of déjà vu swept over her. Here she was, less than forty-eight hours later—only this time the circumstances were entirely different.

Who would have imagined that the man she had visited, a man she really didn't even know, would be the one person she turned to for help?

Ainsley tightened her grasp on the steering wheel. What if Dare couldn't help her? Joel had found her once; what would stop him from finding her again? This was a ridiculous idea. She should just leave, drive far away and start fresh somewhere new.

Ainsley reached for the gearshift to put the car back into drive when she noticed Dare standing in the front doorway. Arms crossed over his chest, head tilted slightly to one side, he stood there staring at her expectantly.

Shit.

Part of her had hoped he would still be asleep. From the look of his drenched T-shirt, it appeared he'd not only been awake for a while, but had been working out.

She drummed her fingers on the gearshift for a moment, then finally turned off the ignition, fingers shaking as she palmed her keys. The dog was nowhere in sight, but she kept her eyes peeled as she cautiously climbed out of the car.

Ainsley drew in a deep breath and plastered on a smile as she approached the front porch. "Hey. Sorry to show up so early."

"No problem." His gaze flickered over her shoulder for a moment before returning to hers. "Wanna come in?"

"Um..."

Dare seemed to read her thoughts as she paused near the base of the stairs and glanced around again. "Sarge is in his room. I put him away when I saw your car."

Relief rushed through her. "Thanks."

He dipped his head in a nod and opened the door wider. "I've got coffee on if you want some."

"Sure, thanks."

She barely refrained from glancing over her shoulder at the driveway. No one had followed her here; no one knew where she was. She was safe.

CHAPTER
SEVEN

Dare studied her where she stood frozen next to the steps of the porch. Her fathomless blue eyes held wariness but also... fear? She couldn't possibly be afraid of him, could she?

Of course, she could. People either wanted to be his best friend to avoid legal troubles, or they avoided him like the plague. Because of his position, he didn't allow most people to get close to him. He was well aware that he came off as an asshole sometimes, and some people—women, mostly—found him unapproachable.

He hadn't gotten that vibe from her the other day, though, so what had changed? And what in the hell would prompt her to show up out of the blue without even a phone call? There had to be more to the story.

Ainsley bit her lip and toyed with the hem of her shirt. "Um... If you don't mind, I need to use the bathroom. Then maybe we can talk inside?"

He fought to keep his expression neutral. There was definitely more here than met the eye. What was going on?

He debated pushing her for more information, but instead let it slide for the moment. He would let her calm down a little and get comfortable. Then he was damn well going to get her to talk.

"Come on in." He stepped aside and let her enter. As he closed the front door, he quickly scanned the area. Nothing seemed to be amiss, but he locked the door behind them just to be safe.

Ainsley's gaze followed his movements, and some of the tension drained from her body as the lock clicked into place. He almost laughed out loud at the look of relief on her face. Most women would be running for their lives being locked inside a house with him. Clearly, she found him to be the lesser of two evils compared to whatever, or whomever, was bothering her.

"The bathroom is down the hall on the right. Meet me in the kitchen when you're ready."

She nodded her assent, slipping like a shadow into the bathroom, and Dare made his way down the hallway toward the kitchen, pondering her demeanor. She didn't appear to be hurt in any way, although it was difficult to tell. She still wore the black shirt and pants he assumed she'd worn to the bar last night, judging from the sweet smell of alcohol emanating from her.

Something was wrong, though. She'd told him she worked at a bar about a half hour north. If that were the case, she must have come here almost directly after closing. The question was—what had caused her to leave town in the middle of the night?

The question plagued him as he waited for her to appear. The sound of the bathroom door opening tore him from his thoughts, and he busied himself by grabbing a mug from the cabinet. Ainsley padded into the kitchen just as he closed the door.

Dare poured her a cup of coffee and slid it her way. "Sugar's on the counter, cream is in the fridge."

Ainsley waved him off as she settled on a stool. "This is great, thanks."

"So." Dare took a sip, then regarded her over the rim of his own cup. "You decided to make the move."

Her hands tightened around the mug, causing her knuckles to turn white with tension. "Yeah. I mean, if that's still okay," she rushed to add.

"Of course. I took the ad down after we talked." He sensed she would be back, though he'd assumed she would call first.

The whole situation bothered him immensely. Whatever was going on, it was serious. If she was in some sort of trouble—and it was looking more and more as if that were the case—then Ainsley clearly needed somewhere safe to land. Dare wanted to make sure it was right here, where he could keep an eye on her.

Her gaze dropped to the coffee cup clutched between her palms, and she cleared her throat. "I kind of forgot to ask... Do you want first and last month's rent up front? I'll have to look for a new job, so I might be a little short. But I promise I'll try to find something right away."

Dare lifted a hand to alleviate her concern. "Just first month's rent is fine. It's just a small place, so if it works for you, we'll work on a month-to-month lease."

"That sounds great, thank you."

His gut told him she would balk if he asked for her to

sign a lease binding her here for an extended period of time. Why, he wasn't quite sure. Her family lived here, so it only made sense that she would want to be close by.

But Dare was damn good at reading people, and everything about her mannerisms told him she would run at the drop of a hat. Getting answers out of her wouldn't be nearly as easy as he'd assumed. She was like an oyster, clamped down to protect herself. Ainsley needed time to get comfortable with him before she could trust him. He decided to offer up a little bit about himself.

Dare tipped his head her way. "I was just getting ready to make breakfast when you showed up. You hungry?"

She shook her head. "Really, that's not necessary. I'm fine." As if on cue, Ainsley's stomach rumbled and her eyes jumped to Dare's, her cheeks turning bright pink.

He fought the urge to smile. He had a feeling it would somehow make her feel bad, and the last thing he wanted was for her to pull away from him. "Maybe just something light?"

"That would be great, thank you."

Dare nodded, then began to pull ingredients out of the fridge, studying the woman across from him as he worked. She was unfailingly polite, and he wondered exactly how far he could push her before she cracked. He wanted to ruffle her feathers and pull back the layers, find the real woman beneath the timid exterior.

Dare plated the food, and Ainsley smiled appreciatively. "This looks great, thanks."

They ate in silence for several moments until they'd cleaned their plates. Though Dare tried more than once to initiate small talk, Ainsley was infuriatingly succinct. She refused to offer up anything about herself except the most inane information, most of which he'd already ferreted out on his own. By the time he pushed his plate away, he was ready to snap at her.

Clamping down on his control, he gathered the plates and set them in the sink, then turned to face her. "Ready to see the suite?"

She nodded. "Sure."

Striding over to the very last cabinet, he pulled open a drawer and retrieved a key, then nodded his head toward the back yard. "Come on, follow me."

He strode through a wide arched doorway into a small, formal sitting room, then crossed to a set of patio doors. Light streamed in through the windows, spilling squares of sunlight over the rich, honey oak floors. "This is the quickest way. Unless you want to grab some of your stuff first?"

She shook her head, answering a little too quickly for his liking. "No. That's okay. I'll grab what I need later."

Dare just nodded and made his way across the patio to the corner of the house. The large plantation-style home had been built nearly two hundred years ago, and at some point one of the late owners had divided the house into sections, creating a mother-in-law suite.

The suite was accessible only from a set of stairs that ran up the side of the house. At the top, a narrow deck ran the length of the building. Two small patio chairs sat in the corner, the perfect place to watch the sun set.

Ainsley paused, staring out over the lake with wide eyes. "Dare, this is beautiful."

He couldn't help but smile. "You haven't even been inside yet."

Unlocking the door, he pushed it open then stepped back to allow Ainsley to enter first. He flipped on the light but left the door open. "Sorry. I haven't turned on the air yet, so it's a little stuffy in here."

"Wow." Ainsley's gaze flitted around the small room. "I wasn't expecting it to be furnished."

His grandfather had left more than enough furniture, and Dare had moved some of it into the suite. "You'll probably want to clean it for yourself, but I did set out fresh sheets and towels so it's at least livable. Are you sure you don't want help with your stuff?"

Ainsley waved a hand dismissively but didn't make eye contact. "I didn't bring much, so it won't take too long. Thank you, though."

"So, anyway," he said, changing the subject. "I'm sure you noticed there's no TV in the suite yet, but we can get one for you if you'd like. Otherwise, you can watch whatever you want in the house."

She waved the offer away. "A TV is the least of my worries."

He nodded. "There's an oven and a small fridge, but no laundry room. You're more than welcome to use the one in the house."

"If you don't mind..."

She trailed off, and he shook his head. "You're welcome to use the house as often as you like. Here's your key for the suite, so you can come and go as you please. I'll get you a house key, too."

Ainsley studied him, confusion tugging at the space

between her brows. "That's really nice of you. Thank you."

She was obviously concerned about his motives, and he wondered once more exactly what had happened to make her so wary. He offered her a smile, needing to reassure her. "I'm glad you decided to take the suite."

"Me, too." A shy smile curved her full lips and she dropped her gaze to the floor, suddenly very interested in her feet. "I really appreciate everything you've done."

He dipped his chin in acknowledgment. "My pleasure."

She fiddled with the key, turning it over in her hands, shifting from one foot to the other. He took her discomfort as his cue to leave, and he cleared his throat. "I've got to leave for work here soon. Is there anything you need before I head out?"

She shook her head. "No, thanks, it's been a long day. I think I'm just going to crash for a few hours."

"You have my number, right?" She nodded, and he continued, "I'll be home around five or so. Call me if you need anything."

He headed back to the house and changed into his uniform. Movement from the driveway caught his eye as Ainsley retrieved her belongings from the car. His eyebrows drew together as he watched her pull several grocery-type bags from the backseat, but no luggage. Not the strangest thing in the world, but... who moved into a new place with no luggage? That couldn't possibly be everything she owned.

He waited for her to come back for more stuff, but after about twenty minutes he finally gave up. She had either taken all of her stuff up with her in the grocery bags, or she would go back to get the rest later. Memories of her behavior this morning left him strangely unsettled, and he wondered if that was truly all she owned. The pieces of the puzzle didn't fit yet, but he was determined to figure out what was going on.

Sarge practically bolted out of his room the moment the door was open, and he darted toward the kitchen, eagerly sniffing Ainsley's lingering scent.

He whistled for the dog. "Come on, boy. We've got some work to do."

CHAPTER
EIGHT

Things had been slow all morning, and Dare decided to take the time to check on the one thing that had been weighing on his mind since the moment Ainsley had pulled into his driveway at the crack of dawn. There was a chance his questions might throw up some red flags, but he couldn't help it. He needed to know exactly what he was dealing with if he was going to help her.

Tapping the car's plate number into the database, he watched as Patricia Fullerton's information popped up on the screen. Dare bit back a growl.

Damn it, Ainsley.

Considering her wariness, it wasn't exactly surprising that she hadn't registered the car in her name. Still, it was illegal and she ran the risk of getting pulled over and fined —if not arrested—every time she got behind the wheel.

He cleared the search, then entered Ainsley's information into the database. Anger surged through him as the information populated on the screen. Her license had expired in October on her last birthday. While some people genuinely forgot to renew their license despite the reminders that came in the mail, he was certain this wasn't an oversight. For some reason, she'd chosen not to renew it.

Because she couldn't afford to? Dare steepled his fingers and clenched his molars together. Ainsley struck him as the type of woman who would follow every law to the letter. So why blatantly choose to ignore this?

Dare knew the car was registered to Patricia Fullerton, but he didn't have access to the title, so he couldn't verify the true owner. If Ainsley had purchased the car legally, that meant the title hadn't been transferred properly. If she hadn't purchased it by legal means...

His stomach flipped violently. Was Ainsley capable of stealing a car? Possibly. It was evident that she was low on cash. And the fact that she appeared to be on the run bothered him immensely.

He switched databases, then entered Patricia Fullerton's name into the search bar. The hairs on the back of Dare's neck lifted, and every cell seemed to freeze in place when the word "deceased" jumped out at him. He stared at the screen for several moments, contemplating the implications.

Mrs. Fullerton had passed away five months ago, apparently from natural causes. The older woman had lived alone until her death when she'd been found by a relative, her daughter, Tess Newman. The local medical examiner had declared cause of death cardiac arrest, so an autopsy was never performed.

If the woman had, indeed, died of natural causes, it was possible the family had sold off her assets—including the car. But if her death only appeared to be natural...

Everything inside him revolted at the idea. There was no way Ainsley could have anything to do with the woman's death. He'd stake his life on it. But the question remained—how had she acquired a car that technically belonged to a dead woman?

His lips pressed together in a firm line. He didn't like any of the options that came to mind. He scrolled until he found the woman's next of kin, Tess. Dare found her number easily enough in the White Pages, and he punched in the number, then waited for the call to connect.

The phone rang nearly a dozen times before rolling over to voicemail, and Dare left his name and number with a request for her to call him back at her earliest convenience. Frustrated and angry, he threw himself back in the chair and glared at the computer screen.

Nothing about Ainsley made sense. She was polite almost to the point of subservience, yet she was driving a car that didn't belong to her with an expired license. He recalled her reaction every time he got near—the way she would shy away from him or duck her head as if to make herself less visible. He'd seen this before, and his suspicions only grew stronger with every passing moment.

If the situation was truly as dire as he expected, she would be safe at his place. But he would need her to trust him enough to stay there. At least she wasn't driving to and from work somewhere. He had a plan for that, too, and he needed to talk with Marley.

Dare gathered up the paperwork on this desk and shoved it into his bag. Typically he worked at the station through dinner, but since Ainsley had just moved in, he wanted to get home in case she needed anything. He left his office and cut across the bullpen toward Detective Sawyer Reed. "I'm headed out. Yell if you need anything."

"You got it, boss." The man tipped his head, and Dare strode out into the warm sunshine.

Fifteen minutes later, he pulled up to the Premier Packaging facility just outside of town. He made his way into the lobby and lifted a hand in greeting to Marley, who was on the phone with a customer. She waved her fingers at him, and Dare idly skimmed a magazine while he waited for her to wrap up the call.

Once she'd hung up, Marley stood and rounded the desk with a grin. "Hey, stranger. What brings you by?"

She opened her arms to him, and he pulled her into a bear hug. "I can't come see my big sister from time to time?"

Marley snorted as she leaned back to study him. "You could, but you won't pry yourself away from your desk long enough. Must be serious if you came by in the middle of the day. Am I under arrest?"

"Very funny." Dare rolled his eyes. "Actually, I'm here to help you. You still wanting to go paperless?"

"We keep talking about it, but there just aren't enough hours in the day." Marley let out an aggravated sigh and swept an arm around the front desk. "I can barely keep up with orders as it is."

Marley and her husband, Troy, owned and operated Premier Packaging, a plant that manufactured multi-use plastic boxes. Troy had expressed an interest in going paperless a few months ago at dinner. Though Marley could do it a bit at a time around her regular duties, it would take her forever to scan seven years' worth of documents into their system.

"I might have a solution for you." Dare propped an elbow on the desk. "I have a friend who's looking for some work."

Her gaze narrowed suspiciously. "Who is it?"

Dare rolled his eyes heavenward with a sigh. "Does it matter?"

"It's a woman, isn't it?" she exclaimed. "Are you dating her?"

Ainsley's pretty face flashed before his eyes, and Dare's stomach tightened. He didn't want to think about Ainsley in that capacity, because he'd be lying if he said he hadn't noticed just how beautiful she was. "If you must know, she's my new tenant. She's renting the suite."

Marley's brows drew together. "Do I know her?"

"Doubtful. It's the Laynes' oldest daughter, Ainsley. She just moved back to town, and she needs a place to stay."

Marley tapped her lip. "The name sounds familiar, but I can't place her. I've seen the other two around—is she as pretty as they are?"

Dare shot her a look. "Mar..."

She rolled her eyes. "Fine. If you think she's up for it, I'd love the help. She can stop by tomorrow, and—"

"Actually..." Dare cleared his throat. "I was thinking she could work from home."

Her gaze narrowed, taking on a protective edge. "Is she in some kind of trouble?"

That was one of the things he loved most about his sister. She was incredibly intuitive, and she fought to protect those close to her. "I'm honestly not sure," he admitted, "because she doesn't talk much. But if I had to guess... yeah. All the signs are there."

"Damn." Marley let out a harsh breath. "Is she safe?"

"She's with me, of course she's safe."

"You know what I mean." Marley turned her green gaze on him.

Unfortunately, he knew exactly what she meant. If someone was after Ainsley, it wouldn't matter that he was Sheriff. They would wait until she was alone, then strike. He would need to be extra vigilant and keep an eye out for any strangers in the area.

His gut twisted into a tight knot at the thought of someone hurting her. No one deserved that, least of all Ainsley, who was one of the sweetest, most reserved women he'd ever met. He was glad she'd trusted him enough to come to him; whatever was going on, he'd make sure she was safe.

Dare dipped his chin. "I'll protect her."

His sister studied him for a second before nodding. "Why don't I bring some files over later this evening? I can get her set up, show her the basics."

Dare pointed a finger her way. "Don't get any ideas."

"Me?" Marley affected her most innocent expression. "I have no idea what you mean."

"You know exactly what I mean," he said caustically as

he strode for the door. "Just bring whatever she'll need, and I'll see you at six."

"Seven," she called after him, a teasing note in her voice. "I wouldn't want to intrude on dinner with your guest."

He pushed outside, feeling both relieved and more disgruntled than when he'd entered a few minutes prior.

Big sisters were such a damn pain.

CHAPTER
NINE

The knock startled Ainsley, and she momentarily froze, heart pounding wildly in her chest. Who could it be?

The obvious answer was Dare, but after her recent scare at the bar, she wasn't taking any chances. She crept across the floor on tiptoe, keeping close to the wall as she angled toward the door. Her heart beat so hard she was sure the person on the other side could hear her coming.

There weren't any windows in the door, so she stealthily crept to the window over the kitchen sink and peered down the deck toward the front door. A relieved breath rushed from her lips when she saw Dare's broad form standing there. She quickly crossed the room, flung open the door—and froze.

A bouquet of red roses greeted her, and her heart almost stopped as memories flooded her brain. For a second she couldn't move. Though her mind knew it was Dare holding them, instinct prodded her to run.

Her muscles trembled, her mind a hazy, muddled mess

as she stared at the red blooms. Dare's deep voice jerked her from her thoughts.

"I'm sorry. I know they're a little formal." He rubbed the back of his neck self-consciously as he regarded the roses wryly. "I wanted to get you something to brighten the place up, but this was all they had, and..."

He cleared his throat and extended the roses her way. "Anyway. These are for you."

Ainsley made herself reach for them. Dare had no idea what the roses meant; it would be rude not to accept them.

"Thanks." She forced a smile as she extracted them from his fingers, then set them on the counter, turning the blooms away from her line of sight.

Dare shifted from foot to foot. "I was wondering if you'd eaten yet. I ordered a pizza, and it should be here in just a few minutes."

Ainsley bit her lip. She'd fallen into bed this morning after Dare left and had woken less than an hour ago. She'd taken a shower to clean away the grime from the bar, and Dare had knocked on the door just moments after she'd finished dressing.

Almost on cue, her stomach rumbled. Dare smiled. "I'll take that as a yes. Pepperoni and cheese okay, or do you want something else?"

"That sounds great, actually." She glanced behind her. "Let me clean up a bit and I'll be down in a few minutes."

He stepped away with a nod. "I'll be in the kitchen. Just come on in when you're ready."

She started to close the door, then yanked it open and stuck her head out. "Dare?"

He glanced over at her. "Yeah?"

"The dog." She swallowed hard. "Is...?"

"I'll make sure he's in his room."

She offered a small smile, grateful for his understanding. "Thanks. I'll be down in a minute."

Ainsley closed and locked the door, then strode toward the bedroom. She took a moment to straighten the sheets, then put her dirty clothes in the hamper. She paused next to the mirror and did a quick once-over. For a brief moment she regretted not buying any makeup.

Almost immediately she admonished herself. Dare was her landlord, nothing more. She had no desire to draw any more attention to herself than necessary, especially a man like the sheriff. She had a feeling he saw far too much as it was.

As she turned to leave, her gaze slid over the room once more. She cocked her head as she stared at the bed, amazement snaking through her. For the first time in weeks she'd actually slept well. It could be, of course, that she'd been exhausted when she'd fallen into bed this morning, but Ainsley suspected that wasn't the only reason.

She felt safe here, in this house tucked away by the lake. She felt safe... with Dare. That thought alone terrified her. She'd trusted a man once, and look how that had turned out. She couldn't afford to get too close to him, to put her faith in him.

She thought briefly about telling him she'd changed her mind about dinner, but she hadn't picked up food this morning, and she was certain Dare hadn't stocked the cupboards.

Ainsley shook off the thought. She was being

ridiculous, overthinking the entire thing. He'd asked her to come share pizza, not go on a date.

Snatching up her keys, Ainsley locked the door behind her, then made her way down to the main house. She knocked lightly before slipping through the French doors that opened into the sitting room.

Dare stuck his head out of the kitchen. "What do you want to drink?"

"Whatever you're having is fine." Ainsley padded toward him, nervously rolling the hem of her shirt.

Dare stared at her for a long moment. "How about whatever you want?"

Those intense hazel eyes made her stomach quiver, though out of anticipation or fear, she wasn't sure.

He tipped his head toward the fridge. "Soda, water... something stronger?"

"I'll have a soda, too," she replied as he pulled a Coke from the fridge. He retrieved a second one, then passed it her way. The metal was cool under her fingertips, and she fought the urge to squirm as he turned to face her.

Dare cracked the can, then leaned back against the countertop. "Did you manage to get some rest?"

"I did, thank you."

He nodded. "I'll give you a tour of the house later so you can find everything. Feel free to come and go as you please."

She dipped her head. "Thank you."

As heavy silence stretched between them for several seconds until the doorbell rang, making Ainsley jump.

Dare flicked a look her way. "That's the pizza. I'll be right back."

Ainsley blew out a deep breath once he was gone and pressed one hand to her chest. Dare was so... intense. Every time he was near she felt lightheaded, like he sucked all the oxygen out of the room.

She'd barely recovered when he appeared once more, pizza box in hand. Ainsley forced herself not to flee back to the safety of the suite. She was hungry and besides, she didn't want to show Dare how much he intimidated her, even if he didn't mean to.

"Want me to get the plates?"

"Only if you want one." Dare plucked the roll of paper towels off the holder, then tipped his head her way. "Let's head into the living room."

Dare strode out of the room, leaving Ainsley to follow him at her will. She kept plenty of distance between them as she skirted the coffee table and settled at the end of the couch where she could keep an eye on both the window and the doorway.

Depositing the box and paper towels on the coffee table, Dare grabbed the remote and flicked on the TV. "What do you like to watch?"

"No preference. Whatever you like is fine."

Dare flipped through the channels for a few minutes before finally landing on a crime show. He leaned forward and snagged a slice of pizza from the box, then turned it toward her. "Help yourself."

She followed suit and gingerly plucked up a slice of pizza, cradling her hand under her mouth as she took a bite. Both of them fell silent for several minutes as they demolished half the pizza.

When the show rolled into a commercial break, Dare

picked up the remote to mute it, then turned to face her. "I hope you don't mind me asking, but you said something this morning about looking for work?"

She nodded. "I wanted to start looking today, but..." She lifted her hands in a shrugging motion. "I slept longer than I planned."

"You don't have to look for anything right away, if you don't want."

Ainsley froze, dark thoughts ricocheting through her mind. It was eerily similar to what Joel had told her when he'd asked her to move in with him. She stared at Dare, every cell of her body hyper alert.

He seemed to sense her unease, because he continued, "My sister and her husband own a packaging company outside of town. They've been looking for someone to do some data entry for them. I asked Marley to stop by tonight, run it by you."

Ainsley was stunned. It was a bit presumptuous of him, but her gratitude outweighed her annoyance. She couldn't believe he'd done that for her. Actually, she could. So far Dare had gone out of his way to help her several times. "That... that would be great, thank you."

Dare watched her with those intense gray-green eyes, and she fought to keep still. She felt marginally better knowing that his sister was coming over. It would at least provide a buffer between her and Dare. She didn't like that he was so intuitive, like he seemed to read every thought that zipped through her mind.

She would have to be more careful in the future not to give anything away. If he knew she'd lied to him about her reasons for moving back to Brookhaven he might kick her out. She liked it here, felt safe here. She didn't want to give him a reason to make her leave.

She studied Dare from beneath her lashes. He was twice her size, standing taller than her by a full foot. He was big and broad, his body so very different from Joel's lithe form. She'd noticed a slight limp when he walked, though it didn't seem to hinder him much. His hands were large and powerful, and Ainsley shivered. She could only imagine the damage he could do.

It occurred to her again that she should be scared of him—but she wasn't. Dare's every movement was deliberate and tightly controlled, and strange as it was, he seemed to want to protect her. Ainsley didn't know how she felt about that. On one hand, she liked that he looked out for her and wanted to keep her safe. On the other hand, it was the same kind of overbearing behavior Joel had exhibited.

She hated to compare the two men, but she'd learned the hard way that appearances could be deceiving. No matter how much she wanted to trust him, she couldn't afford to let down her guard. She would keep her distance so she couldn't—wouldn't—be hurt again.

CHAPTER
TEN

A sudden commotion rose from the front of the house as the front door opened, and a woman's voice lilted on the air. "I'm here!"

Ainsley glanced over at Dare, eyes wide. He didn't seem like the type of person to just let people walk into his home. Was this the sister he'd talked about, or did Dare have a girlfriend he hadn't mentioned?

Ainsley braced herself as the woman's clipped footsteps drew closer, and Dare let out an exasperated sigh as he pushed to his feet. "In case you're wondering, that's the sound of hell on wheels."

Ainsley didn't have time to process Dare's wry statement, because the woman appeared in the arched frame of the living room just a moment later. Her eyes swept over the room, immediately locking on Ainsley.

Dare gestured with one hand. "Ainsley, this is my sister, Marley."

Marley ignored him completely, her focus riveted on Ainsley, who popped up from the couch. She forced herself to remain still as the woman strode toward her and stopped barely a foot away, a wide smile on her face. "It's so nice to meet you. Dare told me all about you."

"He did?" Ainsley barely tamped down the urge to slide a look his way. Instead, she turned her attention to the woman in front of her.

Her dark brown hair and green eyes were almost identical to Dare's, but that was where the similarities stopped. Marley was petite, shorter even than Ainsley herself. Her hair was an explosion of riotous curls, and her eyes danced happily over cheeks that glow pink with happiness, her sunny disposition a complete contrast to Dare's far more stoic nature. The difference between the two was almost startling.

Marley took Ainsley's hands in her her own. "Goodness, you do look just like your sisters, don't you?"

Ainsley jerked a little. "You know my sisters?"

Marley nodded and released her, then dropped onto the couch cushion and gestured for Ainsley to join her. "My son, Owen, had Kinley as a teacher last year. He just adored her."

Ainsley couldn't help but grin, pride for her younger sister suffusing her heart. "That doesn't surprise me at all. I've heard she's an amazing teacher."

Marley nodded. "She's wonderful. I bet your family is glad to have you back in town."

Guilt rippled through Ainsley. Everything had happened so quickly that she hadn't even had a chance to tell her parents and sister she was back in Brookhaven.

She could feel warmth creeping up her cheeks under the weight of Dare's intense gaze. "We were always very close," she said by way of reply. "Kinley and Brynlee were my best friends growing up."

Marley smiled. "Dare and I are that way too. Except when he's grouchy. He can be awfully moody sometimes."

"Mar..." came Dare's warning.

Marley grinned, and Ainsley couldn't stop herself from returning the smile. It was impossible not to like Dare's sister. Ainsley was incredibly curious to know more about her. "Do you live close by?"

"About twenty minutes north. My husband, Troy, and I own Premier Packaging. Did Dare tell you that?"

Ainsley nodded. "He said you might be looking for someone to help out with office work."

"That's right." Marley briefly explained what needed to be done. "Do you think you might be interested?"

"It sounds great. I really appreciate this."

"You're helping me, trust me." Marley tipped her head at Dare. "There are a few boxes in my car. Can you get those?"

Dare sent a quick look toward Ainsley, silently asking if she would be okay alone with Marley. She gave a slight dip of her chin and he reluctantly disappeared from the room.

Marley continued, "Let's talk about the important stuff. I brought an application for you to fill out, but that's just a formality. I'll add you to payroll first thing and get everything filed tomorrow so you can start whenever you're ready. We can deposit the money directly into your account if that's easier for you."

Humiliation, sharp and hot, rolled through Ainsley, and she swallowed hard. "Actually, ma'am..."

Marley laid a hand over Ainsley's. "Call me Marley—

please. You're a friend of Dare's and, by extension, a friend of mine."

Saying she was a friend of Dare's was overstating their relationship astronomically, but she wasn't going to argue with the older woman. She focused on the issue at hand. "It's just... I don't have a bank account at the moment."

The admission escaped on a whisper. She'd been paid under the table at the bar, and she hadn't had control of her own bank account for years.

Something flickered in Marley's expression but was gone a second later. "That's right. You just moved. Well, we can just cross that bridge when you're ready."

Ainsley was certain Marley knew she was lying, but she was acutely relieved that Marley hadn't made a huge deal of it. Ainsley needed this job—everything depended on it. "I just need a few days to get it set up. I'll try to take care of it tomorrow."

"Take your time." Marley gave a little wave of her hands. "Once everything is ready, you can fill out the form."

She outlined the pay schedule, and gratitude rushed through Ainsley. "That sounds amazing, thank you."

Dare returned a moment later, boxes in his arms. "Is this all?"

"For now. I didn't want to overwhelm you," she said to Ainsley. "Do you have a computer?"

Ainsley felt the heat creep up her cheeks once more. "Not yet, but I can get one."

It would seriously cut into her savings, but it would be worth it if the job paid well enough.

"She can use mine," Dare cut in.

Ainsley snapped her head his way. "You don't have to do that. I—"

Dare shook his head, alleviating her concern. "There's no sense in you buying a computer when I have one right here."

Marley turned toward him. "Do you have a scanner?"

He nodded, though his attention and words were directed at Ainsley. "Everything is in the office. You can either move it up to the suite, or you can work from here."

Ainsley rolled the hem of her shirt between her fingertips. Working from Dare's office meant spending more time in his house, being in closer proximity to him. She swallowed hard, indecision twisting her stomach into a tight knot.

"I'm gone half the time," he said quietly. "You won't have to worry about me bothering you."

"It's true. I practically have to pry him out of the office sometimes." Marley rolled her eyes, then glanced at Ainsley. "Is that okay with you?"

"Sure." Ainsley avoided Dare's penetrating gaze as she stood and followed Marley down the hallway. Dare fell in behind her, boxes in hand, and she could practically feel the weight of his gaze boring into her back.

Marley stopped next to a room with wide French doors, then stepped inside and flipped on the light. Her glance roved over the computer situated on the desk, the combo printer/scanner on a table off to the side.

"Perfect." Marley grinned at Ainsley. "I think we've got everything you need."

She dropped into the chair and plugged in the external

hard drive, then walked Ainsley through the process to upload and save the files.

Ainsley discovered she was a quick study, and Marley grinned at her. "That's it. Pretty boring, but a necessary evil. The most important part is categorizing them and making sure the date is correct."

"Thanks again," Ainsley said as she stood. "I appreciate everything. I'll get the paperwork filled out and..."

She trailed off, thinking about her banking options. She'd have to go into town, but it was inevitable. She'd have to show her face sooner or later. And really, what were the odds that Joel had followed her here and would still be hanging around by tomorrow?

Marley seemed to read her mind, because she shot her an encouraging nod. "If you need help with anything, don't hesitate to call."

"I will, thanks."

Dare, who'd been silently watching them up until this point, nodded toward his sister. "Thanks, Mar."

Ainsley fell into step behind them as Dare saw Marley to the door. On the porch, Marley paused and tossed a smile at Ainsley. "Glad you're back in town. I hope everything works out for you."

Dare seemed to tense next to her, but Marley's smile only grew as she tossed one last wave their way and headed down the stairs toward her car.

Then she was gone, leaving Ainsley alone with Dare once more.

CHAPTER
ELEVEN

The moment Marley's taillights disappeared from view, Dare let out a deep breath. Movement from his peripheral vision caught his attention. A few feet away, Ainsley fidgeted nervously, anxious once more at being alone with him.

Keeping his movements steady and slow, Dare turned toward her. "Sorry about that. My sister can be a little overbearing. And bossy."

Ainsley offered a tiny smile. "She said she's your older sister. I think that comes with the territory."

Dare chuckled. "That it does. I don't remember a time when she wasn't trying to push me around."

Taking care to keep a healthy distance between them, Dare headed down the hallway toward the kitchen, shortening his stride so Ainsley could keep up with him if she chose. As he suspected she would, she stayed behind him and slightly to the left, out of arm's reach.

When he reached the kitchen, Dare retrieved the paper bag he'd dropped on the counter when he got home.

Reaching inside, he extracted the key and held it out to Ainsley. "I had the hardware store cut a spare key so you can come and go as you please while I'm gone."

Her bright blue gaze darted up to his before dropping to his outstretched hand. Hesitantly, she reached out and slipped it from his palm, fingertips barely grazing his skin. Her flesh was warm, and he curled his hand into a fist, tucking it close to his side.

"Thanks."

"No problem." He cleared his throat. "Tomorrow's my day off, so I thought we could go into town. Get your banking stuff done and get some groceries. I know the suite's empty, and my cupboards are pretty much bare."

Ainsley stood deathly still, and Dare swore he could see the myriad doubts flickering behind her expressive eyes. Finally she nodded. "Sure. I could use some stuff."

Dare nodded. "We'll meet up in the morning whenever you're ready."

"Great." She offered a tiny smile. "I think I'm actually going to head up to bed if you don't mind. It's been a long day."

"Sure thing. I'll walk you out."

She shook her head. "Oh, that's okay. You don't have to go out of your way—"

"No problem at all. Things can look different at night, especially here on the lake, so I'll go with you until you're comfortable."

"Okay." She dipped her head, giving in much more easily than he'd expected.

He led the way out to the patio, holding the door for her as she passed. Dare walked beside Ainsley, the cool evening air whispering through the trees surrounding his property. The path to her suite was dimly lit, but as they approached, a bright security light flicked on, casting a bright halo around them. Ainsley flinched, her eyes darting to the source of the sudden illumination.

"It's okay," Dare reassured her softly, his voice calm and steady. "It's just the security light. It's motion-activated, so you'll be able to come and go safely. Plus, you'll be able to tell if something's moving around outside."

He slid a sideways glance at her, studying her reaction. Ainsley offered a tight, almost imperceptible nod, but her body remained tense. She didn't acknowledge his statement, but her eyes continued to rove the darkened lawn. Was she watching for someone?

A chill slithered down his spine. He didn't like this— not at all. He desperately wished she would open up to him. But it was too soon. She'd barely known him for twenty-four hours. Earning her trust was going to be a gradual process.

"We get a lot of wildlife around here," he said conversationally. "Deer, raccoons, squirrels... Sometimes they'll set it off, so don't worry too much if it kicks on."

They reached the steps that led to her suite, and Dare gestured for Ainsley to precede him. She dipped her head as she slunk around him, careful not to touch him, and quickly climbed the stairs.

Upstairs, Dare reached out and gently tried the door handle, finding it locked. Good. He was glad she was taking precautions to keep herself safe.

"Let me just check inside," he said. "Make sure everything's all right."

Ainsley hesitated, her fingers curling into the sleeves of her oversized sweater. "Okay," she murmured, stepping back to allow him access.

"Key?" She passed him the key and Dare unlocked the door, then stepped inside. He flipped on the lights, making sure that the living area was empty before motioning her inside and locking the door behind her.

"Stay here for a second."

"Of course."

He methodically checked each room, ensuring the windows were locked and there were no signs of tampering. The hum of the air conditioning mingled with the soft scuffle of his footsteps as he moved from room to room.

He quickly cleared the rest of the suite, checking every possible hiding place before returning to Ainsley where she stood just inside the doorway, her posture still stiff. "Everything looks good," he said, offering her a reassuring smile. "Just make sure to lock up after I leave."

Ainsley nodded again but didn't move. Dare could see the wariness in her eyes, the way she kept herself on high alert. It broke his heart a little each time he saw her like this, a young woman so clearly haunted by her past. But he couldn't push her. He had to let her come to him in her own time.

He sensed she wasn't comfortable being in his house either, and a small part of him regretted talking her into it. "I know you said it was okay, but... if you're not comfortable working from my office, I can bring everything up here."

"No, really. It's fine." She gave him a small, fleeting smile, a glimmer of gratitude in her eyes. "I really appreciate everything you've done for me. Both of you. It means a lot."

"I'm happy to help. I just don't want you to feel like you're being forced into it."

Her head tipped slightly to one side as she studied him, her eyes conveying surprised curiosity, like she wasn't quite sure what to make of his words. It only served to solidify his opinion that someone hadn't treated her well.

"I'll be right next door if you need anything," he said gently. "You can call or come over anytime, no matter how late."

"Thank you," she whispered, her voice barely audible. She stepped farther into the room, and Dare could see her starting to unwind, if only just a little. "For everything. I don't think I've said that enough."

"You don't have to thank me," Dare said gently. "I'm just glad everything worked out."

She looked at him for a long moment, and Dare could see the internal struggle in her eyes. She was fighting to trust him, to let down the walls she'd built around herself. It wasn't easy, but he knew she was trying.

He studied her for a moment, then nodded. "We'll go shopping for groceries in the morning. Just come get me when you're ready."

She gave a tentative smile. "Okay."

"I'm going to let Sarge out, so you'll probably want to stay inside."

She nodded, eyes wide. "I will."

"Goodnight, Ainsley," he replied, stepping back towards the door. He paused before leaving, giving her one last reassuring look. "Sleep well."

As he closed the door behind him, Dare couldn't help but feel a mixture of frustration and hope. Frustration because he wanted so desperately to help her, to ease her fears and make her feel safe. Hope because he knew that with time, patience, and kindness, she might one day trust him enough to open up about her past.

He waited until the lock slid into place before starting back down the steps toward the house. He made his way back inside, his thoughts lingering on the woman upstairs.

He put Sarge outside to use the bathroom, then tossed his favorite ball a few times. All the while, he imagined he could feel Ainsley's eyes on him from the suite, boring twin holes into his back. He petted the dog's head, then headed back inside and locked up for the night.

Grabbing a beer from the fridge, he cracked it open and dropped into his favorite armchair. But instead of turning on the TV, he stared out the window, watching the play of moonlight over the lake.

Sarge slunk into the room and flopped down next to Dare's feet. He closed his eyes and pictured Ainsley on his doorstep just two days ago. He could still see that wild look in her eyes, like a frightened animal ready to bolt at the drop of a hat.

Within the space of a few minutes, he'd decided he would offer her the suite, no questions asked. Whatever she needed from him, he would do it. He wanted her to see that not all men were to be feared, that there were still good people in the world. He would do whatever it took to help Ainsley heal, to show her that she could trust him and that she didn't have to face her fears alone.

As the hours passed, Dare found himself unable to sleep. He kept thinking about Ainsley, about the shadows in her eyes and the way she seemed to flinch at the slightest noise. He knew trauma like that didn't heal overnight. It took time, patience, and a lot of love. And while he couldn't offer her love in the romantic sense—not yet, anyway—he could offer her unwavering support.

For now, though, he was content to take things slowly, allow her to come to terms with everything. And maybe, just maybe, one day she would open up to him about her past so they could face it together.

CHAPTER
TWELVE

The phone vibrated on the nightstand, yanking Dare from a restless sleep. His bleary gaze landed on the clock and before the predawn hour even registered, the swirling sensation in his gut told him something was wrong. Grabbing up the phone, he bit back a curse when saw Yvonne's name.

"Yeah?"

He didn't bother with formalities, and he was grateful his dispatcher didn't beat around the bush. "Hey, Sheriff. We just got a call for a 1020 in the park."

Damn. A grimace pulled at his mouth as he rolled from the bed. "Any details yet?"

"Woman was found on a bench. Shawn Ashmore found her just a few minutes ago. I dispatched your men on duty, but I figured you'd want to be there, too."

"You figured right." Dare wanted to be present for anything that even resembled a homicide. "Can you give the ME's office a call—see if Doc Seidel's available."

"You got it." Yvonne hung up, and Dare released a

sigh. Death was unavoidable, even in a small town like Brookhaven, where most of the calls tended to be mostly domestic disputes or traffic citations.

He quickly dressed and grabbed his gear, then headed toward the west side of town.

A man sat on the curb, head hanging low, elbows draped on his widespread knees. Dare knew most of the residents, at least by sight, and Shawn Ashmore was Brookhaven High School's football coach. An avid runner, the man could be seen running through town each morning.

Dare tipped his head at the man as he climbed from the cruiser. "Hey, Shawn."

The man glanced up at him, his face pale. "Hey, Sheriff."

He looked like he might cast up the contents of his stomach, so Dare stayed several steps away. "You good?"

He nodded shakily. "Yeah, sorry. Just..." His gaze shifted away for a second. "First time seeing something like that."

Dare understood that completely. It was hard for first responders to experience death firsthand, let alone civilians. He nodded and pulled out the small notepad he kept in his jacket. "Can you tell me what happened?"

"I was out for a run—same as usual." The man swallowed hard. "I didn't even notice her at first. When I got closer, I saw her looking my way, so I waved. But she didn't wave back. She didn't even move."

He closed his eyes and gave a little shake of his head. "I could tell her eyes were open, but I thought she was just ignoring me. She was so still..."

Dare glanced at him. "Did you touch anything?"

"No." He shook his head emphatically. "I thought it was odd, the way she was sitting there. I cut across the sidewalk to check on her, and that's when I realized..." He gave a little shudder.

"Do you recognize her?"

Shawn made a face, then shook his head as if doing so would clear the image from his mind. "No, I don't think so. She looks young, so I thought she might be a student, but I don't remember ever seeing her before."

"Did you see anyone else around?"

Shawn pointed across the town square. "Bill Mahle pulled in behind the hardware store about the same time I saw her. But that was it."

Dare jotted down the information. "Do you know who might have done this?"

"I appreciate your help." Dare closed his notebook, then glanced at his watch. School started in less than an hour. "Do you need a ride home?"

Shawn glanced up at him, uncomprehending, and Dare elaborated, "I can have one of the patrolmen give you a ride so you're not late for work."

He nodded a little dazedly, then slowly pushed to his feet. "I think I might take the day off."

Dare didn't blame the man. It was a lot to process. He waved over Evan Landry and asked him to drive Shawn home. Once the man was ensconced in the cruiser and on his way, Dare turned his attention back to the scene. Yellow tape was strung around the park, and several of his deputies milled about, bleary-eyed from having dragged out of bed at the crack of dawn.

He could tell by the way the woman had been painstakingly positioned and cared for that she'd been killed elsewhere and transported here under the cover of darkness. The woman reclined against the bench, her vacant eyes staring out across the playground. She would have been beautiful, but someone had stolen her vivacity, leaving her with the waxy look of death.

If Dare had to guess, she'd probably died sometime in the last twenty-four hours. Dr. Seidel would be able to better estimate the time of death. As if the thought had summoned him, Dare's attention was drawn to the medical examiner's van as it pulled up next to the park. He lifted a hand in greeting as the older man climbed out, then ducked under the tape and approached the scene.

Dare turned his attention back to the woman again. She'd been posed here sometime during the night, he supposed, hands folded primly at her waist, feet crossed at the ankles. Her long blonde hair was combed perfectly into place, a slight curl at the ends, almost as if someone had styled it before placing her here.

He quickly briefed Doc Seidel on what they knew so far, then stepped away to let the man work. Dare glanced around. The park was only a block from the center of town, and he could see the flag of the courthouse from where he stood. Who the hell would be brazen enough to leave her here, where he could have been seen at any moment?

He didn't like what that implied. The killer was confident, and this most likely wasn't his first time. They would need to check the cameras from the city buildings and surrounding businesses, see if they'd picked up any activity during the course of the night.

Dare gave Dr. Seidel a few minutes to get settled, then crossed over to where the medical examiner was examining the young woman. He didn't glance up as Dare reached his side. "What do we know?"

Dare quickly briefed the medical examiner, who nodded along, asking questions intermittently. "Anyone touch her?"

"Not that I'm aware of. Shawn Ashmore found her like this during his morning jog. Said he approached her but called it in as soon as he realized she was dead."

Doc Seidel picked up one of the woman's hands. "Her nails are extremely clean."

Dare leaned closer and examined her fingers. There was no polish on her nails, and they looked as if they'd been freshly scrubbed and manicured. He scowled. "He wanted to get rid of any evidence."

"Probably." Doc Seidel replaced her hand and continued to peruse her still form. "If he left something behind, I'll find it."

Dare watched on broodingly. He doubted they'd get any DNA off this girl and probably very little in the way of evidence. Dr. Seidel completed his work, then loaded the victim to take her to the morgue.

With the body removed, the deputies moved in to process the scene. Dare headed to the station where he dropped Sarge off, then walked the few blocks to the courthouse. Unsurprisingly, news of the murder had already spread, and he put in a request to review the footage from the previous night.

He did the same with the businesses surrounding the park, hoping they would catch a break. It was a long shot, especially since it'd been dark, but they needed to cover all their bases.

Dare returned to the station to find an email from Peggy at the courthouse. She'd attached two files, one from each camera that faced the park, and he settled in to watch. Several hours later, he sat back in his chair, frustrated. Their system hadn't caught a damn thing.

The cameras were decent quality, but they were too far away to pick up any movement near the park. He'd noted all the cars that had driven past and jotted down their license plates. He would have one of his deputies run those, check with the owners to see if they'd seen anything.

Lieutenant Campbell McCoy knocked on the doorjamb, and Dare glanced up at him. "Anything yet?"

Cam shook his head. "Not yet. We printed everything and sent the evidence to the lab, so we'll see if we get any hits."

"Maybe the autopsy will turn up something worthwhile." Dare scrubbed a hand over his face. "You headed out?"

Cam glanced at his watch, then nodded. "Yeah. I reached out to the surrounding departments to see if anyone matching her description has been reported missing. Maybe we'll get lucky."

"Do me a favor and have one of the guys run these." He passed the list of vehicles and plate numbers to Cam. "We need to see if anyone passing through last night noticed anything."

"You got it."

Cam disappeared, and Dare ran a hand through his hair. Hopefully they'd have some information tomorrow so they could ID the victim and figure out who the hell had done this.

It still pissed him off that the killer had left her out in the open like that, right in the center of town. Dare took pride in keeping the town safe, and for something like this to happen right under his nose... That wasn't acceptable.

Dare's foul mood hadn't lifted by the time he got home. Grabbing up the empty bag from the fast food place he'd stopped by on the way home, he crumpled it in his fist and slid from the car. He let Sarge out of the back seat, and the dog immediately bolted toward the freedom of the backyard.

The burger and fries sat like lead in his gut, making him feel even worse. He strode around the corner of the garage toward the trash cans. He lifted the lid and froze when a bright flash of red greeted him. The roses he'd bought for Ainsley last night lay on top of the black trash bags.

CHAPTER
THIRTEEN

A litany of curses hovered on his tongue as he stared at the red blossoms. He should have seen it coming; she'd done everything but tell him flat out she wanted nothing to do with him, and this was the final red flag waving in his face.

Goddamn it.

He pitched the fast food bag on top and slammed the lid, then stalked back through the garage and into the house. It wasn't anger he felt, he acknowledged as he stepped inside. It was her blatant refusal to accept his help, or anything else from him.

He was honestly surprised she'd accepted the offer to work in his home office. She probably would have dug in her heels had Marley not convinced her otherwise. He shook his head. She was far too skittish. How the hell could he convince her he was only trying to help?

He blew out a harsh breath. Whatever she'd been through had affected her deeply, and it was going to take more than a few days to overcome her fears. He would just have to respect the line she'd drawn in the sand—for now.

Eventually he was going to earn her trust and get her to open up to him. He couldn't keep her safe if he didn't know what—or who—she was running from.

And she was most definitely running. The more he watched her, the more he saw the obvious signs of distress. Dare had been trained to keep a keen eye on his surroundings, but his awareness was nothing compared to Ainsley's. Her eyes never stopped moving, even inside the house. She always had one eye on the window or door, almost like she was waiting for someone to walk through and grab her.

The thought made him sick to his stomach. He wanted to reassure her, promise she would be safe, but she wouldn't believe him. All he could do was wait, give her plenty of time and space to settle in and figure it out for herself.

The moment he stepped into the house, every nerve ending tingled with awareness. Less than a second later, the savory smell hit him full force. Dare toed off his boots, then cautiously made his way through the laundry room and down the hallway to the kitchen. He paused just outside and peered around the doorway.

Everything inside him softened when he spotted Ainsley in front of the stove stirring something in a large pot. Dare took the moment to study her. Her blonde hair had been pulled away from her face except for a rogue curl that hung down the nape of her neck. Her movements were fluid as she opened the oven door to check on what smelled like garlic bread.

Well, she was certainly making herself at home. Dare quietly retreated several steps down the hallway, then opened and closed the door again, this time more forcefully, sending the sound echoing down the hallway. "Ainsley?"

"In the kitchen," she called out.

When he reached the kitchen this time, she stood facing him, her fingers nervously fiddling with a dish towel. "I hope you don't mind," she apologized. "I heard about..."

She trailed off, and her gaze darted away for a second before meeting his again. "I figured you'd had a long day and might be hungry."

His ire from earlier melted away. How could he be upset with her when she'd done something so thoughtful? He was an idiot. She wasn't putting distance between them because she disliked him; she did it to protect herself. Even though he'd just eaten on the way home, he couldn't refuse her offer.

"I didn't realize you'd heard about it." He shot her an apologetic look. "Sorry for bailing on you. I know we were supposed to go into town this morning."

"It's fine," she quickly replied. "You had way more important things to take care of."

"I should have at least left a note. But it looks like you've been finding your way around okay."

A scarlet flush swept over her cheeks. "I promise I wasn't snooping or anything."

A pang moved through his chest at her obvious discomfort. He hated seeing her like this, hated more the person who'd stripped away her confidence. But she'd evidently experienced enough anger for one lifetime; she didn't need it from him too.

Instead, he forced a smile. "I know it's going to take some getting used to—for both of us. But you're always welcome here. I trust you."

Her gaze snapped toward him at that, and she stared at him for several seconds, seeming to weigh his words. Finally she gave a tiny nod. "Thanks."

He moved deeper into the room, intrigued by the delicious scent wafting from the oven. "I didn't know I had any thing edible left in the house. What are you making?"

"Just spaghetti. I found some noodles and a can of tomatoes in the pantry. I figured I couldn't go wrong with pasta."

"You made that from scratch?" he asked as he peered into the simmering pot.

A blush stole over her cheeks. "I just added some spices I found in the cupboard."

Dare pulled out a spoon, dipped it into the sauce, and took a small sip. Flavor burst over his tongue, sending his tastebuds into a euphoric bliss. "That's delicious."

"I'm glad you like it." A slow smile unfurled over her lips, and it hit him like a sucker punch to the gut. The timer went off, and Ainsley turned off the oven before glancing his way. "The bread needs a few minutes to cool down if you want to change first."

"I'll be right back." He hustled upstairs and changed into a pair of sweats and was back less than five minutes later.

On his way back he detoured to check on Sarge and found the dog happily lounging near the lake watching the birds. Dare filled his food and water bowls then carried them out to the patio. Sarge's ears perked up at the sound of the door opening, and he loped toward the house. Dare scratched him behind the ears as he dug into his food, then headed inside for his own dinner.

Ainsley had already set the table, and Dare stopped next to the fridge. "Soda?"

"Water, please. I've probably had enough caffeine today."

Dare made a face. "I haven't had enough. I think I could fall asleep standing up at this point."

Ainsley paused, dish in hand, and turned a pair of concerned eyes his way. "I can leave you alone."

"No." He shook his head. "I'd like you to stay. Please," he said at her dubious look. "We haven't had much chance to get to know one another."

Dare recognized that, while he wasn't in the best headspace after the events of the morning, he needed to reassure her. Besides, he liked having her here. She exuded a quiet peacefulness that made him appreciate her all the more. Right now he just wanted to focus on her and put the murder from his mind for a bit.

He reached for the plate, but she waved him off. "I can get it."

He pulled out a seat and dropped into the chair. "What did you do today?"

"Not much." She loaded up a plate and set it in front of him. "I got some files uploaded and filled out the paperwork for Marley."

Dare picked up his fork, but Ainsley stood there, her gaze riveted on him. He glanced up at her. "Aren't you going to eat?"

"Oh. I... Yeah." Her gaze dropped away and she quickly turned back to the stove. Dare waited until she'd made up her own plate and slid into the seat across from him before scooping up a bite of food. It was just as delicious as he remembered, and he forked up another bite.

Across from him, Ainsley still hadn't moved. He sensed her watching him from beneath her lashes, and the hairs on the back of his neck lifted. Had she done something to the food while he was gone?

His nerve endings prickled and he studied her surreptitiously. She gripped her fork tightly, her body tense. Suddenly it hit him. She was waiting for his approval.

A wave of compassion washed over him, and he gestured toward his plate. "This is the best pasta I've ever had."

He could practically see the tension drain from her body as relief flooded her features. "I'm glad you like it."

She finally scooped up a bite and lifted it to her lips. Dare ripped his gaze away and forced himself to focus on his food. With each passing moment his curiosity about Ainsley's past increased. He wanted to know who'd hurt her. He wanted to make sure it never happened again.

CHAPTER
FOURTEEN

Humming to herself, Ainsley let herself into the house and headed straight for the kitchen. Dare had given her his blessing to come and go as she pleased, and she was in desperate need of coffee this morning.

As promised, Dare seemed to have kept the dog locked up, because there was no sign of him when she entered the kitchen. She'd explored the kitchen a bit yesterday, and she moved from memory, quickly gathering all the necessities to start her coffee.

Turning on the coffee maker, she scooped coffee into the filter, then hit the button to dispense the largest amount possible. Within seconds the hot brew streamed into her cup, the pungent aroma permeating the air.

Dare had rescheduled their shopping trip for this morning, so she pulled a pad of paper from a drawer in front of her and started a list. At the top of the page, she wrote down her favorite creamer and other groceries she wanted to have on hand.

Ainsley planned to cook dinner for both herself and

Dare, at least when he was around. She hated cooking for just one person, and this way, she could stash leftovers and eat in the suite if Dare wanted privacy.

The brewer spit out the last bit of coffee and Ainsley spooned sugar and milk into her cup, breathing in the sweet and savory smell. She took a sip and closed her eyes, humming in pleasure. Turning, she caught sight of a figure in the doorway.

Oh, God. He'd found her.

Coffee sloshed over the rim of her cup, splattering her hand and the tiled floor as her heart lurched into her throat. The mug slipped from her grasp, and it shattered on the floor at her feet.

Almost immediately, she realized the man's build was all wrong. Instead of Joel's trim build, Dare's broad shoulders took up a large portion of the archway. Her heart still hammered in her chest, and her gaze dropped to the mess at her feet.

"Oh! I'm so sorry." She grabbed up the dish towel hanging near the sink and dropped to her knees. "I'll get it cleaned up right away."

Dare took a step forward. "It's—"

"I know. It was all my fault." Tears blinded her eyes as she mopped up the brown liquid. "I can't believe I was so stupid."

He dropped to a knee next to her. "Ainsley."

Her hands shook as she scrambled to pick up the pieces. "I—I wasn't paying attention. I'm sorry, I should have—"

"Ainsley."

She bit her lower lip and fought to blink the tears away

as she continued to gather the splintered porcelain. He was going to send her away. Or worse, he would—

Dare grasped her hands, halting her movement, and every cell of her body seemed to freeze in place as she waited for the inevitable. For several seconds, nothing happened. Finally, she lifted her gaze to Dare. He watched her intently, his expression giving nothing away.

Finally, he broke the tense silence. "Are you okay?"

Ainsley gave a jerky nod, heart still lodged firmly in her throat.

"Don't worry about the mug. I can get a new one. It's no big deal."

She watched as he slowly turned her hands over in his. His thumbs lightly stroked over her knuckles before he released her. "Doesn't look too bad. Run it under some cold water and it should be okay."

He slowly unfolded from the floor then extended a hand her way, and she tentatively slipped her palm into his. He drew her to her feet and she allowed him to pull her toward the sink. He turned on the faucet, checking to make sure the water was cold, before tipping his head her way.

Her hands trembled as she held them under the tap, the cold water soothing the sting of the burn. Ainsley watched Dare in her peripheral vision, but he remained still, watching her.

After what felt like hours, he spoke. "I smelled coffee and came running."

Turning slightly, she met his eyes. Dare gave her a small smile, silently conveying his forgiveness and understanding. Relief rushed through her. "I actually just got here. I was going to do a quick stock check of the fridge before we make our grocery run, if that's okay."

Dare laughed. "You've got a lot to learn about cops. Our diets generally consist of fast food and stale coffee."

Ainsley smiled at his joking tone. "Let me brew up some fresh coffee for you and we can make a list."

Several minutes later, they'd cleaned up the broken mug and Dare was seated at the island, a steaming cup of coffee in hand.

Ainsley added a few last items to her list, then folded it up and tucked it into her back pocket. "Do you need anything else from town? We may as well get everything in one trip."

"Sounds good. Let me grab my keys, then we can head out."

He unfolded from the chair, his large form towering over her. Ainsley swallowed hard, unable to speak over the lump that had formed in her throat. The thought of being trapped in a vehicle with him, completely powerless and at his mercy...

Her lungs felt too tight, and she forced herself to draw in a much-needed breath. Dare was naturally powerful and assertive and, though her heart knew that he was sincere, her mind fought to separate the two. Ainsley wondered how long it would be before he pressed for more details. He was a smart man—he knew she was hiding something. Did she dare tell him? And what would he say?

Dare was different, she knew that, but betrayal was a lesson hard-learned. She couldn't afford to let him in any more than she already had. She'd made the mistake of trusting a man once. She couldn't—wouldn't—do it again.

CHAPTER
FIFTEEN

Dare had always considered himself an attentive man. But the way Ainsley watched her surroundings put him to shame. Her eyes never stopped roving her environment, watching everything and everyone.

Searching for threats? The thought didn't sit well with him. He'd asked her to come into town today to push her a little out of her comfort zone. So far, he wasn't sure if was a good idea or not.

Dare loaded the groceries into the backseat of the truck, then tipped his head toward the plaza. "I need to grab a few things from the drug store, then we can head to the bank."

Ainsley followed a few steps behind as he made his way into the store to pick up some toothpaste and shaving cream. After he'd grabbed what he needed, he made his way to the checkout counter and met her there. Once they'd paid for their items, Dare paused near the door, holding it wide for an older woman entering the store.

Ainsley shifted closer to him to allow the woman to

pass, and he automatically settled a hand low on her back. She stiffened slightly bit didn't pull away, and he bit back a smile as he guided her out of the store and onto the sidewalk. As soon as they were outside, he let his hand drop.

From their left, Dare watched a beige sedan slowly approach, presumably looking for an open parking spot. Bright sunlight glared off the windshield, obstructing the driver's face. Instead of stopping and allowing Dare and Ainsley to cross, the driver continued to creep forward.

Something about the situation didn't feel right. Every cell of Dare's body tightened with warning, and he quickly memorized the numbers on the license plate—just in case. He grabbed Ainsley's arm, shifting her slightly behind him as the car pulled even with them. The passenger side window had been rolled down, and alarm bells began to ring in the back of his mind.

Dare's eyes swept over the man behind the wheel. The driver's hooded black sweatshirt was out of place in the sweltering heat of the summer afternoon, his face obscured by a ball cap and sunglasses. Sunlight glinted off the black object as he lifted his hand toward them, and Dare's heart stopped.

"Get down!" A loud crack broke the stillness of the calm morning just as he threw his weight into Ainsley, forcing her to the ground.

"Fuck!" He let out a terse expletive as a second crack split the air and shattered glass rained down around them.

Ainsley shifted below him, craning her neck toward the car. "Wh—"

"Stay down!" Dare pushed her head back down, tucking her further into the protection of his large body. Tires squealed loudly as the driver took off down the row and turned sharply at the end, heading out of the parking lot. The sedan fishtailed onto the main road, heedless of oncoming traffic, and a cacophony of blaring horns filled the air.

Cries of fear and outrage rose around them, but Dare tuned them out as he shoved to his knees and dug his phone from his back pocket. His pulse thrummed as he dialed the department, and his dispatcher answered a moment later.

He didn't give her a chance to get the full greeting out before he was speaking. "Yvonne, this is Sheriff Jensen. I need you to send all available units down to the plaza. There's been a shooting."

"Copy that, boss," came her no-nonsense reply. "I've got them en route."

"D-Dare..."

He glanced down at Ainsley, who had rolled to her back, her big blue eyes wide and unfocused with shock. A small gash on her forehead sullenly oozed blood and a bright red abrasion marred the right side of her face, covering part of her cheek and temple.

He shifted the mouthpiece to the side as he directed his words to her. "Don't move. Looks like you hit your head when you fell. Does anything else hurt?"

She automatically lifted a hand to her forehead. "I— I'm not sure." She struggled to sit up, then fell to her back once more.

"Just stay where you are," he commanded, flicking a

glance around the parking lot. "The car's gone, but there's glass all over the damn place."

"Dare..."

He continued to scan their surroundings. "Yeah?"

Her features contorted into a grimace. "I think I cut my arm."

His gaze swept over her and the phone fell from his fingers as he seized her left arm, his features twisting into a grimace at the sight of the maroon blood trickling down her bicep. "Shit!"

Glass tinkled and crunched as Dare shifted into a crouch beside her. He reached behind him and grasped the collar of his shirt, then stripped it over his head. He tied the fabric around the wound like a tourniquet, then scooped up the phone. "Yvonne, send an ambulance, too."

He ended the call and shoved his phone into his back pocket before turning his attention back to Ainsley. "Don't worry, looks like the bullet just grazed you."

"*What?*" Her voice rose several octaves, fueled by indignation and bewilderment.

"Hold on, hold on." Dare slid a hand beneath her back and levered her to a sitting position, taking extra care with her arm before placing it gently in her lap.

"Did you see—"

Her words were cut off as a middle-aged man ran toward them. "Hey, are you all right, Sheriff?"

Dare nodded and pushed to his feet. "I think we're both okay, just a little banged up."

The guy scowled. "Who would do something like that?"

Unfortunately, Dare had a pretty good idea. Bending

down to Ainsley, he laid a gentle hand on her shoulder. "You doing okay?"

She struggled to sit up, then shifted her body so she leaned against the building. "I'll be fine."

Dare captured her chin, forcing her to look at him. "Ainsley..."

She shook her head furiously, and he tamped down the frustration that swelled in his chest. He couldn't blame her. She didn't know him well enough to trust him. Yet.

He settled for touching her cheek, just briefly. "All right, honey. As long as you're okay."

His leg was starting to feel the effects of the fall and it was aching like a son of a bitch. He collapsed against the wall next to her, trying to relieve some of the pressure.

Sirens blared out on the main street, and the accompanying blue lights soon came into view as two deputies pulled into the lot and parked along the side. Moments later an ambulance turned into the lot, and the first responders made their way over to them.

Dare glanced at the paramedic. "Thanks for getting here so quick. Looks like the bullet grazed her left bicep. She hit pretty hard when we fell, so we'll need to check for a concussion."

"Yes, sir." Antonio helped Ainsley to the back of the ambulance to begin his ministrations.

Deputy Evan Landry studied him. "You okay, Sheriff? You want them to take a look at your leg?"

"Nah. Just make sure she's good." He regarded the other man. "Car had an Illinois license plate." He rattled off the number. "Beige, older style Chevy."

Landry nodded. "I'll run it as soon as I get back to the station."

Dare made his way to the ambulance where one of the paramedics was loading Ainsley and preparing to transport her to the hospital. Antonio had removed Dare's t-shirt from her arm and replaced it with a temporary bandage.

Dare scooped up the shirt and slipped it over his head, his jaw clenching at the sight of Ainsley's blood streaked across the fabric. He leaned over the gurney and took her good hand in his. "They're going to take you to the hospital."

"Will you... meet me there?" Her voice cracked a tiny bit, and he squeezed her hand tighter. He'd originally thought she might want her privacy, but it was obvious she didn't want to be alone.

"I'm going to ride with you if that's okay. I'll send someone to get my truck later." The look in her eyes told him she'd very much prefer he ride with her, and it made his decision that much easier. Before she could say anything else, he hauled himself into the back of the ambulance and settled in next to her.

CHAPTER
SIXTEEN

Several hours later found them in a partitioned room in Danbury Memorial's ER. Ainsley had a butterfly bandage taped over the laceration above her right temple and her other, smaller scrapes had been cleaned and covered as well.

Unbidden, Dare's hands curled into fists at his sides. He couldn't get the sight of her ragged, torn flesh out of his mind. It replayed on loop over and over, serving only to increase his fury. Thank God she'd taken a step to the side when she had. Just a few inches to the side and the bullet would've pierced her heart instead of grazing her arm.

Dare wasn't a fool; bad things happened everywhere. But this was *his* town. Over the past couple of hours he'd played several possibilities through his mind. It could've been a random drive-by shooting, though he seriously doubted it. The bullet could've been intended for him, but that didn't quite feel right, either. Which left one option: that Ainsley had been the intended victim all along.

His focus returned to Ainsley, who listened intently as the nurse held out a sheet of instructions to care for the wound. "No showers for twenty-four hours, and make sure to check for infection when you change the bandages."

"I appreciate it." She offered a smile that didn't quite reach her eyes.

Dare glanced at the nurse. "Will she be okay?"

"No major injuries, just a laceration along with some bumps and scrapes." The nurse directed his words at Ainsley. "Keep your abrasions covered for the next week or so and you'll be good as new. If you have some at home, Neosporin will help the healing process and minimize scarring."

He turned back to Dare. "Your girlfriend will be fine in a few days, just make sure she takes it easy in the meantime."

He didn't bother to correct the guy and instead offered a small nod. "Thank you."

The nurse smiled. "I'm going to get her aftercare instructions, then you two can get out of here."

Dare thanked the nurse and made sure the curtain was pulled shut before turning back to Ainsley. Her gaze was focused on the industrial-style linoleum floor, and he watched her for a long moment before speaking. She looked utterly calm. Too calm. "You holding up okay?"

She nodded listlessly. "I'm fine."

Stepping forward, right into her field of vision, he squatted in front of her, then waited for her to meet his gaze. She blinked at him, her expression carefully blank, mask back in place. He recognized that look already, and he hated it. "The truth."

She lifted one shoulder. "Just tired. And sore. I'll be okay."

He captured one small hand and drew it between his own. "I know you'll be okay; you're strong," he acknowledged. "But if you ever need anything... I'm here. You can always come to me."

For a moment, her eyes filled with pain so acute that he could feel it as it sliced through his heart. In those bright blue depths, he saw fear and worry and something else he couldn't quite name.

Dare gritted his molars together. Goddamn it. If there was ever a woman who needed support, it was her. He wanted so fucking badly to pull her into his arms and hold her tight. But he couldn't.

Ainsley would never ask for help, and he had a feeling that any sort of physical intimacy—innocent or otherwise —would drive her further away. The last thing he wanted was for her to pull away from him. She was in danger, and he needed to keep her with him, where she would be safe.

He settled for resting one hand on her shoulder and giving her a gentle squeeze. "Everything's going to be okay. I've got my guys working on it. We'll figure out what happened."

As he knew she would, she dabbed at her eyes with her fingers as she leaned away, distancing herself both physically and emotionally.

Despite every instinct screaming not to, Dare allowed her to retreat. For now. There was a lot going on in her head and her heart at the moment, and she needed time to come to terms with all of it.

He pushed to his feet. "We'll get those prescriptions filled on the way home. Then you can get some rest."

She didn't look at him, and Dare's gut twisted. He hated seeing her like this. He hadn't yet brought up the possibility of who might be responsible, and he didn't want to upset the fragile balance they'd achieved.

"I'm going to go wash up. Will you be okay 'til I get back?"

She smiled a little. "Take your time."

In the small bathroom, Dare splashed cold water over his arms, scrubbing away the dirt and grime from the sidewalk, and the small smears of Ainsley's blood that clung to him. A few small scratches stung as he soaped them, but it was nothing that required medical attention.

He gripped the edges of the sink and drew in a deep breath. Ainsley had been through so much, and the last thing she needed was to see the anger simmering just beneath his calm exterior.

He dried his hands and face, then made his way back down the hallway. As he approached Ainsley's room, he moved quietly, not wanting to disturb her if she was resting. He peered around the curtain, and the sight that greeted him stopped him cold.

Ainsley was standing in front of the small mirror above the sink, lifting her shirt to check the bruises along her ribs and back. Dare's breath caught in his throat as he saw the dark, mottled marks that stood out against her pale skin.

A grimace pulled at his lips. She'd apparently fallen a lot harder than he'd initially assumed. As he studied the bruises, he noticed something strange. The marks seemed to be grouped together, placed almost strategically, as if—

Good Christ.

His heart slammed against his ribs. As he looked closer, the suspicion twisting in the back of his mind intensified. The colors were all wrong. These weren't fresh bruises; they were old, faded to a sickening palette of yellow and green.

Rage surged through him as the truth solidified in his mind, hitting him like a punch to the gut. Each mark on her body was a testament of the pain and fear she'd been living with for far too long. Dare dropped the curtain back into place and clenched his fists, tamping down the fury that threatened to erupt.

When he had his emotions firmly under control, he called out softly to get her attention. "Ainsley?"

"Come in."

He forced a smile as he pulled back the curtain and stepped into the room. Ainsley turned to face him, her eyes wide with a mix of embarrassment and fear that she'd been caught.

"I'm surprised the nurse isn't back yet," he said conversationally. "Hopefully we'll get out of here soon so you can go home and rest."

She hesitated for a moment, then nodded. "I hope so."

Dare swallowed hard as he studied her. He wanted to reach out, to comfort her, but he held back, giving her the space she needed.

He busied himself instead with arranging for one of his deputies to bring his truck to the hospital. It was ready and waiting for them a half hour later when Ainsley was finally released. They made a brief stop at the pharmacy to get her prescription filled, then headed out to the parking garage.

Ainsley stuck close to his side as he guided her toward the truck and unlocked the door. Her mobility was hampered by the injury to her arm, so Dare opened the passenger door for her, then lifted her easily into the passenger seat. In this position their faces were almost even. He studied her surreptitiously as he reached across her torso and buckled her into the seat. She twisted her hands in her lap, looking everywhere but at him, and Dare closed the door with a sigh.

He'd give her some space for now, certain that was what she needed. He hoped that once this blew over, she'd come clean with him and tell him the truth.

CHAPTER
SEVENTEEN

As soon as they got home Dare led Ainsley inside the house, then settled her on the couch in the living room and handed her the remote. "I'll get your prescription."

She waved him away. "I'm fine."

"Ainsley..."

"Fine." She rolled her eyes.

He poured a glass of water in the kitchen and took two tablets to Ainsley. He waited until she'd swallowed them down and he set the water on the coffee table. "I'm going to go unload the car. Rest here for a few minutes and let the painkillers start to kick in."

"I can help, it's no big deal."

She moved to get up, but Dare gently pushed her back on the couch. "Nope. You're staying right here."

That stubborn little chin of hers notched up as her lips turned down in a frown, and Dare bit back the urge to smile. She was such an enigma—so independent at times, yet borderline submissive other times.

He gave her his most exaggerated stern expression. "I'll be back in a few to check on you. Don't move."

"Fine." With a huge sigh, Ainsley flopped into the corner of the couch.

He had no idea how she could be so damn calm about everything that had happened today. He felt like his pulse hadn't slowed since the moment he'd seen the gun leveled her way. The memory caused the hairs on the backs of his arms to stand on end, and fury raced through him. He needed to touch base with his men and see if they'd found anything.

After retrieving the groceries from the truck, Dare carried them into the kitchen. He sorted all of the frozen and refrigerated items, tossing several that would no longer be edible.

One hip propped against the counter Dare stared out the window, a dozen scenarios running through his head. Who would shoot at Ainsley, and why? While it could have been random, he seriously doubted it. He knew she was running from someone. Was this the person who'd caused her to flee in the middle of the night?

Needing to check on Ainsley, he headed back into the living room and he stopped dead in his tracks as his gaze settled on her. She was curled up in a tiny ball on her side, sleeping soundly.

Blood thrummed through his body and his chest tightened at the sight of her. Soft afternoon light from the large bay window spilled over her slight form, bathing her in an ethereal glow.

Her cheeks were flushed and her head was turned to the side, partially hiding the bandages covering the abrasions from where she'd scraped the pavement. Her lips were slightly parted, her breathing soft and even. His eyes strayed farther down her body. Her left hand rested on her stomach and the right extended over the edge of the couch, curled slightly in repose.

The fact that she could relax enough to fall asleep after this morning's episode meant that she felt safe here. She trusted *him* to keep her safe. And he would. Whoever the hell was after her would have to come through Dare first, because there was no way in hell he would let this woman be hurt again.

A small movement from Ainsley drew his attention back to her face. Even in sleep she looked disturbed, eyebrows drawn slightly together. Her long eyelashes fluttered several times before finally resting against her cheeks. A shiver racked her body and she curled more tightly into herself, pillowing her hands under her chin.

Dare pulled a fleece blanket from where it was folded at the end of the couch and tucked the soft material around her. She looked so tiny and fragile lying there, and his anger flared anew. How could anyone hurt this woman? The urge to protect her swept through him, sharp and fierce. He wanted to pull her into his arms and promise to shield her forever, but she would never let him.

With one last look at Ainsley, Dare headed down the hall to the office. He settled behind the desk, his gaze scanning the surface. Ainsley had been busy, and it looked like she was settling in well. Paperwork was sorted into neat piles, everything organized and in its place.

He pulled out his phone and hit speed dial, hoping

Cam was available. The lieutenant answered on the fourth ring. "Hey, Boss."

His tone was laced with a combination of exhaustion and frustration that Dare recognized from having worked similar cases. "How's everything coming along?"

"We requested footage from the supermarket but haven't gotten approval yet. Hal Fromeyer is being a dick about it." Cam let out a beleaguered sigh. "We questioned two dozen people, but none of them could remember seeing the driver."

That didn't surprise Dare in the least. Most people tended to ignore their surroundings unless the incident directly impacted them. "So we've got nothing on him yet."

"Nothing conclusive. A few said they noticed he had on a hooded sweatshirt and hat, but with the sunglasses..."

The lieutenant trailed off, and Dare bit back a growl. Someone had to know who the hell it was. "Stay on Fromeyer. If he gives you any shit, let me know. I'll get Judge McCallister to sign off on the warrant."

Some people—men like Hal Fromeyer—would fight law enforcement just because they thought it was within their rights to do so. The asshole was either too stupid or full of himself to realize he was potentially jeopardizing an investigation.

One of the local judges was a good friend of Marley's husband, Troy. Dare was sorely tempted to reach out to the woman tonight just to put Hal in his place.

"Will do. How's Ainsley?"

"As good as can be expected." Dare rubbed a hand along the back of his neck. "She's taking a nap right now."

"Kinley is gonna be pissed when she finds out."

Cam was friends with Ainsley's younger sister, Kinley, and the two spent most of their time together. Dare suspected that, in her early-morning flight, Ainsley had neglected to tell her family and friends of her arrival in Brookhaven.

"Keep it quiet for a bit if you would. I'm sure Ainsley would like to tell them herself."

Cam let out a disgruntled sound on the other end. "I'll try, but you know how fast news travels in this town."

Yeah, he did. That was both good and bad. Maybe word would get back to someone who knew the shooter and they would finally get a lead.

"Let me know if anything else comes through."

Dare hung up and stared at the wall for several minutes, lost in thought. He grabbed his work laptop and pulled up the browser, then typed in Ainsley's name and waited for the search results to populate. He needed to know more about her—where she'd lived, what she'd done for the past few years. Who she'd dated.

He ground his molars together as he skimmed through her information, scrolling back to several years ago. He knew she'd grown up here in Brookhaven, but they'd either never met or she'd left before he moved to town. Most of the documents listed her parents' address here in town. A few showed an address in Minneapolis.

Curiosity piqued, he dug deeper. Dare discovered she attended college in Chicago but had never officially graduated. After she left campus, she seemed to just... disappear. Her name wasn't listed on any official documents, and there was no address listed for the past several years. The puzzle that was Ainsley Layne grew more complex by the minute.

Dare sat back in his chair and contemplated the implications. More than likely she'd lived with someone— probably the person she was currently evading. But who was it?

He recalled the bruises that riddled her body, and he clenched his hand into a fist. Her driver's license was expired, which solidified his theory that whoever the man was, he'd very obviously wanted to control her.

Fury rolled through him. He was going to get to the bottom of this, and soon. Because he'd be damned if he let the man near Ainsley ever again.

CHAPTER
EIGHTEEN

The first thing Ainsley noticed when she blinked her eyes open was the pain—an intense, searing pain that covered her entire body. Her head throbbed as if someone were using it as a makeshift drum, and her muscles felt like she'd been hit by a freight train.

Her eyes closed again of their own volition, and she rubbed her temples, the blood pulsing rhythmically under her fingertips. Every cell of her body ached, and her mind felt foggy.

With Herculean effort, she managed to roll to her back, barely managing to suppress a groan. Her neck was stiff, and she rolled it side to side, trying to relieve the pressure from the tense muscles.

Her skin felt too tight for her body, like it had shrunk around her bones. The fabric of her clothing scraped over her abraded flesh as she stretched, and she hissed out a breath. Her body was covered with a mixture of abrasions and bruises, compounded by the fall she'd taken earlier.

Ainsley managed to raise her head just enough to see

the huge dog curled up on the floor next to the couch, and her heart constricted at the sight. Sarge, sensing she was awake, stood then stretched, and a low whimper escaped her throat.

"Dare..."

Sarge turned to peer at her but didn't move otherwise. They remained like that for several seconds, just staring at one another. Ainsley's pulse raced almost out of control, and her breaths came hard and fast. It was too close.

"Dare!"

The dog cocked his head, then turned and trotted from the room, toenails clicking softly on the hardwood floor. Dare strode through the doorway several moments later, his gaze immediately zeroing in on her. "Hey. You're awake."

He moved forward and settled on the coffee table in front of her. His gaze swept over her face, down her arms and legs, then back up to her eyes. "How are you feeling?"

She grimaced. "Sore."

"I'm sure." He nodded empathetically. "Dinner's almost ready. You can take a couple painkillers after you've eaten."

Her mind latched on to the first part of his statement. "You cooked?"

The corner of his mouth quirked up in a smile. "I'm not completely useless in the kitchen."

Her eyes widened and she sat up straighter, worried she'd offended him. "Oh, that's not—"

"Of course, it's not nearly as good as your cooking," Dare continued, cutting off her protest. "But if you're drugged, maybe you won't notice."

Ainsley stared at him. Why was he doing this—all of this? He'd only known her for a few days, yet he was going out of his way to help her. He'd been by her side practically every minute of the day, keeping a close eye on her and making sure she was safe.

While she appreciated it, she didn't understand his motive. Was he trying to earn her trust so he could reel her in the way Joel had? Or was he truly worried about her? As a police officer, it was his job to take care of people. But he'd taken his duties to a whole new level today. Some of the most influential people hid their true characters behind well-cultivated façades.

Dare's smile faltered when she didn't respond. "Sorry. Cop humor's not for everyone."

"Sorry, I'm still just..." Ainsley shook her head and pushed the dark thoughts away. "My head is a little fuzzy. You didn't have to cook for me."

"You've been through enough today." Dare's piercing gaze met hers. "Making dinner should be the least of your worries."

He leaned closer, his gaze sweeping over her. "Are you hungry?"

"Now that you mention it..." She scooted to the edge of the couch. "I'm starving."

Ainsley pushed to her feet and the room swam before her eyes. Dare was next to her a moment later, one strong hand curled around her elbow. Her first instinct was to pull away, but she stopped herself just in time.

His touch was firm yet gentle, his hold supportive rather than commanding. A dozen conflicting emotions roiled in her stomach. She'd been conditioned to be wary of a man's touch, but with Dare she couldn't seem to summon the same reservation.

Once she'd regained her balance Dare released her, keeping his hands at the ready in case she stumbled again. "You good?"

Ainsley pressed one hand to her temple. "Just got lightheaded for a second."

Dare nodded, concern etched in his expression. "Maybe you'll feel better after you've had something to eat."

He watched her carefully as he shadowed her into the kitchen. Her stomach rumbled as a delectable scent teased her nostrils, and she sniffed the air appreciatively. "That smells good."

"Stir fry." He grinned at her. It's about the only thing I can make without burning."

"You won't hear me complain if it tastes half as good as it smells."

Dare plated up the food and slid it her way. A comfortable silence settled between them as they ate, and Ainsley watched Dare from beneath hooded lashes.

She couldn't quite figure him out. Was he really as kind as he seemed? Or, like Joel, would he pull the rug from beneath her feet once he'd earned her trust?

A memory tickled the back of Ainsley's mind. "Oh!"

She froze, her fork hovering in midair. "I never made it to the bank. I promised Marley I would get over there today. She's going to be so upset."

Dare shot her a bewildered look. "That's the last thing she'll be concerned with. You were shot at. Your safety trumps going to the bank."

Ainsley bit her lip, unease swirling in her stomach. "But..."

"Ainsley." Dare dipped his chin and leveled a look at her. "All that matters is that you're okay. Trust me. I can give her a call if you want me to, let her know what happened."

She barely resisted the urge to squirm under his intense stare. "It's just..." The tortuous admission ripped from her lips. "I really need this job, and I don't want to disappoint her."

His expression immediately softened. "You might be able to set up an account online. Do you want to try after dinner?"

She glanced across the table at him. "You don't mind me using your computer?"

"Of course not. Think of this as your house, too."

But it wasn't her house. Just as Joel's house had never really been hers, either. Though she'd lived there, she'd never been allowed to make any decisions aside from what to make for dinner from his pre-approved list of meals. In the years she'd lived under his roof, he'd never even allowed her to so much as hang a single picture. Joel had hired someone to furnish the home according to his taste, never once asking her opinion. The most say she'd had was in what kitchen appliances she used since she made dinner for him each night.

Ainsley mulled over Dare's offer as she scooped up another bite. She'd lost access to her money once; she wouldn't make the same mistake again. This time she would use a new password—something no one would ever guess. And she wouldn't save it anywhere but in her head.

"If you really don't mind…"

"Take your time." Dare waved her off and she headed down the hallway to the office.

Setting up the account was remarkably easy, but she made a mental note to get new copies of her birth certificate and social security card. She'd had to leave those behind in Joel's safe. He'd refused to give her the passcode, and she had no idea where he'd put the key.

Once she was done, she stood and shook out her hands. Anxiety clung to her, like she was once more a little girl wary of being caught with her hand in the cookie jar.

Ainsley swallowed down the tightness constricting her throat and drew in a deep breath. This was the first step to moving on and putting the past where it belonged. Every step forward, no matter how small, was a victory.

She left the office, scanning for the dog as she retraced her steps through the house. Dare was in the living room watching TV, and she shot him a small wave before slipping out the back door and up to her suite.

Ainsley locked the door behind her then checked the windows before dropping to the edge of her bed. She pulled her cell phone from her pocket and fiddled with it for a moment before pulling up her call log. She tapped the button and held her breath until the call connected.

"Hello?"

Confusion saturated Kinley's tone, and Ainsley couldn't help but smile at the welcome sound of her voice. "Hey, sis. It's Ainsley."

"Oh, my God! Are you okay? Cam said—"

"I'm okay." Ainsley cut her off. "I have a couple scratches, but it's nothing major."

Thank God Dare had been there. If she'd been just inches to the side, she might not be here right now. Her heart raced at the memory of the incident, the events unfolding in startling clarity before her eyes.

She could still hear the sound of people's voices carrying on the air, smell the faint scent of exhaust fumes mixed with grease from the fast food place one block over.

"I was so scared," she admitted.

Kinley was silent for a minute before responding. "Tell me what happened."

Ainsley flopped back on her bed and stared at the ceiling. "It's kind of a crazy story…"

CHAPTER
NINETEEN

Dare pushed from his chair and moved to the glass wall surrounding his office, his gaze sweeping the bullpen. He caught Cam's gaze and tipped his head, indicating for the lieutenant to join him.

He settled behind the desk just as Cam entered the office, and Dare gestured toward the door. Brows drawn, Cam did as requested and closed the door before dropping into the seat across from him. "What's up?"

"Any news on the murder from the park?"

"Not yet." He shook his head. "We're still waiting on the lab results, and no one has identified her yet."

"Keep running down leads." Dare glanced at the woman's picture pinned to the whiteboard. "Someone has to know who she is. Autopsy is scheduled for 2:00. I'll have Doc Seidel send dental impressions to the lab, see if we can ID her that way."

Cam ran a hand over his dark blond hair. "I'll see what I can find in the meantime. I'm going to call around, see if anyone has missing persons matching her description."

"Do that." Dare rested a hip on the corner of his desk. "Where are we on the incident from yesterday?"

"They were able to retrieve a slug from the drug store. It came from a 9mm."

That was promising, at least. "Anything in the system?"

"Not yet." Cam ran a hand through his hair. "We got the footage this morning, too, but it's a clusterfuck."

Dare lifted a brow, and the lieutenant continued, "You described the car in the parking lot as a late-model beige Chevy sedan. The plate on the car is registered to a white BMW."

Dare scowled. It didn't surprise him that the perp had swapped plates, but it made their job that much harder. "Owner?"

"Diana Morris. According to the system the vehicle hasn't been reported as damaged or stolen, so Reed and Forester are on the way to her house as we speak."

"Keep me posted."

"You got it." Cam eyed him shrewdly. "Anything else?"

Dare mulled over his request for a moment before speaking. "I have a favor to ask."

Cam nodded readily. "Shoot."

Dare shot him a look. "This stays between us."

Cam's expression turned wary. "Okay?"

The anger Dare felt yesterday had only compounded over the past twenty-four hours. He was certain Ainsley's ex had something to do with the shooting yesterday morning. He wanted to find the man and nail his ass to the wall, rip him limb from limb for ever daring to lay a hand on Ainsley in the first place.

Dare steepled his fingers as he regarded his lieutenant. "What do you know about Ainsley?"

Cam's face went turned blank as he stared at Dare. "What do you mean?"

A scowl pulled at Dare's lips. "Now's not the time to play dumb. I need to know where she's been the last few years."

"I don't think I ever heard. If Kinley knows, she never said anything. I know she never went to visit her, and Ainsley rarely came home." Cam shrugged. "Apparently she was busy with school or work or whatever and never made it a priority to visit."

The anger simmering in his gut rolled to a boil. "I don't think that's what happened."

Cam's gaze narrowed. "Why?"

"None of this leaves this office," Dare repeated. At Cam's terse nod, he continued. "Ainsley doesn't know, but while we were at the hospital yesterday, I came back to the room just as she was changing. Her back and ribs are covered in cuts and bruises. I initially figured they were from the fall, but these look like they're half-healed."

Cam's expression turned lethal as understanding dawned. "You think he hit her."

It was a statement rather than a question, but Dare nodded regardless. "She showed up at my place just after dawn a few days ago, like she'd literally fled in the middle of the night. She brought almost nothing with her, flinches every time you so much as raise your voice..." He shook his head. "And then she just happened to be shot at yesterday? That's not a coincidence."

"Goddamn it." Cam scrubbed one hand over his face. "Have you asked her about him?"

"No." Dare shook his head. "I worry she'll try to leave if I push too hard."

He told Cam what he'd discovered about the car she'd shown up in and that fact that Ainsley had basically been a ghost for the past few years. "Can you find out where she was living or who she was dating? See if Kinley knows, and I'll work on Ainsley."

Cam's jaw tightened. "If it really is her ex, he might target her family members to get back at her. I don't want Kinley involved in any of this shit."

"I get that." Dare ran a hand through his hair. "Is she seeing anyone at the moment?"

"Not since she broke things off with that tool, Ted."

"What about you? You're with her enough to keep an eye on her, right?"

"Maybe." Cam shot him an unreadable look. "What about you? You gonna take care of Ainsley?"

Dare went rigid. "She's safe enough at my place until we find this guy."

"Uh huh." Cam nodded slowly. "I think we both know that's not what I meant."

A prickling sensation swept up the back of Dare's neck. He knew exactly what his lieutenant was implying. As if it weren't the same thing that had crossed his mind every minute of the past two days. If Ainsley were his...

He shook the thought from his head. Ainsley wasn't his, and she never would be. She'd been through far too much, and she didn't need the added pressure of attraction. "She has nothing to worry about."

His voice was gruff, and Cam pushed to his feet with a little nod. "Shame," he said, pausing next to the door. "Seems like she deserves someone solid after everything she's been through."

He was gone a moment later, the door closing softly in his wake, and Dare dropped his head back. Cam was assuming a lot—like the fact that Ainsley would want to date again, let alone someone like Dare. If he were in her shoes, he probably wouldn't want to get close to anyone again, either.

CHAPTER
TWENTY

Ainsley's ears perked up at the sound of the feminine voice, and she jolted from the chair. She rounded the doorway of the office at a near run and immediately slammed into a huge body.

Her breath momentarily suspended in her lungs, her heart stalling. The fear that rolled through her dissipated as the familiar feel and smell of the man penetrated her brain. "Oh! I'm so sorry."

Dare caught her easily as she bounced off his chest, and he waited until she was steady before releasing her. "No harm done."

Ainsley glanced over his shoulder then back up at his face. He appeared to read her mind because he cracked a smile as he stared down at her. "Your sister's in the living room."

Ainsley couldn't contain the smile that broke across her face at the news. "What's she doing here?"

Dare fell into step next to her as they made their way

down the hallway. "Probably wants to check on you. She and Cam are both here."

Ainsley nodded at the mention of Kinley's best friend, Campbell McCoy, who worked with Dare. Kinley's gaze immediately zeroed in on Ainsley as she approached the living room, and she popped up from the couch. Kinley threw her arms around Ainsley and hugged her tight. She pulled back a moment later and shot Ainsley a concerned look. "How are you feeling?"

"I'm fine. Really."

Kinley released her and dropped back to the couch, shooting a dirty look Cam's way as she did so. "He wouldn't give me any details, and I know you told me everything was okay, but... I wanted to see you for myself."

Cam nodded Ainsley's way. "Glad to see you're feeling better."

"I am, thanks."

Dare gestured with his chin. "We'll leave you ladies alone. I'll be in the office if you need anything."

Ainsley smiled in acknowledgment. "Thanks."

Dare snapped his fingers, indicating for Sarge to follow. The dog lifted his head briefly to send an insouciant look Dare's way, then flopped back down again.

Dare made an impatient sound in the back of his throat. "Sarge."

"He's okay." Anxiety twisted Ainsley's stomach into a knot as she regarded the dog, then Dare. Since yesterday, Sarge had kept her within his sights at all times but hadn't ventured closer. He seemed to sense Ainsley's reticence, and he respected her space while still protecting her. It was oddly touching. "I don't mind if he stays."

Dare flicked a look her way. "You sure?"

"No problem." She forced a smile. It was time for her to get over her ridiculous fear anyway.

"All right. If you change your mind..."

"I won't." She waved off his offer, and the men disappeared. Ainsley turned back toward Kinley only to find her sister studying her intently. "What?"

"Just thinking." Kinley shrugged. "I was a little surprised to hear you were moving back."

Ainsley dropped her gaze away. "I missed it here. And you know I hated being so far away from you guys."

"I'm glad you're home. Have you found a job yet?"

"Actually, yeah. Dare's sister was looking for someone to help with some office work, so he suggested me. It's worked out really well so far. It's not hard work, but it keeps me busy. Plus, any paycheck is better than none at all."

Never again would she rely on a man to take care of her. Even if she eventually married, Ainsley would never allow a man to have full control again. She wanted her own money, her own safety net.

She'd emailed Marley her information this morning so she could set up her direct deposit, and she was ridiculously excited at the prospect of receiving her first check. She would finally be able to pay Dare for the suite and have a little left over to put into savings.

She would eventually need to go back to the bar to get her things, but she had enough now to get by. For now, she needed to lie low just a bit longer. Until Joel stopped looking for her.

"The company is just outside of town," Ainsley

elaborated, "but I work from here. Dare lets me use his office while he's at work."

Her sister nodded slowly. "That's nice of him. Do you rent a room?"

"It's a full suite adjacent to the house. The stairs are out by the patio, so I can come and go as I please. I was worried about the arrangement at first," Ainsley admitted, "but he's been really great."

"That's good. So, what happens when he gets home? Do you go back to your suite?"

"Sometimes." Ainsley shrugged. "Usually we make dinner and we'll talk for a bit before bed."

"Well, he moves quickly," Kinley said dryly, a hint of humor in her tone.

Ainsley felt her cheeks go up in flames. "It's not like that. I'm sure he's just being nice because I'm new. Not new to Brookhaven." She waved a hand in the air. "But you know. Because I'm renting the suite. He's just being... neighborly."

Kinley studied her, the blue eyes so similar to her own seeming to delve deep into her soul. "He does seem protective of you."

Ainsley didn't know how to reply to that. In truth, she'd never felt safer than when she was with Dare. Despite her fear from yesterday, Ainsley knew he would keep her safe. He'd stuck by her side every waking moment, made sure she was taking her medicine and eating to keep up her strength. He'd been absolutely amazing and he put her at ease in a way no one else ever had.

It was strange because he was so intense, his attention like a laser beam focused on her, scanning her every thought. As she had last night, she found herself contemplating what it might be like to have Dare view her not with sympathy, but with desire.

She wanted so badly to ask Kinley for advice, but she bit back the urge. There was no sense in contemplating something that would never—could never—happen.

"Remind me to show you around before you go."

Kinley stared at her for a long moment before accepting the abrupt change of subject. "Sure. So, tell me what happened yesterday."

Ainsley recounted the details of yesterday's shooting at the plaza. "Dare has everyone trying to track down whoever it was, so I'm sure they'll find him soon."

"I'm sure they will," Kinley said. "Do they have any leads yet?"

Ainsley had her suspicions, and she bit her lip. She couldn't reveal the details of her past, even to Kinley. She was too ashamed. "I don't think so. I haven't heard anything yet."

"We've never had anything like that here before." Kinley eyed her for a moment. "It's so strange... Like, the moment you show up, someone shoots at you. I swear, the world is going crazy."

"It is." Ainsley nodded, ignoring Kinley's implication that Ainsley's arrival had somehow precipitated the shooting. There was no way her sister could possibly know about Joel.

She picked at her thumbnail. "They're still trying to figure out exactly what happened. There were a lot of other people around, too, so who knows?"

But no one close to her. The knowledge sent chills

down her spine. Though she'd tried to dispel the thoughts that had plagued her for the past twenty-four hours, she knew... Joel had found her.

And this time, he wouldn't let her go.

CHAPTER
TWENTY-ONE

Dare dropped into his chair. "Got an update for me?"

"With the homicide, no." Cam shook his head. "But Reed stopped by after they visited Ms. Morris's house, so I figured I'd pass it along."

Dare flicked a look at Cam. "They find the car?"

He'd specifically requested to be updated ASAP but hadn't heard anything yet. He was going to throttle Reed if he was withholding information on a case.

"Reed and Forester stopped by her house this morning, but she was out of town. Morris's next door neighbor said she was traveling for work and wouldn't be back until this weekend."

Dare lifted a brow. "We know for a fact she's gone?"

"Yep." Cam nodded the affirmative. "He spoke with her employer, who confirmed that she's currently in San Diego at a conference. She's not due back for another couple of days."

"So someone either stole her plates or swapped them."

Cam grimaced. "Looks that way. They haven't spoken

with Ms. Morris yet, but as soon as they find the car we'll know for sure."

Dare nodded slowly, then tipped his head toward the living room where the two Layne sisters sat catching up. "And Ainsley? Were you able to find out where she's been?"

"Not where, no. Kinley doesn't seem to know exactly where they were." Cam held up a hand at Dare's growl of frustration. "But I did get a name for you."

"You could have led with that, asshole," Dare grumbled.

Cam didn't take offense and instead just laughed good-naturedly. "Yeah, but where's the fun in that?"

His smile dropped away as quickly as it had come. "I think the man you're looking for is Joel Parsons—Dr. Parsons."

A tingling sensation swept up the back of Dare's neck. Ainsley had been covered in bruises that he knew for a fact had been obtained long before the incident at the plaza.

He steepled his fingers and regarded Cam for a long moment. "I don't recall seeing any hospital visits in her file, do you?"

Cam's face was grim. "No. But he's a doctor, so..."

Dare drew in a deep breath. He knew exactly what Cam was implying. If Parsons had inflicted the wounds, he could have mitigated the damaged himself. And even if Ainsley had gone to the hospital to report him, would they have believed her over an esteemed colleague? Doubtful. Dare knew all too well how many of these situations played out, and more often than not they didn't work in the woman's favor.

He cleared his throat, shoving down the fury that had risen at the thought of Ainsley at that monster's mercy. "I think we need to find Dr. Parsons."

"Shouldn't be too hard to find him. If she did leave him..." Cam shook his head. "Shooting at her in a public place is pretty damn extreme, but I can't say it would surprise me."

"Me either. And I have a feeling it's not the first time he's done something like this."

Dare strongly suspected the man had driven Ainsley from her previous residence and followed her to Brookhaven. Good. Better for them to be on Dare's turf. He almost wished the asshole would try something again, but it was too soon.

Unfortunately, there wasn't much he could do at this point. No one had gotten a look at the driver, and the plate was registered to a completely different vehicle. Maybe they would get lucky and get something, but until then he had little evidence to work with.

Dare barely repressed a snarl. "I'm going to make damn certain that prick doesn't get close to her again." He gestured to the computer. "She's working for Marley now, and I told her to use my office. It's easier that way, so I can keep an eye on her."

Cam's lips lifted in a speculative smirk. "I'm sure."

"Not like that, asshole." Dare rolled his eyes even as a surge of desire shot through his chest.

"For what it's worth, I think she likes you."

The force of his words struck him in the heart. Did she? He shook the thought away. Ainsley probably wouldn't have let him within ten feet of her if she hadn't been injured. "She appreciates my help. That's all there is to it," Dare replied flatly.

Cam gave a slow nod. "If you say so. You deserve to be happy, too. I saw the way she looked at you."

Dare's hand tightened into a fist where it rested on the arm of the chair.

"I'm not telling you what to do. I'm just telling you what I see. Maybe there's a reason she's here."

"Yeah," Dare remarked dryly. "She ran from her home in the middle of the night just to see me again."

"Don't be a dick." Cam flipped him off. "Just think about it." Spreading his hands over his knees, he pushed off the chair. "Anyway, I better get Kins out of here before she takes over your house."

Dare chuckled. "If it makes Ainsley feel better, she's welcome to stay."

"Better not take any chances." Cam laughed as he stood, but it had a strained quality to it.

Dare studied him as he pushed from the chair, then rounded the desk. "Maybe you should follow your own advice."

Cam's laser-like gaze slid his way. "Don't know what you're taking about."

Dare nodded and let the conversation drop. It wasn't any of his business what happened between Cam and Kinley.

He followed his lieutenant out of the office, turning Cam's words over in his mind. Did Ainsley actually care for him? He didn't think it was possible. She'd just showed up a few days ago, and their interactions had been limited, not to mention fraught with tension.

Dare fixed his gaze on Ainsley as they entered the living room, his gaze sliding over her pretty features. As if she could feel him watching she turned toward him, and a soft smile curved her mouth.

A vise tightened around his chest and his blood warmed, sliding slow and sluggish through his veins. He meant what he'd told Cam. He would keep her safe. Earn her trust. Be her friend. And if it eventually turned into something more... Well, only time would tell.

CHAPTER
TWENTY-TWO

Both men's heads swiveled his way as Dare strode into the office. Sawyer Reed tipped his head in greeting as he wrapped up a phone call. "Thank you, ma'am. I'll be in touch if we need anything else."

He hung up, then turned his attention to Dare. "Sheriff."

Dare dipped his chin at his newest hire, then gestured toward the whiteboard that took up the wall behind the men. "How are we coming on the homicide?"

"We're not," Cam groused. "We interviewed everyone who was out that morning—all four of them—but no one heard or saw a damn thing. No prints in the system, nothing from the footage. We questioned the drivers who were out that night, but no one saw anything out of the ordinary. The asshole didn't leave a damn thing for us to work with."

Dare glanced back to Sawyer. "What about the car from the drive-by at the plaza? Did you find the owner?"

"Just got off the phone with her, but it wasn't her. She

left the car at the airport Monday morning when she flew out."

He glanced down at a note stuck to the corner of his computer. "The car is located in the Gold Lot, Row J. She didn't have a space number, but it should be easy enough to find."

Dare nodded. "Reed, you're with me today. We're going to the airport."

"Yes, sir." He popped up from his chair and grabbed his phone and keys.

Dare waved for him to follow. "I'll drive."

He glanced toward Sarge who lay sprawled on his pillow beside Yvonne's desk. The dog might as well stay here and get spoiled.

He tipped his head toward his dispatcher. "We'll be back in a bit. Watch him for me, would you? And easy on the treats this time."

The older woman tossed him a sly grin as she reach down to pat the dog. "But he's such a good boy."

Sarge rolled to his back, exposing his belly and Dare rolled his eyes. It was a losing battle; the dog had everyone wrapped around his paw and there was no undoing it now.

Outside, he and Sawyer climbed into the cruiser and headed toward the airport. He glanced over at his new hire. "Settling in okay?"

"So far." The man nodded. "It's pretty quiet compared to my last position."

Dare snorted. That was a huge understatement. Reed had come from Minneapolis where their departments dealt with multiple homicides every day. "This is the first violent death we've had in several years," Dare admitted. "It's not usually this exciting."

"That's okay, I don't mind," Reed replied. "The slower pace doesn't bother me in the least." He gestured toward the fragrant, freshly tilled fields. "Besides, the view is better."

"I'm probably biased," Dare said, "but I'm pretty damn partial to Brookhaven myself."

Sawyer glanced his way. "You live here your whole life?"

"Nah. I took off at eighteen, joined up and put in eight years. Saw enough of the world to hate most of it."

Sawyer nodded in commiseration. "Military will do that to you."

They chatted until they turned into the Gold Lot of the airport, and Sawyer pointed. "There's row J. We're looking for a white BMW."

It wasn't hard to find. Dare pressed a button on his radio to call Dispatch. He rattled off the plate number, then waited for Yvonne to run the information.

After a few minutes, the radio crackled to life. "Sheriff, that license plate is registered to a beige Chevrolet reported missing from Riverside two days ago. The vehicle is marked as stolen."

"Copy that," Dare replied, biting back a sigh. He turned to Sawyer. "We need to check with the airport security to see if they have any footage."

"Good idea. Let's head over to the security office."

They made their way to the airport security office, where they introduced themselves to the head of security,

Carl Thompson. The older man nodded their way. "Afternoon, Sheriff. Lieutenant. What can I do for you?"

"We've found a BMW in the parking lot with plates that belong to a stolen Chevy." Dare explained the situation. "We need to check your security footage to see who tampered with the plates."

Thompson grunted in acknowledgment. "Come on, I'll take you to the surveillance room."

The large room was filled with monitors displaying live feeds from various parts of the airport. Thompson directed one of his staff to pull up the footage from the long-term parking lot.

"Ticket says she clocked in at 5:52. Let's start from there and see if we can spot anyone near the BMW," Thompson suggested.

They fast-forwarded through the footage, watching cars come and go. Several dozen people passed, but none slowed next to the car. After nearly a half hour of scanning, they finally found what they were looking for. A beige Chevrolet pulled into the lot and navigated slowly down the aisle. The timestamp indicated it was shortly after noon three days ago.

Anyone watching would assume the driver was looking for a spot to park, but Dare's nerve endings went on full alert as the car pulled into a spot across the row and parked. A minute later, the driver exited the car and glanced around, checking to make sure the coast was clear.

"Can you zoom in on the driver?" Sawyer asked.

Thompson zoomed in, but the image quality was grainy. On the screen they watched a man wearing a baseball cap and sunglasses make quick work of swapping the plates. Once he was done, he climbed back into the Chevy then disappeared as quickly as he had come, his features obscured by the low resolution of the camera.

Dare bit back a curse. He hadn't truly expected much more than that. "Thanks for your help." He nodded to Thompson as he and Sawyer moved toward the door. "We'll be in touch if we need anything else."

Silence stretched between them as they left the office and climbed into the cruiser. Once inside, Sawyer spoke. "So the guy boosts the Chevy and chooses the airport because there are a thousand cars to choose from. And how many people check their license plates before getting in the car?"

"Pretty much," Dare confirmed. "Probably picked the BMW thinking it was a businessperson who would be traveling most of the week and wouldn't notice right away. He swaps the plates, then leaves. So where the hell is the Chevy now?"

"I'll get a BOLO issued and find out."

CHAPTER
TWENTY-THREE

Dare and Sawyer drove along the winding roads leading to Riverside, the late afternoon sun casting long shadows over the landscape.

Pulling up to a modest house at the end of Maple Street, Dare turned off the engine and glanced at Sawyer. "Let's hope he can give us something to go on."

Sawyer nodded in agreement, opening the passenger door and stepping out onto the gravel driveway. They approached the front door, and Dare knocked firmly. Moments later, a man in his late forties answered, his expression wary. "Can I help you?"

"Mr. Carter? I'm Sheriff Dare Jensen, and this is Detective Sawyer Reed. We need to ask you a few questions about the car you reported stolen."

Carter's shoulders sagged. "I already told the other officers everything I know."

"I understand that," Dare said gently, "but we'd just like to confirm a few things. When did you report the car missing?"

"Three days ago. I called as soon as I realized it was gone. The police came and looked around, said they would look for it." He scowled. "It's been hell the last few days, dealing with the insurance agency and everything."

Dare and Sawyer exchanged a glance before Dare spoke again. "We understand that, Mr. Carter. We actually found the vehicle in question."

"You did? That's great," Carter said, his voice tinged with relief. "When can I get it back?"

"Before we can discuss that, we actually have a few questions for you," Sawyer replied.

Carter nodded. "Whatever you need."

"Sir, can you tell me precisely when you noticed your car was missing?"

"Tuesday morning," he said decisively. "When I got up to leave for work, I noticed it was gone."

"Do you typically park in the garage or outside?"

"In the driveway," the man stated. "My wife and daughter park their cars in the garage, so mine is outside every night."

"And when did you report it stolen?"

Carter's brows drew together. "As soon as I noticed it was gone. Why?"

"We have reason to believe this car was involved in a drive-by shooting recently," Dare cut in.

The man's eyes flared wide. "Oh—Oh, my God!"

"I need any information you might have. Do you know anyone who might harbor ill will towards you or have a reason to use your car for such a crime?"

"A drive-by shooting? N-no, I can't think of anyone.

My life's pretty quiet. I go to work, come home, and that's about it."

Dare studied Carter's face for any sign of deceit but found none. "Are you familiar with a woman named Diana Morris?"

Carter shook his head slowly, confusion evident in his expression. "No, the name doesn't ring a bell. Who is she?"

"She's connected to the case we're working on," Dare replied, jotting down Carter's responses. "It's crucial we find out how your car ended up at the crime scene. You sure there's no one you can think of who might want to set you up or use your car?"

Carter shook his head, eyes wide, his expression adamant. "Honest, Sheriff. I don't know anyone who would do this."

"We're hoping you might have seen or heard something unusual around the time the car went missing."

"Not that I can remember. Like I said, I noticed it was gone early Tuesday morning, but I don't remember seeing or hearing anything unusual during the night."

Sawyer took a small step forward. "Did you notice anyone hanging around the neighborhood recently? Maybe someone who didn't belong?"

Carter shook his head. "No, nothing like that. It's usually pretty quiet around here. You may want to talk to my neighbors, though. Maybe they saw something I missed."

Dare nodded, appreciating Carter's cooperation. "Thank you. I'll do that. And if you remember anything, no matter how insignificant it might seem, please contact me immediately."

Leaving Carter with his information, Dare moved toward the neighboring houses, Sawyer by his side. "You take this side. I'll question the others."

Dare crossed the street and knocked on the door of a small yellow house with peeling paint. An elderly man answered the door a moment later. Dare posed his questions, but the man hadn't seen anything strange. Dare thanked him and moved on.

The first few houses he visited yielded no new information. Most of the neighbors were either not home or hadn't seen anything out of the ordinary. As he approached the last house on the block, an older woman answered the door.

"Good afternoon, ma'am," Dare greeted her with a warm smile. "I'm Sheriff Jensen. I'm investigating a car theft that happened a few days ago. Did you happen to see or hear anything unusual?"

The woman, Mrs. Hendricks, thought for a moment. "I did hear some noise late Monday night. I remember because it woke me up. Sounded like a car door slamming and then an engine starting. I didn't think much of it at the time."

Dare took notes. "Did you see anyone, or perhaps notice which direction the car went?"

Mrs. Hendricks shook her head. "I'm sorry, dear. I just heard the noise. By the time I got to the window, it was quiet again."

He thanked Mrs. Hendricks and crossed over to where Sawyer stood next to the cruiser. "You get anything?"

"Nope."

"Me either." Dare sighed as he slid behind the wheel and started the engine. "Not much to go on."

"Maybe not," Sawyer agreed, "but at least we know when the car was likely taken. It's a start."

CHAPTER
TWENTY-FOUR

Dare had just rinsed the last dish and set it aside when a soft buzzing drew his attention. He dried his hands on a towel then scooped up Ainsley's phone.

"Ainsley, phone call."

Hearing her name, she darted into the kitchen from where she'd been working in the office. He extended the phone her way, and a bright smile lit her face when she saw Tess's name. She answered quickly, bringing the phone to her ear. "Hey, Tess! How are you?"

He watched surreptitiously, observing the interaction. He'd recognized the woman's name the moment he saw it pop up on the screen. This must be the same Tess related to the older woman whose car Ainsley now drove. Judging from the exuberant look on her face, the two of them were close.

Would Ainsley be so upbeat if she'd stolen a car from the woman's mother? He seriously doubted it. Every thought that moved through Ainsley's head flashed across her face like a light-up billboard. She wasn't a good enough actress to pull off that kind of deception.

A twinge of guilt moved through him. He regretted doubting her in the first place, but there was much more to the story that he didn't know yet, and he needed to get to the bottom of it.

"Hello?" She waited a beat, then pulled the phone away from her ear and looked at the screen again. Dare watched as Ainsley's brows drew together in confusion.

"Everything okay?" he asked.

Ainsley looked up at him and lifted one shoulder. "The call must have dropped."

He slid into a stool across from her. "Maybe it was a bad connection," he suggested. "Why don't you try calling her back?"

Ainsley nodded as she dialed Tess's number and turned on the speakerphone function. It rang several times before someone picked up. This time, instead of silence, the faint sound of breathing came from the other end. It was slow, deliberate, and the sound sent chills down Dare's spine.

"Tess?" Ainsley's gaze darted up to Dare, her voice tinged with worry. "Can you hear me?"

The breathing continued, but there was no other response. Suddenly, the call dropped and the screen returned to the home page. The hairs on the backs of his arms stood on end.

Ainsley turned her big blue eyes up at him, a question he didn't want to answer in the depths. Before she could ask, Dare forced a smile that he was far from feeling. "Sounds like a bad connection. Sometimes service is spotty out here by the lake. It cuts in and out from time to time."

She nodded, not appearing convinced by his explanation.

"Is Tess a friend of yours?" Though he already knew the answer, he wanted to hear it from her.

She nodded. "We've known each other since college. We kind of... lost touch for a few years," her gaze darted toward the wall as she spoke, "but we reconnected recently."

"I don't think I recognize her name. Is she from around here?" Dare prodded.

He watched as Ainsley swallowed hard and drew in a fortifying breath. "No, she lives a couple hours away, near St. Cloud. She's a good friend. Always looking out for me." She smiled a little and gestured toward the front of the house. "She even let me borrow the Honda to drive for a bit."

"That was nice of her." Dare's heart rate kicked up. Finally, they were getting somewhere. "Tess lent you her car?"

"It's actually her mother's car." Ainsley looked down at her hands, twisting the fabric of her sweater nervously. "My car... wasn't running, and I didn't have the money to get it fixed. Tess understood and helped me out."

Dare's suspicion grew. There were gaps in her story that he couldn't ignore, but he decided to press gently. "What happened to your car?"

"It just stopped working," Ainsley said quickly, avoiding his gaze. "Tess's mom passed away several months ago, so Tess offered to let me use it until I could sort things out."

Dare leaned back, his eyes never leaving her face. He

could tell she was holding something back, but pushing her too hard could make her retreat further. "I'm glad everything worked out."

Ainsley nodded, her expression still tense. "Me, too."

Dare pointed to the cell phone. "Maybe it's a tower issue or something. Try her again tomorrow and let me know if you're still having trouble reaching her."

She shot him a bland smile that didn't reach her eyes. "Thanks. I think I'm going to head to bed."

Dare's gaze sharpened on her as she fidgeted with her keys for a moment. "I was going to let Sarge out anyway. Want me to walk you out?"

Her teeth sank into her bottom lip and her gaze darted away before she finally shook her head. "No, thanks. I'll be fine."

Dare watched her go, a prickly sensation sweeping up his spine. One way or another, he was going to find out what was really going on.

He just hoped it wouldn't lead to more trouble for Ainsley.

CHAPTER
TWENTY-FIVE

Ainsley's revelation the night before sat in his gut like lead. Now that she'd admitted that Tess had allowed her to borrow her deceased mother's car, he felt a little better.

At least Ainsley had someone to look after her. But the fact that Tess hadn't returned his call from last week bothered him. Coupled with the fact that the call last night had come from Tess's phone but they'd never spoken with the woman directly, it didn't bode well.

Anxiety churned in his stomach as he looked up her information. There was nothing listed in the database, but that didn't mean anything. His instinct told him something wasn't right. Dare dialed the woman's number and waited impatiently as it rang. His unease grew with each grating ring of the phone until it finally rolled over to voicemail.

Double checking her address, he called the local police in her area and explained his concerns. The patrolman promised to do a well check, then advise what they found.

Dare pushed from his chair, grabbed up his keys and

phone, then headed outside, leaving Sarge with Yvonne. The autopsy was complete, and he was champing at the bit to see the results.

Thirty minutes later, Dare exited the highway and pulled up to the building housing the Burnett County Medical Examiner's office several minutes later. Inside, he greeted the receptionist and made his way down the hallway toward the morgue.

Dr. Seidel nodded at Dare as he entered. "Sheriff. Let me get our Jane Doe."

He stood from the computer where he'd been inputting data and moved to the small freezer where the body was stored. A moment later, he rolled out the table and flipped on the light overhead for better visibility.

"What's COD?"

Seidel pointed to a collection of fibers. "Pulled those from her airway. Official cause of death is asphyxia. Fibers are small and white, probably cotton or something similar, but I can't say for sure until we have them processed. I lifted a few hairs, several of which are probably hers, but also a few shorter ones. We'll see what the lab comes back with."

He lifted the woman's hand from the table. "Mild abrasions around her wrists indicate she was bound at the time of death. I checked under the nails, but they appear to have been freshly groomed."

Dare bobbed his head in acknowledgment. No big surprise there.

"As we suspected, there are signs of sexual assault."

"Semen?"

Doc Seidel shook his head. "Unfortunately, no. But

there are definite signs of trauma, bruising to the vaginal walls."

Dare grimaced. "What the hell is wrong with people?"

The ME leveled him with a look. "It gets worse."

Dare braced himself as the doctor cleared his throat. "Whoever killed her wanted to make sure any evidence linking back to him would be eliminated. He—or she—cleaned up after themselves. I found traces of bleach in her throat and vagina."

Dare couldn't stop the forceful shudder that racked his body as he snapped toward the doctor. "Jesus Christ."

"I know." The doctor looked sick himself. "I've heard of it, but to see it firsthand..." Dr. Seidel shook his head. "I lose faith in humanity a little more every day."

It was a sentiment Dare agreed with wholeheartedly. "Were you able to find anything else?"

"Unfortunately, no. I'll send over my report by tomorrow."

The doctor shook his head, and Dare pursed his lips. He'd pull some of the old missing person's reports for young blonde women within the last year and check for any similarities in the cases. "I appreciate it. And if anything else jumps out at you, let me know ASAP."

"Will do."

Dare made his way to his car, his mind whirling with possibilities as he left the ME's office.

His phone rang, tearing him from his thoughts. He quickly glanced at the strange number, a sense of foreboding slithering through him.

"Sheriff Jensen," he said.

"Sheriff, this is Clint Montgomery from St. Cloud PD. We checked on Tess Newman, like you asked."

Dare felt his stomach tighten. "And?"

Clint took a deep breath. "I'm sorry to report, Sheriff. We found Tess Newman dead in her home. The place was completely tossed, and there were clear signs of a struggle."

Dare closed his eyes, taking a moment to process the information. "Damn it," he muttered under his breath. "Any leads on who might have done this?"

"We're still investigating," Clint replied. "At this point, it looks like a burglary gone wrong. Maybe the perp didn't expect her to be home."

"I seriously doubt that," Dare's replied. "Last night, Ainsley Layne received a call from Tess's phone."

He briefly explained what he'd overheard, and what had precipitated Ainsley's arrival the previous week. "Ainsley leaves him, then her friend turns up dead? I don't think this is a coincidence."

"We'll dig into Joel's background and see what we can find," Clint replied, his tone hard. "Do you have any additional information on him that might help?"

"Unfortunately, no. Just speculation," Dare said, frustration saturating his tone. "He's a respected surgeon, practically a pillar of the community. Everyone who works with him seems to like him, but something about him just doesn't feel right."

"We'll make sure to look into him," Clint reiterated. "If he's involved, we'll find out."

"Thanks, Clint," Dare said. "And please, keep me updated on any developments. I need to make sure Ainsley stays safe."

"You have my word, Sheriff," Clint assured him. "We'll get to the bottom of this."

"Appreciate it," Dare said. "And, Clint, I know this is asking a lot, but I need to know everything as soon as you find it. Ainsley's been through enough. She can't handle any more surprises."

"Understood, Sheriff," Clint said. "We'll keep the lines of communication open. You'll be the first to know if we uncover anything."

"Thank you," Dare said, dread sitting like lead in his stomach. "I'll be in touch."

As Dare ended the call, he leaned back in his chair, his thoughts racing. He had to protect Ainsley and ensure that justice was served for Tess. Joel wouldn't get away with this. Not on his watch.

CHAPTER
TWENTY-SIX

She knew something was wrong the moment she laid eyes on him. Her heart tumbled into her stomach, and her words jammed in her throat as she stared at Dare's stoic expression.

He paused in the doorway, his face inscrutable as he studied her. "Ainsley... I need to tell you something."

It felt as if a vise had clenched around her lungs, making it hard to breathe. Something had happened, something bad. She had just spoken to Kinley yesterday. Had something happened to her parents? Was it Brynlee?

"My family," she managed to choke out. "Are... Are they okay?"

Dare gave a tiny nod and stepped farther into the room, closing the distance between them. "Your parents and sisters are fine as far as I'm aware."

Still, the tension pulling at his features didn't abate, and her pulse kicked up. "What is it?"

The sympathy in his gaze tore at her soul, and his next words ripped at her heart. "It's about Tess."

Oh, God. Ainsley pressed one hand to her chest. "What happened? Is she hurt?"

She should have known something was wrong when she got that phone call last night. She blamed it on the connection, but now she had a horrible feeling that wasn't it at all. What if Tess needed her help and Ainsley hadn't been able to reach her?

"Where is she? I need to see her."

Dare took another tiny step forward and shook his head. "Someone broke into her house. It looks like she was sleeping at the time."

Ainsley blinked at him, not comprehending the strange undercurrent of his statement. "So she scared them off?"

Dare stared at her for a long moment before shaking his head again. "I'm sorry. She didn't make it."

"No." Ainsley shook her head. Everything inside her revolted at the thought. "That's impossible. She just called. I just talked to her."

"You never actually heard her voice," Dare said softly.

Ainsley refused to believe it. "No. You're wrong. I'm going to call her right now. You'll see."

"Ainsley..."

"No!" She grabbed up her phone and dialed Tess's number. She kept her eyes glued on the screen, heart pounding furiously as she waited for the call to connect. Before it even had a chance to ring, Tess's voicemail message kicked on.

Ainsley stabbed the button to end the call, then redialed, fingers shaking uncontrollably. It immediately rolled over to voicemail.

"I'm sorry," Dare repeated softly.

The room swam before her eyes, and it felt like the floor had dropped out from under her feet. The phone slipped from her fingers and she grabbed the edge of the desk as she fought to stay upright. Dare's strong hands wrapped around her biceps.

"No." She pressed her hands against his chest. "She can't be gone. She..."

Her voice cracked, and Dare eased her closer. "I'm sorry, honey. I wish I was wrong."

Ainsley closed her eyes against the scalding tears and allowed herself to lean into Dare's solid body. He didn't say anything else. He just wrapped his arms around her and gently stroked her back, holding her as she cried.

Ainsley wasn't sure how much time passed as they remained that way. Her eyes and throat burned, and she felt numb from the top of her head all the way down to the tips of her toes. Her muscles felt leaden as she peeled away, extricating herself from Dare's grasp.

She kept her chin down as she swiped away the moisture that clung to her cheeks. "Thank you for telling me."

She stood there for a moment, unsure what to do now. She still couldn't believe it, didn't want to believe it was real. But Dare had no reason to lie to her, and he would never have told her unless he was absolutely certain.

"Do you want some coffee? I might have some tea somewhere..."

She hated the pity that underscored his softly spoken words. Ainsley shook her head. "No, thanks. I just... I need a few minutes to... process everything."

Dare hesitated for a long moment before nodding. "If you need anything, I'll be right here."

"Thanks." She forced a smile she didn't feel and woodenly made her way out of the house and up to the suite.

Tears blurred her vision once more as she flipped the lock into place, then crossed to the bedroom. She didn't bother to kick off her shoes or undress. She just curled up and let the tears come once more.

Ainsley jerked awake, her eyes flying wide. They felt gritty and sore, and it took a moment for her vision to adjust. Day had given way to night, the dark lapis of evening sky visible through the window. She blinked again and stretched, every muscle protesting violently.

Memories from earlier came flooding back, and she flopped back to the bed, squeezing her eyes shut. Poor Tess. She still couldn't believe her best friend was really gone.

A soft knock came from the direction of the front door and she jackknifed to a sitting position, heart leaping into her throat. Had Joel come for her too?

She shook the thought away. She was being ridiculous. Joel couldn't get to her; Dare wouldn't let him get close.

She slipped off the bed and padded toward the small kitchen area. She glanced out the window just in time to see Dare turn and head back toward the stairs. Ainsley rushed toward the door and yanked it open. "Dare?"

One foot on the first step, he paused turned at the sound of her voice. "Hey. Sorry if I bothered you."

"You didn't." She cocked her head. "Did you need something?"

"I just came to see if you'd eaten yet."

He didn't mention Tess, and for that she was grateful. She wasn't ready to analyze her feelings just yet. "I'm not sure I can eat anything," she replied honestly. Her stomach still felt like it was tied in one giant knot.

"I made soup," he said quietly, his gaze roving over her face. "I can bring some up if you'd like."

She deliberated for a moment before nodding. "Actually, I'll come down if you don't mind."

Right now she didn't want to be alone. She took a moment to lock up, then followed Dare downstairs.

"Can you grab us something to drink?" he asked once they'd entered the kitchen.

Dare moved away to fill two bowls with fragrant soup, and Ainsley's stomach rumbled. Even if she didn't quite feel up to eating, her body needed the nutrients. They sat at the table and tucked into their food, a comfortable silence settling over them.

Ainsley glanced at Dare from beneath her lashes. He was so different from her ex. She was touched that he'd come to check on her and had been concerned enough to make her dinner. Even now he was caring for her, though he tried not to be obvious about it. She could feel him watching her when she wasn't looking, his intent gaze sliding over her from head to toe.

For a moment she wished he was watching her not because she was injured, but because he truly cared about her. It was irrational, but a small sliver of her wondered what it would be like to be with a man like Dare. He was solid and steadfast, and he cared deeply for those close to him.

She bit back a sigh. It didn't matter how she felt. She was not only his tenant, but now he viewed her as a victim. She hated that. She hated feeling broken and helpless.

Joel may have stripped her independence away, but this would be a fresh start for her. From now on, nothing and no one would hold her back.

CHAPTER
TWENTY-SEVEN

The time for truth was now.

"Ainsley." Dare dipped his chin and narrowed his eyes at her, willing her to come clean. "I need you to tell me what's going on."

She licked her lips, her shoulders curling inward. "It's nothing, really. I—"

"I know about Joel."

She flinched slightly, her gaze dropping away. Still, she didn't say a word, and the silence grated on Dare's frayed nerves. "I can't help you if you don't talk to me."

She needed help and, quite frankly, he didn't give a damn if he hurt her feelings as long as she was safe. "Did he come after you? Is that why you came back here?"

With a heavy sigh, she turned back toward him and met his eyes. "I'm not sure."

Her fingers curled into the hem of her shirt, nervously twisting the material as she spoke. "I never actually saw him, but... I have good reason to believe it was him."

Striving for patience, Dare nodded slowly. "Why don't you start from the beginning?"

"I..." She swallowed hard, her gaze dropping to the table. "We met in college. He got an offer in Minneapolis and... I followed him. After we moved, things changed. He didn't want me to go to school or work. Wouldn't let me have a car or cell phone. One day..."

Her breath hitched, and Dare's hand curled into a fist.

Her gaze darted up to him before sliding away again, and she licked her lips. "I... couldn't stand it anymore, and I left. Tess called an Uber for me, and I went to her place. That's when she let me borrow her mother's car."

Her eyes glazed with tears at the mention of Tess, and she hastily swiped them away. "I couldn't stay there. I didn't want to put her at risk."

Her voice cracked at that, sending a pang of regret through Dare's chest. He was sorely tempted to stop her, but she continued. "I drove until I found a small town in the middle of nowhere. I asked around and found a bar looking for a waitress. Marv, the owner there, let me move into the apartment over the bar."

Her expression tightened a fraction as she continued, "Everything was fine at first. Then I started having these feelings like I was being watched. That night at the bar... I knew he was there. I knew he'd found me. So I did the only thing I could think of and came here."

Dare remained quiet, taking a moment to process everything. Where was the asshole now? And when would he show up? Because Dare had watched this same situation play out time and time again. It wasn't a matter of whether Joel would come looking for her, but when.

Apparently he'd been quiet far too long, because she bit her lip and pushed back her chair.

"I'm really sorry." She swallowed hard as she stood and threw an apologetic glance his way. "I'll understand completely if you don't want me to stay."

"You're not going anywhere." It was evidently the wrong thing to say, because Ainsley's eyes flared with fear and she pulled back a bit. He quickly amended his statement to allay her anxiety. "You're safer here than you will be anywhere else. He didn't follow you, did he?"

Ainsley shook her head and some of the tension melted from her body. "No, I don't think so. I didn't see any familiar cars behind me."

"Is he dangerous?"

"He's a little... protective."

Dare raised an eyebrow at that. Typically, *protective* was code for *possessive*. Some men went crazy when their women left, taking a personal affront to it, and it sounded like her ex was just that type. The asshole was pissed that she'd left, and he'd resorted to intimidation tactics, hoping to scare her into coming back. Her behavior made complete sense now.

"Are your things still at his house?"

Ainsley shook her head. "I took what I needed. I don't want anything else from him."

"Ainsley—"

"No." She drew in a deep breath. "He liked to buy me things. After... After we fought."

Dare briefly closed his eyes as pure, unadulterated rage washed over him. Oblivious to his inner turmoil, Ainsley spoke, her voice soft. "I sold off some of the designer stuff and hid the money away. I did that for about a year and a half. I was so scared he'd find out, but I had to do it. It was better than the alternative. And it wasn't much, maybe a couple thousand dollars. Just enough so that I could get away."

A sudden calm descended over him. Those things were better left in the past. Dare would buy her whatever she needed, use every connection he'd ever made to ensure she never had to go through something like this ever again.

He wasn't even sure he wanted to know the answer, but the words slipped out before he could stop them. "What made you leave?"

She was silent for so long he thought she might not answer him. Finally, she sighed. "The very last argument we had was over a pair of pants. He was looking for a specific pair of dress slacks, but they were still in the laundry. I was trying to hold off until I had a full load to wash so it wouldn't be wasteful, but he would've been upset either way, I guess."

She shrugged nonchalantly, but the torment in her eyes tore at his soul. "But that morning after breakfast he went upstairs to get dressed and couldn't find them. He flipped out, started screaming and throwing things..."

Her voice trailed off, and Dare studied her as her gaze took on a faraway quality. Her hands ran briskly over her arms to ward off the goosebumps that had popped up at the memory. A wave of fury threatened to consume him, beaten back only by Ainsley's soft voice as she continued.

"After he left, I cleaned up the mess and showered. I got dressed, packed a small bag of clothes, and reached out to Tess."

She picked at her thumbnail. "I even made his favorite dinner before I left so he wouldn't think anything was out of the ordinary when he got home. I wanted to put him off until the last possible moment. I thought I'd gotten away with it... Until I found the roses in the apartment."

At Dare's questioning glance, she elaborated. "He always brought home red roses after a fight."

Dare barely repressed a groan. The roses. No fucking wonder she'd looked terrified when he'd shown up with them. "I'm so sorry. I had no idea. No wonder you threw them away."

She blushed furiously. "I'm sorry. I—"

"No need to apologize." He held up a hand to stall her. "Lesson learned. No more roses."

She offered a little smile, but it slipped away again almost immediately. "It was late when I finished my shift, around 3 or so, when I went up to the apartment and saw a huge bouquet sitting on the counter. I didn't even go inside. I just hopped in the car, stopped at a WalMart on the way, and... came here."

"You'll be safe here, I promise. I won't let him bother you."

Ainsley searched his eyes as if weighing his words. Finally, she nodded. "Thanks."

Dare nodded. "Speaking of, we should go back and get your stuff soon so you have it."

"Oh, it's okay," she replied. "Marv will keep an eye on the place and let me know when it's safe to come back and get my things."

He lifted an eyebrow. "*We* can go when you're ready. You're crazy if you think I'm going to let you go alone."

She flushed. "You really don't have to do all this. It's... too much."

The woman triggered every one of his protective instincts and Dare fought the urge to pull her into his arms. "No, Ainsley, I really do. You deserve to be taken care of, and I'll do everything in my power to keep you safe."

CHAPTER
TWENTY-EIGHT

Dare strode up the bricked pathway leading to the stately colonial house, its white columns and pristine façade giving it an air of timeless elegance. The lawn was meticulously kept, and the landscaping was immaculate, the flowers expensive and well-groomed, not a single weed to be seen.

Beside him, Cam made a little sound in the back of his throat. "Not a thing out of place."

Dare had the same thought. He punched the button to ring the bell, and they waited. The chirping of birds and the distant hum of a lawnmower filled the silence, grating on his nerves.

His heart rate ratcheted up at the sound of approaching footsteps, and a moment later the front door swung open. Dr. Joel Parsons stood there, his expression morphing from curiosity to recognition and concern as he saw the uniforms. "Can I help you?"

Dare dipped his chin. "I'm Sheriff Jensen with the Brookhaven Sheriff's Office. This is Lt. McCoy."

Parsons's expression didn't change. "What brings you by?"

Cam gestured to the house. "Do you mind if we come in for a minute?"

Parsons stepped aside to let them in, and they entered the spacious foyer, the cool air a welcome relief from the May heat outside. Paintings of serene landscapes adorned the walls, and the scent of fresh roses permeated the air.

Ainsley's admission flashed in his mind, and Dare's stomach roiled. His fist clenched of its own volition, and he forced his muscles to loosen, swallowing down the urge to wrap his hands around the man's neck.

"Dr. Parsons, we have some news to share," Dare began, his voice steady despite his inner turmoil. "Your ex-girlfriend, Ainsley Layne, was shot at in the parking lot of the grocery store in Brookhaven."

Joel's eyes widened, genuine shock washing over his face. "My God, is she okay?"

"She was treated and released at the local hospital," Cam assured him. "But, as I'm sure you understand, this is a very serious situation. We need to know if you have any information that might help us."

"I haven't seen Ainsley for weeks." Joel ran a hand through his hair, exhaling slowly. "Not since she broke things off."

He was a good actor, Dare would give him that. "Have you spoken with Ms. Layne recently?"

"Unfortunately, no. I came home from work one day and found her bags packed by the door. She told me she wasn't happy anymore and that she needed some space. I...

I thought about reaching out to her, but I wanted to respect her wishes."

Liar. Dare bit his tongue to keep from calling the man out as he continued, "I blame myself for that. I've been so busy recently, and..." He glanced up at Dare with a shrug. "Well, I'm sure you know what it's like. Ainsley must be terrified. I should reach out to her."

Not on his life. Dare was certain Joel was fishing for information, but he'd be damned if he would indulge the asshole. "Did she mention where she was going?" Dare asked, ignoring the man's implication.

"No, she didn't," Joel replied, shaking his head. "We agreed it was best not to stay in touch. She wanted a clean break."

Every cell of Dare's body vibrated under the fury coursing through his body. Before he could say anything else, Cam cut in. "Are you familiar with Ainsley's friend, Tess Newman?"

Joel's brow furrowed in confusion. "Detective Montgomery stopped by to ask me the same thing. He said she'd recently been in contact with Ainsley and thought she might have some insight. Apparently she hasn't updated her address yet."

He glanced up at Dare, who stared back silently. On the off chance the asshole wasn't responsible for the shooting, he now knew she was back in Brookhaven. Dare wasn't going to give him anything else to use against her.

Undaunted, Joel continued, "I'm sorry to hear about the woman's death, but I'd never heard of her until the detective mentioned her."

"She was a close friend of Ainsley's," Dare said. "We're

trying to piece together if there's any connection between the two incidents."

Joel's face was a mask of concern and puzzlement. "I wish I could help more. I'm truly sorry for what happened to Ainsley and her friend."

"We appreciate your cooperation," Cam said, his tone deceptively conciliatory. "Would you be willing to provide your schedule for the past week, particularly during the time of the shooting?"

"Of course." Joel nodded, moving towards a sleek glass console table. He retrieved a tablet and pulled up his calendar. "I had surgeries scheduled all day. You can check with the hospital; they'll confirm I was in surgery during that time."

Dare took note of the times. "Thank you, Dr. Parsons. This will help us narrow down our search."

Joel emailed over a copy of the schedule, his expression earnest when he spoke. "I want to help in any way I can. Ainsley and I may not be together anymore, but I still care about her."

Dare was certain of that. Joel cared about getting her back, and he would stop at nothing to accomplish it.

"We appreciate that," Cam said, exchanging a glance with Dare. "If you think of anything else, anything at all, please contact us immediately."

Joel nodded, accompanying them to the door. "I will. And please, keep me informed about Ainsley's condition."

"Sure thing," Dare lied. He turned toward the door then paused, his gaze drawn to a handbag hanging on a hook on the wall behind the door. Ainsley's?

Joel's expression slipped the tiniest bit as Dare glanced over at him. "That belongs to a... friend."

Dare smiled benignly, gritting his teeth as the obvious lie rolled over him. The sun was beginning its descent, casting long shadows across the yard as they stepped out onto the porch.

"Thank you for your time," Cam added, giving Joel a reassuring nod before they made their way back to their cruiser.

As they drove away, the house growing smaller in the rearview mirror, Dare spoke. "What do you think?"

"He seemed genuine," Cam replied, tapping his fingers on the dashboard. "But something doesn't sit right with me about this whole thing."

"Me either," Dare agreed. "Let's keep digging. Someone has to know more than they're letting on."

Joel Parsons had secrets, and it was only a matter of time before they uncovered them.

CHAPTER
TWENTY-NINE

A quick triple knock drew Dare's attention to Cam, who stood in the doorway. He lifted his chin in greeting, and the lieutenant strode toward him, a sheaf of papers in hand.

"The lab results from the autopsy just come back." He passed the report to Dare, then dropped into the chair across from him. "Name's Jayla Simms, twenty-six, from Milaca."

Dare shot him a questioning glance. "Where is that?"

"Just across the border. A little over an hour away."

Dare's computer dinged with the arrival of an email, but he ignored it. "What else do we know about her?"

Cam leaned back in the chair. "She was reported missing ten months ago when she didn't show up for work."

He nodded and silently perused the report, his mind whirling. How did the woman end up in Brookhaven—and why now?

"I've contacted the locals over in Milaca," Cam

continued. "They're going to apprise the family so they can handle burial arrangements. I've requested a copy of the original report, so I'll see if we get any leads there."

"Let me know if you find anything."

Cam pushed from the chair. "Will do."

He disappeared and Dare opened the email that had come through just a few moments ago from Detective Clint Montgomery from SCPD. His mouth pulled into a frown as he glanced over the information Clint had sent over.

According to their findings, the final ping from Tess's phone had come from a cell tower nearly thirty minutes away from her home, and the call log confirmed that her final contact was the phone call Ainsley had received.

The medical examiner had approximated Tess's death had occurred sometime during the previous weekend. Unless dead women could dial the phone, there was no way that call had come from Tess.

The information gnawed at him; he felt certain Joel Parsons had her phone at some point and disposed of it. And if he'd had her phone... That placed him at the scene of the crime. Despite Joel's insistence that he knew nothing about Tess, the whole thing didn't sit right with him.

Joel was involved somehow—he just needed to prove it.

Dare picked up his phone and dialed Detective Montgomery's number. After a few rings, Clint answered, his voice weary. "Montgomery."

"Clint, it's Dare. Got a minute?"

"Sure, what's up?"

"I've been digging into Tess's phone records. The last ping is from a tower roughly thirty minutes from her place, the night before she was found. There's no way she made that call."

Clint sighed audibly. "I hear you. But we've got nothing to place Parsons at the scene. We found no prints, no DNA—nothing to link him directly."

"I know," Dare said, frustration evident in his tone. "But this whole thing feels off. Parsons is a surgeon, meticulous by nature. He'd know how to cover his tracks."

Clint was silent for a moment. "Look, I get your suspicion. But we need hard evidence. What about the shooting Ainsley was involved in? Any leads?"

"Nothing yet." Dare hated to admit that they were at a standstill there too. Worst of all, that asshole's alibi had checked out. Joel had been in surgery at the time of the shooting, so he wasn't responsible for the attack. But that didn't mean he wasn't involved somehow. "There has to be something we're missing."

"Or it's not him," Clint replied.

Dare bit back a curse. "I know how it sounds, but—"

"Do you?" Clint pressed. "The woman living with you recently lost her best friend and was shot at. Add to that, her ex is an arrogant prick. Tell me what I'm supposed to think."

Anger burned through Dare's blood, and he clenched his molars together in an effort not to snap at the other man. He knew how it sounded, damn it. While he could admit that it was jealousy in part that drove him, there was more to it. He could feel it.

Dare inhaled and forced himself to think rationally. "I

understand where you're coming from. And as much as I despise that asshole, he's the only one with motive. I think Tess's murder was a message. She's the one who helped Ainsley when she left Joel—gave her a place to stay, let her borrow her mother's car. He wouldn't take kindly to that."

Clint seemed to think it over for a moment. "I don't suppose he would."

"I know he wasn't responsible for the drive-by," Dare continued. "Maybe he didn't do it himself. But I'd stake my life that he's ass deep in this whole thing. If we got access to his bank records, we might be able to find the connection."

"He'll never just hand those over, and without something solid..."

Yeah, Dare knew exactly where he was going with that. Without cause, they wouldn't be able to get a warrant. They needed evidence that placed Joel at the scene of the crime.

"I can't make any promises," Clint finally said. "But I'll keep digging and see if I can find anything."

"I appreciate it." Dare ended the call then leaned back in his chair, staring at the ceiling.

He needed to find that one loose thread that would unravel Joel's carefully constructed alibi. He knew he was on the right track. Joel Parsons was meticulous, but even the best made mistakes. He just needed to find the connection that would tie Joel to both crimes.

His phone buzzed, breaking the silence as it rattled across the wooden surface of his desk. He bit back a groan when he saw Marley's name on the screen. Just what he needed. "Hey, Mar, what's up?"

"Dare! How's my favorite brother doing?" Marley's voice was a bright contrast to the restlessness plaguing him.

"Unless something happened that I don't know about, I'm pretty sure I'm your only brother," he replied dryly.

"Details," Marley teased. "So, how's my favorite sister-in-law?"

Dare snorted. "You don't have a sister-in-law."

"Yet," Marley said, a singsong quality to her voice.

"Don't," he warned. "If you're trying to play matchmaker, it's not going to work," he said, unable to keep the exasperation from his tone.

Marley huffed. "You can't tell me it hasn't crossed your mind."

No, he couldn't say that. He couldn't bring himself to lie to his sister. His silence must have given him away, because she pressed on. "You like her, don't you? Otherwise, you wouldn't be going out of your way for her."

She's..." Beautiful. Smart. He could come up with a thousand other words to describe his tenant, though he would never voice them out loud. "Ainsley is off limits, Mar. You know that."

"I saw the way you looked at her."

Dare rubbed the bridge of his nose, already sensing the impending headache brewing behind his eyes. "Mar..."

"I just think you deserve to be happy, too. How about we all meet up for dinner sometime? I really like Ainsley, and I want to make sure she's settling in okay."

He hesitated, the image of Ainsley's sweet smile flashing in his mind. "I'd like that, but not right now.

Everything's too crazy. Once things settle down, we can arrange something."

"Okay, I get it. But how's Ainsley holding up through all this? She must be worried sick," Marley said, sympathy tinging her voice.

"She's good. Stronger than she looks," he replied. "We'll meet up soon, I promise. Just let me get through this mess first."

Marley's tone turned serious. "Just make sure to take care of her, okay?"

"With my life," Dare promised. He'd never meant anything more.

CHAPTER
THIRTY

The sheriff had been a thorn in his side ever since that first visit, probing and questioning, always looking for something Joel couldn't quite hide. By all rights, Dare Jensen wasn't a man to be trifled with. He was well-respected and had earned his job as sheriff after serving several tours as a Marine. It made Joel hate him even more.

He'd covered his tracks well enough. The sheriff didn't have proof of anything, or Joel would be staring at the inside of a cell right now instead of sitting here. And he wouldn't miss this for the world.

He sat in his rental car, parked discreetly on a hill that overlooked the small, somber cemetery. The muted tones of gray and green blended into the overcast sky, creating a solemn backdrop for Tess's funeral. From this distance, Joel could barely make out the faces of the mourners gathered around the freshly dug grave. But he didn't need to see their faces to know who was there. His gaze had instantly been drawn to her familiar curves.

She stood near the grave, her shoulders hunched with grief. But that wasn't what drew his attention. It was the man next to her. He wasn't some chump she'd managed to sweet talk into helping her as he'd first assumed. No, the big man standing next to her was none other than Dare Jensen, the sheriff of Brookhaven.

This was a complication he hadn't foreseen. Joel's mouth twisted into a scowl. Fury rolled through him. It should be him down there next to Ainsley. She should have come back to him by now. Jealousy speared through him, hot and fierce, as Jensen wrapped an arm around her waist and pulled her close.

Joel's heart pounded in his chest and bile crept up his throat as he watched her lean into Jensen, seeking comfort in his embrace. Ainsley's head rested briefly against Dare's shoulder, and a fresh wave of anger surged through Joel. He had once been the one she turned to for comfort, the one she leaned on when the world became too much. Seeing her now, finding solace in another man's arms, was almost more than he could bear.

His grip tightened on the steering wheel as he watched them, the knife of betrayal twisting deeper in Joel's gut. How dare that man touch her? How dare he think he could take Joel's place?

Joel's thoughts spiraled as he imagined them deep in conversation, cuddling on the couch sharing a bottle of wine. In his mind's eye, he saw Ainsley confiding in Dare, opening her heart to him. He saw Dare comforting her, promising to protect her, taking her into his arms... and into his bed.

His stomach revolted. He couldn't stand it. Ainsley was his. She had always been his, and she would always belong to him.

The other mourners slowly began to disperse, offering their condolences and quietly leaving the cemetery. Joel remained in his car, watching as Ainsley and Dare lingered by the grave. He saw the way Dare looked at her, the way his eyes softened with concern and compassion. It made Joel's blood boil.

As the last of the mourners left, Dare and Ainsley turned to walk back to the parking lot. Dare kept his arm around her, and Ainsley didn't pull away.

Rage coursed through him, and his hands clenched around the wheel so tightly that his knuckles turned white under the strain. He wanted to storm down there, tear Ainsley away from Dare and take her home where she belonged. But he knew he couldn't. Not yet.

He needed to bide his time, find the right moment. He would get Ainsley back if it was the last thing he did. No one, especially not Sheriff Dare Jensen, would stand in his way.

For a moment, Joel fantasized about plunging the knife into the sheriff's chest, just as he'd done to Tess. He would make Jensen beg and plead; he'd make him sorry for interfering.

Joel sighed, the daydream dissipating. He'd love to kill the man, but it would be far too risky. His death would raise far too many questions, especially after Ainsley disappeared, too.

As he started the car and drove away from the

cemetery, Joel's mind was already working, plotting his next move. Watching her with Dare had ignited a fire within him, a burning desire to reclaim what was his. And nothing, not even the law, would stand in his way.

CHAPTER
THIRTY-ONE

The past few days hadn't seemed quite real. In some small part of her heart, Ainsley had held out hope that there'd been some sort of mistake, and Tess would suddenly appear with a welcoming smile and a hug, the way she always did.

But today Ainsley had watched them lower her friend into the ground, and that last kernel of hope had dissipated into thin air.

Tess was gone.

Ainsley stared out the window as they drove away from the cemetery. The funeral had been a blur of tears and condolences, and now that it was over, an overwhelming sense of emptiness settled over her.

The image of Tess's grave lingered in her mind, a painful reminder of her own failings. She never should have asked Tess to help her. If she'd just stayed away, none of this would have happened.

Dare pulled into his driveway and turned off the engine. He glanced at Ainsley, concern etched deep in his expression. "Come on in," he said gently. "You don't have to be alone right now."

Ainsley nodded, her eyes swollen and gritty from crying. She followed Dare into his house, glad for once that he was taking charge. She didn't have to think, didn't have to make any decisions. It was all she could do to put one foot in front of the other as she trailed along behind him.

Dare led her to the living room and guided her to the couch. "I'll make us something to drink."

He headed into the kitchen, and Ainsley sank into the couch, hugging a pillow to her chest. The silence of the house was a stark contrast to the chaos of the past few days, and it pressed in on her until she felt like she might fly apart. She closed her eyes, trying to hold back the fresh wave of tears threatening to spill over.

Dare returned a few minutes later, carrying two glasses of amber liquid. He held it out to her and she slipped the tumbler from his hand as he took a seat next to her.

"Whiskey," he said at her questioning look.

She nodded and took a tiny sip, the liquid burning across her tongue and down her throat. For a while, they sat in silence, sipping at their drinks. The warmth of the whiskey spread through Ainsley, tempering the bitter sting of grief.

After a few minutes, Dare broke the silence. "Do you want to talk about it?"

"No, not really. I just... I can't." Her earlier crying jag, coupled with the burn of the whiskey, turned her voice raspy.

Dare nodded, respecting her need for silence. "That's okay. Whenever you're ready, I'm here."

Ainsley drained her glass and rolled it between her hands. "I'm sorry for dragging you into this," she said, her throat tight with tears. "I never wanted any of this to happen."

Dare reached over and gently took her hand. "None of this is your fault, Ainsley. You have nothing to apologize for."

"I keep thinking about Joel," she admitted after a moment. "I can't help but feel like he's involved somehow."

Dare neither confirmed nor denied her suspicions, his expression neutral as his gaze remained locked on hers. "We're looking into everything," he said carefully. "I've been in touch with Clint Montgomery—the detective assigned to Tess's case. You have my word, Ainsley. We'll do our best to find whoever did this and bring them to justice."

Ainsley nodded, and a tear escaped from the corner of her eye before she could stop it. She hastily swiped it away. "I just can't believe she's gone. She didn't deserve this."

Dare extracted the glass from her numb fingers, then set it on the table. Ainsley leaned into him, glad for the solid comfort of his huge body. "No, she didn't," he agreed softly, his breath ruffling her hair. "But we'll make sure whoever did this pays for what they've done."

Ainsley's heart beat hard in her chest as she gave voice to her greatest fear. "This is all my fault. If I hadn't been so dumb, none of this would have happened."

"That's not true." Dare captured her chin and directed her gaze to his. "None of this is your fault."

"You don't understand." She shook her head, tears

burning across the bridge of her nose. "She and I hadn't spoken for years. He only found her because of me. I should have known better than to use his computer, but—"

Her words cut off on a choked sob, and Dare shifted to face her more fully. "If you're going to blame anyone, blame Joel." He reached out and took her hand, his thumb stroking along the backs of her fingers, imploring her to listen. "You had no control over what he did."

Ainsley swallowed hard. "I never intended to drag you into my crazy life. This is way more than what you signed up for and I... I think it might just be best if I leave."

His thumb stilled and her gaze dropped to her hand, still ensconced in his. "Is that what you want?"

"It's just that..." Ainsley bit her lip. "You've already done so much for me, and I don't want to put you through any more than I already have. I'll understand if you'd rather I not be here."

"You're safe here, Ainsley. I promise you that. Can you just give it a little more time? Please?"

She lifted her gaze to his, uncertainty thrumming through her. "Are you sure it won't be a bother?"

He gave her hand one last squeeze before releasing her. "No. It's no problem at all. Actually... I'd like you to stay."

She nodded slowly, something like relief unfurling inside her chest. "Okay."

They sat there for a long time, the quiet ticking of the clock the only sound in the room. Grief hung like a heavy weight around her shoulders, but Dare's presence eased the burden of pain. She closed her eyes, letting herself relax against him, the warmth of his body a reassuring presence.

"Thank you," she whispered. "For everything."

Dare's fingers tightened on her upper arm as he hugged her the tiniest bit closer. "You don't have to thank me, Ainsley. I'm here for you. Always."

Ainsley took a deep breath. With Dare by her side, she didn't feel so alone. She would get through this, and she would demand justice for Tess—no matter what it took.

CHAPTER
THIRTY-TWO

The soft scratching sound brought Ainsley out of a fitful sleep. She blinked rapidly to clear her eyes and glanced at the red numbers on the clock. She hadn't been asleep more than an hour or so. What had woken her?

The sound came again, another metallic scratch that lifted the hairs on the back of her neck. A soft creak reached her ears and she froze in place. Over the past couple of weeks she'd become accustomed to the suite's quirks; the house groaned sometimes as it settled, the old structure contracting and expanding with the weather. But this was the unmistakable sound of the loose floorboard next to the front door.

Someone was in the house.

Fear clutched at her throat as her gaze darted around the room. She had to get away—but how? Going out the window wasn't an option; it was a two-story drop to the ground below. The only way down was the stairs. And to get to the stairs, she had to get past the intruder.

She was trapped.

Ainsley rolled out of bed, landing as quietly as a mouse. Dropping to her knees, she slithered under the bed just as the first footfall echoed through the living area. Little by little the intruder was revealed as he moved toward the bedroom. She could tell from the build that it was a man, but his features were obscured, lit from behind by the moonlight streaming in the windows.

She dropped her head to hide her face, heart beating so hard she was sure the sound would lead the intruder right to her. She remained frozen, listening to every movement as the man drew closer.

Goosebumps prickled over her arms as he reached the threshold of the bedroom. His feet remained rooted to the floor as if he were examining his surroundings, and she pressed a hand over her mouth to control her breathing. She couldn't stay here—she had to find a way to get past him.

Ainsley drew in a slow, deep breath and her heart nearly stopped as the man stepped into the room. She held her breath as he stopped just a few feet from the opposite side of the bed, pulse thrumming rapidly in her ears.

Oh, God. He was probably just now noticing she wasn't in bed. Daring a glance toward the bathroom, she saw the door was partially closed. Hopefully he would think she was in there, and she could escape outside while he was distracted.

She shifted slightly, angling away from him and slowly shuffling out from under the bed. She held her breath and sent up a prayer that he wouldn't check underneath.

Stupid, stupid, stupid. Why had she hidden beneath the bed? She watched in terror, waiting for him to drop to one knee and look right at her. What felt like minutes passed before his feet turned away and he headed toward the closet. The bifold doors slowly slid open and she could imagine him peering inside, searching through the various articles of clothing.

Keeping her head low, Ainsley slid out from under the bed, keeping to the shadows. She paused by the foot of the bed and peeked around. Abandoning the closet, the man moved toward the bathroom. Making sure his back was to her, she crept farther away, praying he couldn't hear her soft movements over the noise of his own.

He reached out and eased the bathroom door open. As the room was revealed inch by inch, Ainsley crawled toward the living room, not daring to take her eyes from the intruder. She felt the lip of the carpet disappear, replaced with the cool tile of the kitchen, and she bit back a sigh of relief. Almost there.

Her gaze flitted to the kitchen counter, her keys gleaming in the moonlight. She closed her palm around them as quietly as possible and winced when the metal clinked together.

The sound echoed in the silence, and the man suddenly spun around. Though his face was obscured, his dark eyes seemed to look right at her, sending her pulse into a tailspin. Abandoning any attempt to remain quiet, she lunged for the front door and bolted down the stairs. Her foot slipped on the dew-slickened wood, and she tumbled down the last few steps. She landed in an awkward heap at the bottom, every cell of her body aching.

Through the haze of pain clouding her mind, noise from the suite filtered down to her. Pressing her palms to the rough concrete, she managed to lurch to her feet. Somehow she'd managed to hang onto the keys, and she fumbled them as she tore across the patio to the back door. Her hands shook so badly she couldn't get the key lined up properly in the dim light. They slipped from her fingers and landed with a clatter at her feet.

Inside, Sarge began to bark madly, nearly drowning out the sound of the man's heavy tread on the stairs. Abandoning all pretense, Ainsley pounded on the door. "Dare!"

Sarge barked louder and she threw a look over her shoulder, straining to see the man through the dense fog that had rolled in over the lake. The man's hulking figure was cutting across the yard now. She pounded on the door, sending it rattling in its frame. "Dare!"

A light flickered to life in the depths of the house and she saw the sheriff's welcome figure a moment later.

"Dare!" She pounded her palm on the glass. "Let me in!"

He wrestled with the lock for a moment before the door swung inward, and she tumbled inside. Dare caught her around the waist, simultaneously closing and locking the door with his free hand. "What's wrong?"

She pointed a shaky hand toward the patio, her body trembling violently. "He's outside! H-he was in my room, and I got out, but then he followed me and I—I don't know where he is now."

"Shh. Everything's going to be okay," he said as he eased her away.

How could be be so calm and collected? She opened

her mouth, but he was already moving, stepping into a pair of boots. "Did you see where he went?"

"N-no." She wrapped her arms around her waist. "He followed me down the stairs and I saw him coming across the lawn. After that..."

He placed one hand on her shoulder. "Stay here. I'll be right back."

He moved swiftly out of the room but was back less than twenty seconds later, Sarge in the lead. Dare threw open the back door and the dog took off like a bullet, both of them plunging into the dark night.

CHAPTER
THIRTY-THREE

Dare burst out of the house, his eyes scanning the darkness for any sign of the intruder. The moonlight cast long shadows across the lawn, but the figure had already vanished into the foggy night. Sarge was a blur of motion as he bolted toward the lake at full speed.

He didn't hesitate as he sprinted after the dog, adrenaline pumping through his veins. He caught up to Sarge at the edge of the lake where he had his nose to the ground, sniffing fervently. A low growl rumbled from his chest, the hair on his back bristling.

Dare's gaze followed the dog's lead, sweeping the area. There was no one in sight—no sign of the man who had broken into Ainsley's suite.

Goddamn it.

Dare gazed out over the lake, and his eyes narrowed as he fought to see through the dense fog. Was that a boat? The ripples in the water suggested recent movement, and Dare could only assume the intruder had made his escape by boat. Frustration gnawed at him; there was no way he could catch up to the man now.

"Sarge, heel," Dare called softly, his voice tense. The dog lifted his head, ears perked, and after one last growl at the water's edge, trotted obediently back to Dare's side.

Sarge on his heels, Dare cautiously climbed the stairs to Ainsley's suite and cleared the small space. He locked up behind him then headed back toward the house. A glint of metal gleamed in the beam of light, and he noticed Ainsley's keys lying on the ground. He scooped them up and pocketed them to return to her, then turned his attention back to the darkness surrounding him.

Just to be certain the man wasn't hanging around, Dare swept his flashlight over the yard as he circled the house. He paused on the front porch, eyes straining as he gazed out over the driveway. He was certain the intruder had arrived by way of the lake, but he couldn't be too careful.

Digging his keys out of his pocket, Dare unlocked the front door then stepped inside, locking up once more behind Sarge. The dog plopped down on the rug and stared up at him, expectantly. Dare brushed a hand over his head, then strode down the hallway toward the kitchen.

Ainsley stood near the sink, staring out the window, her back to him. The soles of his wet boots squeaked softly on the tile floor as he stepped into the kitchen, and she spun around at the sound.

Her face went as white as a sheet, and the shattering of glass filled the air as the cup she'd been holding hit the ground at her feet. Water splashed up over her bare legs, but she didn't seem to notice. Her eyes flew wide with terror at the sight of him and for a second she froze. Then she bolted.

She made a break to her left, attempting to round the kitchen island. "Ainsley!"

He called out to her, trying to break through her haze of fear. Sarge, not to be outdone, gave a loud bark as he bolted forward to cut her off. A bloodcurdling scream rent the air as Ainsley skidded to a stop and tried to reverse directions.

"Halt!" He called the dog off, though he wasn't entirely sure who he was yelling at—her or the dog. Sarge froze and Dare darted toward her, desperate to catch her before she cut her feet on the broken glass.

"Ainsley!" He placed himself in front of her but she fought him off, smacking at his hands as he reached for her. "Ainsley, you're okay. Everything's okay."

His arms closed around her, but she continued to wiggle out of his grasp and away from the dog. "Ainsley."

She shook her head violently, his voice not fully penetrating the fog of fear. He kept talking to her, trying to get her to focus on him. "Ainsley. Look at me."

He grasped her biceps lightly, and her hands came up to cover her face as a sob caught in her throat. His heart twisted in his chest at the sight of her, so visibly shaken. He wanted to help her, but she refused to let him in. She'd kept her walls up, guarding her heart and withholding the truth of the past.

He'd hoped she would come to trust him, but it seemed that every time they took one step forward, she took two steps back. Well, he was done waiting. He couldn't bear to see her like this. He took control then, gathering her into his arms. "I've got you."

He intended to lift her up onto the counter where she would be away from the dog and unable to run. Instead, her arms wrapped around him as she buried her face in the crook of his neck. She clung to him, body trembling, and he clutched her tightly. "You're okay, honey. I won't let anything happen to you."

For what felt like forever he held her, one arm under her legs, the other banded around her back, holding her close. His leg began to ache, and he winced against the pain. Dare turned toward the counter, but when he moved to set her down, she clung more tightly to him.

"He's gone," he whispered against her hair. "No one's going to hurt you."

He settled her on the counter but didn't release her. She didn't cry; she just shook uncontrollably, remnants of fear coursing through her.

Fury billowed up inside him. Though he and Sarge had gone after the man, it was as if he'd disappeared into thin air. Despite the fact that he'd seen no sign of the man, Dare knew she hadn't made it up. It had scared her too badly to be a figment of her imagination. The way she'd screamed for him...

His blood turned to ice as goosebumps sprouted over his skin. He'd never forget that as long as he lived. His arms tightened a fraction, pulling her even closer. He wanted to shelter her from whatever—whoever—was after her.

He needed to check the security cameras, but he didn't

dare let go of her. More than he wanted to find the guy, he wanted to hold and comfort her. Whoever it was had gotten away, and the cams probably wouldn't reveal much anyway. Taking care of the woman in his arms was far more important; Ainsley needed this.

"I won't let anything happen to you." He smoothed one hand over her back. "I promise."

She had gradually begun to relax, and now she nodded against his chest. Her arms were still wound tightly around his neck, and her muscles loosened by degrees until she finally peeled herself away from him.

"I'm sorry," she said, her voice small as she stared at his chest, unwilling to look at him.

"Hey." He hooked a knuckle under her chin and gently lifted her gaze to his. "Don't ever apologize for coming to me. I'll always help you, no matter what you need or what time it is. You call for me, I'll be there. Got it?"

She gave a little nod, her expression conflicted. He barely resisted the urge to pull her back into his arms and cuddle her close. Her reaction to the dog was far worse than he'd suspected, and he needed to get to the bottom of it.

"You're really terrified of dogs, aren't you?" She bit her lip and gave a tiny nod. He studied her for another long moment before speaking. "Did something happen?"

She blinked rapidly, and he braced himself for whatever half truth she was going to offer this time.

Finally, she nodded. "I was… attacked." She swallowed hard. "I never had a problem with dogs until then, but…"

A shudder racked her body. "It was a German Shepherd, too. Just like him."

She pointed at Sarge without looking his way. "He... he grabbed me here." She grasped her left bicep and closed her eyes, as if trying to shut out the memory. "He was put down afterward."

Emotion played over her face, and he watched her carefully. "Can I see?"

She hesitated, then nodded. Ever so slowly he inched up the sleeve of her t-shirt. Just below the more recent gunshot wound, an older scar was just barely visible. Had he not been looking for it, he never would have noticed. Whoever had performed the surgery to correct it had done a good job.

He swept his thumb over it lightly, and she trembled against him. "I'm sorry that happened to you. Not everyone trains their dogs properly."

Her eyes opened then, sad and liquid soft. "No, they don't," she whispered.

She looked so devastatingly heartbroken that he ached to pull her to him. But he'd pushed her enough for one night. "I checked your place before I came back to the house. If you want to go back—"

She was already shaking her head before he'd finished the sentence. "No. I..."

She broke off, teeth sinking into her lower lip, and he nodded. "I think it would be better if you stay here tonight. Okay?"

She nodded gratefully. "Thank you."

"Of course." He wrapped his hands around her torso

so he could lower her to the ground, but her flinch stopped him cold. "Shit, I'm sorry. Did I hurt you?"

She shook her head. "No, it's just... still healing."

He nodded. "Mind if I look?"

She nodded and turned slightly so her back was toward him. He lifted the hem of her shirt, exposing her lower back. The bruises that covered the silken flesh had begun to yellow. Glad she couldn't see him, he shook his head. According to her, it had been nearly a month since she'd left.

Bile rose up his throat at the sight. He couldn't imagine the abuse she'd endured if they were just now starting to heal. He reached out and traced his fingers lightly around the perimeter of one bruise. She tensed ever so slightly but didn't pull away from him. He flattened his palm and coasted it over her back in a slow, comforting sweep.

Her skin was so soft, so delicate. Her body was still just a little too slender, but she was finally beginning to fill out, her waist and hips curving beautifully under his palm. He trailed his fingers down her vertebrae, tracing each bump and marveling at her inner strength. He wished with every fiber of his being that he could hunt down Parsons and give him a dose of his own medicine.

Realizing how intimately he'd been touching her, he allowed his fingers to slide down to the curve of her hip. She seemed to enjoy his touch, leaning slightly into him though he couldn't see her face. Part of him wanted to swivel her around, take her face in his hands and kiss her. But he knew it was too soon. He settled for sliding his hands around her hips and lifting her against his chest.

She sucked in a breath and looped her arms around his shoulders as he carried her away from the broken glass on the floor. Only when they were far away did he put her down, allowing her to slide slowly down his body. He settled her on the bottom step, then toed off his boots so he wouldn't drag glass through the house.

He gently patted her hip. "Wait here."

He strode back to the kitchen then whistled for Sarge, directing him around the broken glass. Once the dog was settled in the living room, Dare returned to Ainsley. Her brows drew low, and she wrung her hands together. "I'm sorry about the glass. I'll clean it up, I promise—"

Dare gently took her hands in his own, stalling her nervous flow of words. "I'll take care of it."

"But..."

Her obvious distress tore at his heart. How many times had she been punished for accidents like the one that had just happened? "Ainsley."

Her tortured gaze met his, and he stared at her for a moment before speaking. "Promise me you won't go back in the kitchen until it's cleaned up." Her mouth parted, and he squeezed her hands the tiniest bit. "Please. I don't want you to get hurt."

She blinked rapidly, obviously unsure how to react. The way she bit her lip and studied him like she was just waiting for the other shoe to drop infuriated him. This woman deserved so much better than what she'd dealt with in the past.

He placed a foot on the step next to hers, bringing them closer together. Her eyes widened slightly as he tucked a lock of hair behind her ear. "I know you don't trust me. But I'm going to change that."

Her lips moved, but nothing came out. The silence stretched between them for several long moments, fraught with tension. There were so many things he wanted to say to her, but they'd been through enough tonight.

There would be plenty of time to discuss everything tomorrow.

CHAPTER
THIRTY-FOUR

Dare's gaze swept over her, still clad in her oversized nightshirt. She'd obviously been sleeping when the man had broken in. Now that he could see her better, the maroon scratches on her knees stood out in stark relief.

His brows drew together. "What happened?"

"Oh." Ainsley shrugged self-consciously. "I fell down the stairs."

His eyes flew up to meet hers. "Are you all right?"

"I'll be fine."

He grabbed up her hands and inspected her palms. The flesh was torn in places, and he gently ran his thumbs around the wounds. "We need to get these cleaned up."

"I think I'll just take a shower—if you don't mind," she hastily added. "And..." She tugged at the nightshirt, wet in places and smeared with dirt from her fall. "I should probably wash this, too."

He settled a hand on her back and gently propelled her up the stairs. "No need. You can use something of mine."

She glanced up at him. "If you're sure you don't mind. Just a shirt is fine."

"Do you mind taking the room next to mine or do you want more privacy? I can put you at the end of the hall."

"The room next to yours is fine."

He nodded. "Come on, let's grab you some stuff."

He led her into his room and yanked open a dresser drawer. Pulling out a t-shirt, he handed it to her then walked into the master bathroom, returning a minute later with a new toothbrush and toothpaste, peroxide for the cuts, and some bandages.

"Towels are in the linen closet." He dug her keys from his pocket and passed them to her. "You dropped these outside."

"Oh, right." She gave a little shake of her head as she slipped them from his fingers. "I completely forgot I'd dropped them."

Dare offered a kind smile. "Do you need anything else?"

"No, this is plenty." Ainsley shuffled her feet as she accepted the toothbrush and toothpaste that he held out to her. "I know it sounds silly of me, not wanting to go back over there, but..."

"I completely understand. You've been through a lot, and I don't blame you for not wanting to go back just yet." He moved in front of her and offered a soft smile. "There should be some soap, maybe some shampoo in the guest bathroom. Let's look."

"Don't worry about it. I can make do with whatever you have." She followed him into the bathroom, then placed her things on the counter and turned to him. "Thank you for everything."

He nodded. "I typically leave Sarge out of his kennel at night. I know you're not comfortable with him, but I think under the circumstances..."

She nodded emphatically. "That sounds good to me. I'm glad he heard me."

"Me too. Is there anything else you need?" Ainsley shook her head, and Dare flashed her a small smile. "All right. Good night, then."

"Good night."

Neither of them moved. They remained that way for several long moments, each studying the other.

"Everything's going to be okay, Ainsley. I promise." His voice was strained, his resolve to leave her alone slowly dissolving.

Dare and Ainsley stood close, the space between them filled with unspoken words. The fear and worry that had gripped Dare's heart since the break-in were finally beginning to recede.

He took Ainsley's hand, giving it a gentle squeeze. She didn't say anything, but the gratitude in her gaze spoke volumes. She was still shaken, but Dare's presence seemed to offer her the comfort she needed.

With his free hand, he cupped her face, his thumb brushing softly against her cheek. Dipping his head toward hers, he breathed her in. His lips skimmed her silky skin as he dropped a soft kiss on her forehead.

She'd been through so much—too much—and he didn't want her to feel like he was pressuring her into anything. He couldn't take advantage of her like that.

When he did finally kiss her, it would be because they both wanted it.

Dare reluctantly released her and stepped away. He tucked a stray strand of hair behind her ear and stroked her cheek with the pad of his thumb. "Good night, Ainsley," he whispered.

Ainsley's eyes were wide as she watched him, poised like a rabbit ready to flee. The fear had receded, and now uncertainty filled the depths as she grappled with her emotions.

Dare forced himself to leave, knowing she needed the space. She was safe, and for now, that was enough.

CHAPTER
THIRTY-FIVE

She couldn't sleep. Silvery moonlight streamed in through the curtains, spilling over the bed, deepening the shadows in the corners of the room. A shiver ran down her spine. Each time she closed her eyes she saw the man who'd broken in.

Was it Joel? What did he intend to do to her? Drug her and take her back to his house? Or worse, kill her?

Knowing she wouldn't be able to fall asleep, Ainsley tossed back the covers and climbed from the bed. On silent feet she glided toward the door, then crept down the stairs. She moved stealthily through the formal sitting room at the back of the house, her gaze drawn to the large patio doors.

Beyond, fog swirled in the air, shrouding the landscape, and goosebumps sprouted over her arms. The silvery glow of the moon broke through the clouds and spilled over the lake. The water rippled as a gust of wind slithered over the land, sending shafts of light splintering over the surface. Leaves danced and branches rubbed against one another, but nothing was out of place.

She wasn't sure whether to be relieved or disappointed. Part of her hoped he would come back, if only to catch him in the act. Ainsley tipped her head against the window and closed her eyes. The glass was cool, the effect almost soothing to her nerves. Her heart felt like it hadn't slowed down, and she couldn't relax.

The soft click of toenails on the floor sent goosebumps prickling along her arms, and Ainsley froze as the dog lumbered toward her. She'd completely forgotten about the giant German shepherd, and for a moment, crippling panic seized her.

She remained rigidly still as the dog padded softly forward, then leaned against her legs, clearly looking for attention. Or... to offer comfort.

A smile tugged at the corners of her mouth as she regarded the large dog. She tentatively ran a hand over his head, and Sarge nuzzled against her as Ainsley scratched behind his ears.

"You're not so bad, you know," Ainsley whispered.

Suddenly a face appeared in the reflection, and she whirled around. A scream caught in her throat as her gaze locked on the broad figure looming in the doorway. She stumbled backward, her shoulder blades hitting the cool glass of the door.

She opened her mouth to scream just as her brain caught up with her eyes and the man's face came into view.

"It's just me."

Her shoulders curved inward and her lungs deflated as

relief rushed through her. She dragged in a shuddering breath and covered her face with her hands.

"I'm sorry." Two strong hands curled around her elbows. "I didn't mean to scare you."

The deep timbre of his voice wrapped around her, and she swayed into him. He took her weight easily, shifting her so one brawny arm banded around her waist. His free hand moved to her back and slid over her spine in a comforting motion.

He was so strong, so solid. For the past few weeks she'd been constantly on edge, leaving her drained both emotionally and physically. She tipped her head against his shoulder and breathed in his masculine scent, soaking up the heat of his body. It felt good to have a shoulder to lean on, someone to hold her when she needed it most.

"I'm sorry." A ragged exhale filtered from her lips as she peeled herself away from him. "I'm a mess."

"You're not a mess. You have every right to be cautious." Dare peered down at her, concern marring his brow. "Are you okay?"

She nodded, and he tipped his head toward the couch. "Do you want to sit?"

"Sure." She reluctantly pulled from his grasp and settled in the corner of the couch.

Dare followed suit, leaving plenty of space between them. "Can't sleep?"

She shook her head. "Every time I close my eyes..."

A shudder rippled down her spine, and Dare settled a hand on her shoulder and squeezed lightly. "You're safe here. I won't let anything happen to you."

He dropped his hand away and she lamented the loss

of his touch. "I know." She swallowed hard then turned to meet his gaze. "I'm sorry if I woke you up."

"You didn't. I couldn't sleep either," he admitted. "I heard you walking around, so I figured I would come keep you company. If you want it," he added.

Ainsley offered a little smile. "I appreciate it, thanks."

Sarge settled next to the couch and Dare gave a little shake of his head. "Looks like he's taken to protecting you, too."

Her smile slipped away as she stared at the dog. "We used to have a German Shepherd just like that. A couple years ago," she said softly. "His name was Ajax. We had to put him down."

"I'm sorry. Was that how you got...?"

She couldn't help her fingers straying toward the scar on her left arm. "Yeah. We..."

Ainsley closed her eyes as the memory of that day washed over her. "We had an argument about something. I don't even remember what. But I was so fed up that I decided to leave. Joel refused to let me go. He..."

Her voice broke, and she swallowed down the bile that rose in her throat. "He sent Ajax after me. It could have been so much worse. He didn't bite me very hard—I don't think he wanted to at all, but Joel kept screaming at him to stop me."

A tear slipped down her cheek as the memory washed over her. She remembered the terror, the pain, as clearly as if it had happened yesterday.

She shivered. "He called Ajax off, then took me to the hospital and told them I'd been attacked. He refused to leave my side, so I couldn't even tell the doctors what had happened. Even if I did, they wouldn't believe me. They were his coworkers; they treated him like a god. When I was finally released, he took me home but Ajax was gone. He'd had someone pick him up and taken away..."

She broke off again, and Dare's hand slid over her knee. He didn't say a word, just sat there in silence until she continued. "It wasn't the dog's fault. He'd never been violent until that day. But just seeing them..."

Goosebumps sprouted over her skin as she shook her head. "I can't help but think about that."

She could feel the tension radiating off Dare's body though he kept his touch light as he gently stroked her knee. "I'm glad you're okay. If you'd prefer I keep him away..."

She shook her head. "I'm getting used to him. It just... catches me off guard sometimes."

Silence fell for several moments, both of them lost in thought. It was becoming increasingly clear that Joel wasn't going to let her go. He'd found her, now he meant to drag her back to hell with him. Why? She wasn't that special. She wasn't particularly beautiful or smart. She was just obedient and naïve enough to fall for his manipulative behavior. She'd been so stupid. But never again.

"Why won't he just leave me alone?" Ainsley asked aloud.

Dare shifted to face her, then gathered her hands in his. "I don't know, but I'll make sure he stops. We'll catch him."

She shook her head. "I could have figured out a different way. I thought I covered my tracks. If I'd never reached out to Tess..."

Her voice broke as another tear leaked from her eye, and she blinked against the burning sensation. Sarge moved as Dare slid to the floor in front of her. "None of this is your fault. Honey, you have to know that. You did what you had to do in order to survive. Most women would have stayed; I'm so damn proud of you for having the courage to leave. What happened to Tess was tragic, but you didn't cause that—he did."

Regret welled up inside her. "I ruined everything. I shouldn't have come here. I—"

"This is exactly where you should be," Dare cut in, his voice harsh. "I always want you to come to me. If you'd stayed... Christ. I don't even want to think of what would have happened to you. I can't stand the thought of losing you."

His eyes blazed up at her, sending a flicker of warmth igniting around her heart. He sounded so sincere, so emphatic. She'd never met a man like Dare before. He was noble and strong, and he believed in what was right. He cared for her.

A dozen emotions ping-ponged through her chest, rapidly changing from grief to despair to need. Dare awakened a long-dormant emotion she hadn't dared to hope for in years. She wanted to feel close to someone, wanted to be desired, even if it was just for tonight. Her gaze was drawn downward to where Dare still held her hands. Was she brave enough to ask for this?

Her hands shook as she drew in a steadying breath before meeting his gaze. "Earlier you said I don't trust you. But... I do. I trust you."

He stared at her for a long moment, his gaze searching.

Ever so slowly, his hand lifted and curled around the back of her neck. "You trust me?"

Her tongue darted out to lick her lips, and she nodded. Her heart felt like it would beat right out of her chest, though not from fear this time. A different anticipation swirled in her stomach, sending fire licking along her nerve endings. Did he feel this thing brewing between them?

His thumb stroked along the cords of her throat. She sensed it was a test. It was such a delicate spot; he could easily hurt her if he wanted to. But he never would. She knew that. Dare would never lay a hand on her in anger.

His free hand moved to her hip and squeezed gently. "Let me show you how good it can be."

His voice was little more than a whisper, barely audible in the stillness of the night. Ainsley nodded, and his grip tightened a fraction. The hand holding her hip shifted to her lower back and pulled her forward, until only a few inches separated them. He gradually increased the pressure on the back of her neck, silently urging her closer.

Her hands moved to his shoulders then slid around the back of his neck as she swayed into him. His lips met hers, just the barest brush of skin on skin. He gave her plenty of time to pull away, to tell him to stop. But that wasn't what she wanted. Tonight, she wanted to be loved.

She pulled him back to her and pressed her lips to his, encouraging him to keep going. His hands moved over her body, their path slow and sure. He traced each vertebrae of her spine, molded his palms to every curve. When his hand slid upward and brushed her breast, she sucked in a breath. Her nipples tightened almost painfully, and warmth flooded her core. He hesitated, and worry crashed over her.

"Don't stop," she breathed against his lips, tightening her hold on his shoulders. "Please…"

"Never," he promised. "We have all night, honey, and I'm going to make the most of it."

He kissed her again, then lifted her into his arms as he stood. She'd never been picked up like this before, carried like she weighed nothing at all. It was scary yet exhilarating. Like this she was completely at Dare's mercy, but she trusted him implicitly. His touch was nothing like Joel's, and she fought to tune out the old memories, focusing instead on Dare's hands cupping her bottom as they moved toward the stairs.

Sarge followed them upstairs, and Dare paused in the doorway of the bedroom. "Sorry, boy. She's mine tonight."

CHAPTER
THIRTY-SIX

He nudged the door closed with his foot, then carried her to the bed and lay her in the center of the mattress. He stroked one finger along her cheekbone. "I'll never hurt you."

"I know." Her voice was barely more than a whisper, the faint trembling of her body belying her confident words.

Moonlight spilled in through the window, lending its dim glow to the room as he stretched out next to her. This thing had been building between them for the past couple of weeks, and tonight he was going to show her how it felt to be loved the way she deserved.

Propped on one elbow, he coasted his fingers down her arm from shoulder to wrist, then back up again. Across her collarbone, up her neck, his fingers blazed a trail over her skin, slowly acclimating her to his touch.

Goosebumps broke out over her skin as he coasted downward, his fingertips gliding over each rib, the dip of her waist, and across her hip. Inching her shirt up, he teased the silky skin of her stomach before slowly making his way up to her breast. A little shudder rocked her body and her head dropped back as he circled her nipple.

"If you want to stop, sweetheart, just tell me."

She shook her head and opened her mouth to speak. Instead of words, a soft moan escaped. Dare bit back a smile. Smoothing his hand over her waist he grasped the hem of her oversized t-shirt, then pulled it upward.

He gently drew the material over her head and off, exposing her exquisite body. His gaze trailed over her torso, examining the indent of her waist where it flared out at her softly rounded hips, then up to the swells of her breasts. He leaned in and dropped a kiss on the arc of one. "Beautiful."

She turned her face away in embarrassment. Cupping her face in one hand, he turned her back to him. Her bright blue gaze met his and held. He wanted her to understand that he meant every single word.

Dipping his head, he took her mouth again. Her lips were full and soft, and they parted slightly to let him in. He swept his tongue over hers, tasting the minty sweetness of her toothpaste and he delved deeper, the kiss nearly sweeping him away with its intensity.

Remembering his vow to take things slow, he gentled the kiss and trailed his lips over her jaw, down her throat, between the valley of her breasts. He resisted the urge to take a gorgeous peak in mouth and moved downward instead. He still needed to earn her trust.

He felt her flinch when he kissed the first bruise. He lifted his head and found her eyes clenched tightly closed, her hands curled into fists by her sides. He dropped another feather-light kiss on the next bruise, and her teeth cut into her bottom lip.

He continued the sensual assault, lightly tracing each rib with the tips of his fingers, his mouth following suit. He tenderly kissed every bruise, wishing he could take away her pain and free her from the tethers of the past.

He kissed his way across the flat plane of her stomach, her muscles contracting under the light touch. Her lungs hitched, and her muscles trembled as he ever so slowly worked his way upward.

From the corner of his eye, he watched her hands fist in the covers. He coasted toward her breast, and she sucked in a breath as he brushed the tip with his nose. Her hand closest to him released the comforter and reached for him. Almost immediately she slapped her hand back down, digging her fingers into the fabric.

Acutely aware of every tiny twitch of her body, he took her nipple in his mouth. Her hands clenched as she writhed beneath him, but she refused to let go. Because she was holding herself back? Or... because it was expected of her? He suspected the latter.

He kissed his way up her throat until his mouth hovered next to her ear. His breath stirred her hair when he spoke. "Touch me."

She went utterly still, barely even breathing. Dare kissed the shell of her ear. "I want to feel your hands on me."

She dragged in a sharp breath. By increments, her hands lifted, hovering over his skin before finally landing on his back. Her touch was light as she ghosted her fingertips over the broad muscles.

Dare dipped his head and kissed her throat. "Good girl."

She grew bolder, her touch becoming increasingly firm as she skimmed over his shoulders and down his back, touching every part of his body that she could reach.

Her explorations drove him nearly mindless with need, and he quickly stripped both of them and rolled on a condom before settling over her.

Sliding one hand up her back, he cradled her head with his large palm. He pulled her closer, their bodies melded together from hip to chest, and slanted his mouth over hers.

Her legs parted wider, and Dare accepted the silent invitation. He slid deep inside her, eliciting a throaty moan from Ainsley. Her arms curled around his shoulders as she gave herself over to him.

Dare clamped down on his control as he took her slowly at first, then more rapidly as he lost himself to the sensation of her wrapped around him. Everything about her made him crazy.

He loved the feel of her next to him, their bodies entwined together. Nothing had ever felt more right.

Ainsley was his. *Forever.*

CHAPTER
THIRTY-SEVEN

Ainsley stood next to the kitchen sink, staring out the window, lost in thought. She didn't hear Dare approach, but she felt his presence the moment before his arms wrapped around her waist. His embrace was warm and secure, and she closed her eyes as a smile curled her lips.

"Good morning, beautiful," he murmured against her temple, planting a soft kiss there. "How did you sleep?"

"I think you know the answer to that," Ainsley retorted, a teasing lilt to her voice. "Someone kept me up way too late."

"Hmm..." Dare made a little humming sound as he dropped his head and kissed her collarbone. "I think he might have to do it again tonight."

When she'd slipped out of bed earlier, leaving Dare peacefully asleep, she'd worried briefly about how he would act around her today. Her fears, apparently, were unfounded.

There was no awkwardness between them, despite the deepening intimacy. She was growing closer to him every day, trusting him not just with her life, but with her heart. She had never felt so comfortable with a man before. Dare accepted her completely, and she loved him for it.

The thought terrified her. She couldn't fall for a man she'd just met—not even a man like Dare. No matter how amazing he was. No one fell in love that quickly.

Except... She was. She'd never felt this way about Joel, and she'd spent years with him. Being with Dare was different. Exhilarating. Not that she would ever admit as much to him. Their relationship was still new, still fresh, and she wanted to savor this newfound joy before rushing to declare her feelings.

Together, they moved to the kitchen table, coffee mugs in hand. Sarge settled at their feet with a contented sigh, and Ainsley reached down to rub between his ears. She smiled when the dog flipped to his back, silently commanding her to rub his belly.

Dare tipped his head at the dog. "Do that and you'll be his slave for life."

Ainsley couldn't help but smile. "He's growing on me."

He gave a slow nod. "So you wouldn't be opposed to having him around all the time?"

Her heart gave a hard thump at his implication. Was he asking her to stay here, in the house? She'd made the mistake of moving too quickly once before. But this was different—Dare was different. Her family was close by, and she knew he would never pressure her into anything she didn't want.

He watched her intently, his gaze never wavering, and Ainsley felt heat sweep up her cheeks. "Maybe."

Dare stared at her for another second before speaking "Maybe we should go to the bar this weekend and pick up your things."

It was a practical suggestion, but she loved what it implied. He wanted to be there to support her, to keep her safe. She blushed, a smile spreading across her face. "That would be great, thanks."

He squeezed her hand gently. "I need to ask you something."

Immediately, her smile slipped away. Before the words left his mouth, she knew what he was going to ask. "The man who broke into the suite last night. Did you get a look at him?"

Ainsley blew out a breath. He hadn't pressed her last night, for which she was grateful, but she knew he needed details now that her mind was clear. "No. I was asleep when I heard the door unlock. At first I wasn't sure what it was. But when I heard the footsteps, I slid under the bed. He was dressed all in black, but I couldn't make out anything else."

"How about his build? Was there anything that stood out?"

"Not really." She shook her head. "He was about average height. Not too thin, but not overweight, either."

He didn't look pleased by this information, and she swallowed hard. "I'm sorry. I—"

"Don't be sorry." He laced his fingers with hers. "I'm just trying to figure out what's going on." He paused briefly. "Do you think it was Joel?"

She'd had the exact same thought. Goosebumps raced over her skin. "Who else could it have been?"

Dare was silent for nearly a full minute. "When did it start?"

Ainsley didn't pretend to misunderstand him. She lifted one shoulder. "I'm not even sure. When he took the position in Minneapolis and convinced me to go with him, it kind of cut me off from all my friends and family. He told me not to worry about school or work, that he would take care of everything so I had a chance to settle in. At first it wasn't so bad. Then, little by little, things shifted."

She swallowed down the bile in her throat at the memory. "I don't even know what our first real fight was about. I was so shocked when he slapped me that I couldn't even believe it. He begged me to forgive him, brought home roses later as an apology. I knew it was wrong, but I didn't have anywhere else to go and…"

She shrugged. "I kind of just let it slide. It got better for a little while and I thought maybe he'd just been stressed out from our argument. But after a month or two, things just got worse."

"I'm sorry, sweetheart."

She twisted the hem of her shirt between her fingers. She felt so stupid. "I… I made a mistake."

She hesitated, the words caught in her throat. But she knew she couldn't keep it inside any longer. "I lost access to my bank account."

Dare's brow furrowed with concern. "What do you mean?"

Ainsley looked down at her hands, ashamed. "I let my computer save my passwords. Joel… He used them to log in and changed everything. He locked me out of my own account."

Dare's jaw tightened. "Have you contacted the bank?"

"I tried." She shook her head, shame flooding her. "They said I need to come in person with identification, but... I don't even know if my ID is valid anymore. He took that, too."

Dare scooted his chair closer and wrapped one hand around the back of her neck. "We'll get your money back. I promise."

She nodded, tears welling up in her eyes. "I lied... About my car. It wasn't broken down. He took my keys so I couldn't leave. The only phone I had was a landline, so he'd know I was home if he called to check in."

She drew in a shaky breath. "He gave me permission to leave the house once a week to get groceries. He would leave the car keys and cell phone when he left for work and check the mileage when he got home. I... I thought about leaving once, but... he had trackers on both of them. He always knew if I went somewhere I wasn't supposed to."

She felt Dare's muscles bunch and tense against her and she knew he was desperately trying to keep himself under control. She continued, needing him to understand. "I knew I had to get out, so I started planning. There was a small resale shop across the street from the plaza where I got groceries. So... Once a month, I would drop off some items while I shopped. I would walk over once I was done, pick up whatever money they offered, and I stashed it away."

He rubbed a hand over his face before clearing his throat. His mouth opened several times as if to say something, but each time he pressed his lips into a firm line before any words could escape.

Ainsley laid a hand on his. "What matters is, I got out. And I'm here now."

He wrapped his arms around her and pulled her close, forehead resting on hers. "You're so strong, sweetheart. So brave. But now you have me. I promise he won't hurt you ever again. And, Ainsley... You can always count on me if you ever need anything."

She bit her lip, trying to stay composed. "I know. I just... I didn't know what to do. He controlled everything. My money, my freedom. I can't ever go through that again."

His hold on her tightened a fraction. "You'll never have to worry about that again. You have an amazing support system: Your family, friends... Me. You're safe here, and I'm going to make damn sure Joel won't hurt you ever again."

Her heart swelled with gratitude. "I don't know what I'd do without you. I feel... better here. Safer," she admitted.

"I'll be here every step of the way." She nodded, and he cupped her face in his hand. "You're stronger than you think, Ainsley. You'll get through this."

For the first time in years, she truly believed that.

CHAPTER
THIRTY-EIGHT

Dare was in a piss-poor mood by the time he got to the station. Ainsley's words had played on repeat in his mind for the past hour, and his ire grew with each passing moment.

He strode inside, his gaze immediately landing on Cam. His eyes widened fractionally and he jumped up from his desk, moving quickly to catch up to Dare as he moved into his office and shut the door behind him.

"What's wrong?"

Dare scrubbed a hand over his face. What wasn't wrong?

He started at the beginning. "Someone broke into the suite last night."

Cam's eyes flew wide. "When? I never heard the call—"

Dare held up a hand. "He was long gone by the time I got there."

The lieutenant's eyes narrowed to slits. "Parsons?"

"Possibly. Probably." Dare growled. "It's worse than I suspected."

He relayed the story Ainsley had told him about locking her out of her account, then taking her phone and keys, effectively keeping her a prisoner in their home. He left out the rest. Cam didn't need to know the other details.

Cam swore. "He's getting brazen."

That was good and bad, in Dare's opinion. "Do you still have his schedule? I'd say we're due for another visit."

Dare followed Cam to his desk, where he scooped up the copy of the schedule Joel had given them last week. Cam checked his watch. "Looks like he went into surgery at eight, but we should be able to catch him as soon as he's done."

They climbed into the cruiser and headed toward Northwestern Memorial. Inside, they flashed their badges to the woman behind the desk and were escorted to a small office to await Joel.

The door swung inward twenty minutes later and Joel stepped inside, his expression shifting from curiosity to something darker as he recognized them. "Sheriff Jensen, Lt. McCoy." False sincerity drenched his tone as he slid into the chair across from them. "What can I do for you?"

Dare didn't waste any time. "Dr. Parsons, we need to talk about Ms. Layne. Her apartment was broken into last night."

Joel's eyes flickered, but his expression didn't change. "That's awful. I'm sorry to hear that."

"I'm sure you are," Dare said acidly. "Where were you last night?"

A muscle ticked in Parson's jaw. "Are you accusing me of something, Sheriff?"

"Not at all. Just trying to figure out what's going on. So I'll ask you again—where were you last night?"

Joel crossed one leg over the other, settling deeper into his chair. "I was home, Sheriff. Alone. As you're aware, I had surgery this morning, and I needed to be well-rested."

"Understandable." Dare glanced across his shoulder at Cam. "How long did it take us to get here? About an hour?" He glanced back at Parsons, whose face burned bright red.

"What, exactly, are you accusing me of?"

"We're not here to accuse you, Dr. Parsons," Cam interjected. "But you need to understand—Ainsley and Tess both have been victims of violent crimes. We need your help."

"I've told you everything I know," Parsons snapped. "I don't have an alibi for the break-in because I wasn't involved."

Cam leaned his elbows on the desk, his tone calm but firm. "Dr. Parsons, you care for Ms. Layne, don't you?"

Dare fought the urge to glare at Cam. What the fuck was he doing?

"Of course I do." Joel's angry gaze moved to Cam. "I think I've made that perfectly clear."

"I would think that, in your position, a man like yourself would harbor a sense of... resentment." Cam tipped his head.

"What's that supposed to mean?"

Cam gestured around the room. "You're successful. Respected by your colleagues and peers—everyone but

Ainsley." Joel's hands clenched around the arms of the chair as Cam continued, "You have everything, yet she still doesn't want you. You must have been furious when she left."

Twin spots of color appeared high on Parson's cheekbones. "How dare you? This is getting ridiculous. I've done nothing wrong, and I won't be interrogated again." Joel's voice shook, his composure slipping further as he stood abruptly, causing the chair to jerk backward. "I've had enough of this. If you don't have anything concrete, I suggest you leave."

Dare nodded slowly as he followed suit and stood. "We'll leave for now."

As they walked back to the cruiser, Cam spoke up. "He's starting to crack."

Dare's mouth pressed into a firm line. "He's too calm. That bastard won't break until he's pushed up against a wall with nowhere to go."

"Then let's put a boot to his throat. We need to get a warrant to trace his phone. If we can place him at the scene, we can nail his ass to the wall."

A heavy exhale filtered through Dare's lips. "As much as I'd love to see that asshole squirm, he's too smart for that. Even if we got a warrant, it probably wouldn't do us any good. I'd wager he left it at home. Ensures reasonable doubt."

"Then we'll keep digging," Cam said forcefully. "Joel might be careful, but everyone makes mistakes. There's a connection here, and we'll find it."

Dare wished he were as confident. But Cam hadn't seen the look on Ainsley's face when she'd told him about everything. He hadn't seen the fear, the shame. Joel was practiced at getting away with abuse of power. He was cold and calculated, and far too sure of himself. Dare could only hope that the man's arrogance would eventually be his downfall.

Ten minutes outside of Brookhaven, Dare's cell rang. Seeing the station's number on the screen, he tapped the bluetooth function to answer the call.

"Jenson."

"Sheriff, they found that car you've been looking for," came Yvonne's voice from the other end.

His hands tightened on the wheel. "Where?"

"Off Bixler Creek Road, in the woods."

"Call Reed, get him over there. We need to print it and search for any evidence."

"You got it, boss."

Cam pointed to a road coming up on the right. "Cut across here. We'll take the back way in."

Less than a half hour later they stood on the edge of a secluded road, the thick canopy of trees overhead casting dappled shadows on the ground. The air was heavy with the scent of pine and earth, and in birds chirped merrily above them, a stark contrast to Dare's mood.

Tucked into the weeds and partially obscured by the underbrush was the beige car they had been looking for.

Dare walked around the car, careful not to disturb anything. The car's once-shiny exterior was now dull and covered in dirt, leaves, and branches. He noted a single set of tire tracks where the car had been driven off the road and hidden in the brush. Whoever had done this had intended for the car to remain hidden.

"Do you think this will give us what we need?" Cam asked, his eyes never leaving the car.

"I hope so," Dare replied. "If we can find something in this car, it might be the piece of the puzzle we've been looking for."

The moment Sawyer swung the door open, though, Dare's stomach dropped to his toes. As dirty as the exterior was, the interior of the car was pristine. The scent of bleach wafted into the air, and he bit back a curse.

Sawyer and Cam traded knowing glances before silently moving forward to collect what they could. They worked diligently, dusting the car for fingerprints and taking photographs from every angle. Dare squatted next to the vehicle and examined an impression in the earth.

"Reed. Check this out."

Sawyer moved next to him and studied the partial footprint and gently tested the solid ground. "When did it rain last?"

Dare mentally drew back. "A few days ago?"

Sawyer nodded. "Looks like this was left right around then, when the ground was still soft."

He measured and photographed the impression, then continued to scour the surrounding area for evidence. After what felt like hours, Cam grimaced. "We've combed every inch of the car inside and out, but there's not a damn thing here."

Dare bit back a growl of frustration. "What about other evidence? Anything inside the car?"

"Not much," he replied. "There are a few personal items, but nothing that looks out of place."

Near the scene, they'd collected a faded candy wrapper,

a rusty Coke can, and a few other bits of debris that appeared to have been there for far longer than the vehicle.

"Got this," Forester said, holding up a bag as he approached. He handed the evidence bag to Dare, who inspected the cigarette butt. "Found it at the edge of the road."

It wasn't much, but it was more than they'd had before. "Send it to the lab for DNA testing, along with everything else."

Forester dipped his chin. "I'll request an expedite and let you know as soon as we have results."

Dare nodded, disappointment and defeat churning in his gut. "Thanks. Catalogue every single thing, no matter how small."

He would keep pushing, keep digging until they found the truth. And he would—no matter what it took.

CHAPTER
THIRTY-NINE

Dare dropped into his favorite armchair and stretched his leg. The muscle felt tight, the old scar tissue hard and unyielding. He dug his fingertips into the muscle, massaging the tissue, and winced as pain shot down his leg.

"Are you okay?"

Dare snapped his head toward Ainsley where she stood in the doorway and forced a smile. "I'm fine. Just sore."

Her brows dipped together in concern. "Do you need medicine? Maybe an ice pack?"

"Nothing to worry about." He shook his head. "Just an old injury acting up."

Ainsley moved closer and settled on the edge of the couch, her gaze sweeping over his leg. "I didn't know you were hurt. What happened?"

It was a long story, and guilt clutched at his throat just thinking about it. He hesitated a moment too long, and Ainsley's expression shuttered as she stood. "I'm sorry, it's none of my business. You don't have to—"

"Ainsley." He reached over, grasping her hand and

tugging her to a stop before she could run away from him again. "You can ask me anything. You know that."

She bit her lip. "I just don't want to make you uncomfortable."

"I'll tell you anything you want to know." He gave her hand a little squeeze, gently pulling her back down to the couch. "You grew up here, didn't you?"

She nodded, and he continued, "You ever hear of the Cottrell boys?"

Her gaze moved to the ceiling in thought even as she shook her head. "I think so, but I don't know them personally."

"They're several years older than you. I graduated with Wade. His brother, Beau, was a few years ahead of us in school. Anyway, as far back as I can remember, they loved to stir up trouble. They were always getting into one scrape or another and it only got worse as they got older."

Their old man, Cy, had served time for a number of things, and the apples didn't fall far from the tree. The Cottrell boys were known for picking fights and stealing anything not nailed down.

"I enlisted after graduation, but I always knew I'd come back. When I did, I joined the sheriff's office. One night, about a year in, I was on patrol." He sighed as the memory of that night filtered back to him.

"It started as a routine traffic stop. I ended up behind this old junk truck, noticed it had a busted taillight. I figured it would be quick, just a warning and he'd be on his way."

Dare ran a hand through his hair. "I recognized Beau right off. He was nervous, jittery... I knew that look. I asked him to step out of the vehicle, but he knew he was done for. Before I could call for backup, Beau panicked and took off. I went after him, yelled for him to stop."

He briefly closed his eyes, remembering the flash of metal as Beau had turned toward him. "He pulled a gun. I barely had time to react before he fired. The bullet hit me in the thigh, and I went down hard."

Ainsley gasped softly, her fingers tightening around his. "Dare..."

He gave her a small smile, but his chest ached. "It hurt like hell, but I managed to get off a couple shots. Hit him twice. Once in the stomach, the other in the heart. He went down, and I called for an ambulance. They took him to the hospital, but it was too late. He died on the way."

A heavy silence fell over the room. Ainsley squeezed his hand, her eyes shining with unshed tears. "I'm so sorry, Dare. That must have been awful."

Dare's throat constricted, and he swallowed down the emotion threatening to choke him. "I still think about it sometimes, wonder if there was something I could have done differently."

"If there's anything I've learned..." Ainsley's gaze dropped to their joined hands. "It's that hindsight is 20/20. You did what you thought was right in the moment. I can't begin to imagine what you went through, but you did what you had to do. You saved yourself."

Everyone had told him the same thing, and logically he knew it was true. He cleared his throat and shifted in his seat, grimacing as the old wound throbbed. "Anyway, the bullet did a lot of muscle damage. I was in the hospital for a while, then months of physical therapy. I healed up, but it still gives me trouble from time to time."

The injury had taken him off patrol, which irritated him to no end. He'd been moved to desk duty and done more paperwork than he ever cared to see again in his lifetime. But he'd excelled at it and had been promoted several times, earning the mens' respect. Eventually, he'd run for Sheriff.

Those giant blue eyes turned up to him, seeming to burn straight to his soul. "I'm glad you're okay."

Dare squeezed her fingers. "Thanks, Ains."

She smiled a little at the nickname, and Dare gave her hand a little tug. With a curious smile, Ainsley stood and moved toward him. He wrapped one hand around the back of her neck and pulled her to him, covering her mouth with his own.

Ainsley melted into the kiss, and he allowed himself to forget all about the pain in his leg, the case, and everything else but the woman in his arms.

CHAPTER
FORTY

Dare stared at the ceiling, unable to sleep. Jayla Simms's case was quickly going cold, though Sawyer and Cam were still looking for leads. The car for the drive-by had been found, but there were too many unanswered questions.

As for Ainsley... For hours he'd lain awake, details of the case taunting him every time he closed his eyes. He couldn't shake the feeling that something wasn't quite right. What if he was wrong? What if Joel really wasn't involved?

The background check they'd run on him had come back clean. A couple years back a local newspaper had featured Parsons in an article, touting his success. Cam had spoken with several of his colleagues and friends, all of whom liked and respected the man.

Parsons had fooled all of them into believing he was a veritable saint. Despite the fact that Dare knew the darker side of his personality that lay hidden behind closed doors, Dare recognized part of the man's statement as truth.

Maybe Parsons wasn't directly responsible for the break-in as he had originally thought.

The bullet retrieved from the store after the drive-by was a 9mm; the man didn't have a single weapon registered in his name. It was possible that Parsons had purchased a pistol illegally or even borrowed one. But without the gun, they couldn't confirm the ballistics. And the asshole would be off the hook once more.

The drive from Parsons's home to Brookhaven took just over an hour and a half, and the break-in had happened just before midnight. Accounting for the time it would have taken to cross the lake and escape, the man probably wouldn't have gotten home until after two in the morning.

Though it was feasible, it seemed unlikely. Parsons had woken early for surgery this morning, and when Dare had seen him, the man's face had been devoid of any signs of sleeplessness.

As much as he hated to admit it, he suspected Parsons wasn't lying about breaking into Ainsley's suite. Still, it didn't eliminate him entirely. He could have hired someone to do it, and they were going to find out for sure one way or another.

Cam was meeting with the judge tomorrow to request a warrant to pull Parsons's phone and bank records. Dare mentally crossed his fingers that she would sign off. They needed a damn lead, and the sooner the better. He would lose his mind if Ainsley were put in harm's way again.

Rolling to his side, he studied Ainsley where she lay next to him. He'd half-expected her to pull away from him after last night, yet she hadn't. She'd moved into his arms and his bed as surely as if she'd been there forever.

He reached out and stroked one finger along the back of her hand where it rested between them. She twitched slightly under the touch and shifted closer to him. He wrapped one arm around her waist and eased her closer, burying his nose in her thick honey-colored locks. He kissed the top of her head and Ainsley burrowed into him, brushing her nose along his collarbone.

His heart ached for her. She had been through so much, more than anyone should have to endure. The story she had shared with him had rocked him to his core. He'd suspected the man was possessive, but never in a million years would he have guessed the depths of the man's controlling nature.

It had taken every ounce of control for Dare not to snap when she'd finally spilled the truth. He'd wanted to hunt Joel down right then and there, make him pay for every ounce of pain he had inflicted on Ainsley. But he knew that his anger would do no good now. What Ainsley needed wasn't his rage; she needed his understanding and support.

The real Ainsley was in there, beneath the layers of hurt and fear. He had seen glimpses of her—a spark in her eyes when she talked about something she loved, a shy smile when she felt safe. She was strong, resilient, and capable of so much more than Joel had ever allowed her to believe.

Ainsley had been under Joel's thumb for so long, conditioned to believe that she was at fault for his abuse.

She had been denied the freedom to be herself, to make her own choices. Dare was going to change that.

As he watched her now, his resolve only strengthened. He would be patient, give her the time and space she needed to rebuild her confidence. He thought back to the first time he had seen her smile, really smile, after she left Joel. He wanted to see that smile again, to watch it light up her face, extinguishing the shadows of fear and doubt that lingered in her eyes.

A fierce protectiveness welled up inside him as he studied the contours of her pretty face, outlined in the pale moonlight. In just a couple of weeks, Ainsley had managed to burrow beneath his skin, imprinting herself on him like she was a part of him.

He wanted to claim her, to own her mind, body, and soul. He would love her, cherish her, and protect her every day. He wanted to be her everything. And though he'd tried not to focus on it, he knew... She was it for him.

Ainsley lay draped over him, her fingers drawing tiny designs across his chest. Dare sifted his hand through the long golden strands, watching as they slipped through his fingers like a waterfall of silk.

His phone vibrated an alert, and a soft growl welled up in the back of his throat. Hoping it was just a message, he ignored it. The buzzing continued, and he shifted Ainsley slightly to the side, swiping a hand at the nightstand. "Sorry, sweetheart. I've gotta get this."

Sawyer Reed's name popped up on the screen, and his

brows drew together as he tapped the screen and lifted the phone to his ear. "Jensen."

"Hey, Sheriff. Sorry to interrupt your day off, but we've got a situation. Just got a report of a woman who appears to have been abducted from her home."

He dropped his feet to the floor, already moving as the words came out. "What do we know so far?"

"Woman's name is Lindsey Gill," Reed replied. "Blonde, blue-eyed. Matches the description of the victim we found just a couple weeks ago—Jayla Simms."

Fuck. That sure as hell put a worse spin on things. Dare immediately transitioned into cop mode. "Address?"

"1270 Harvest Lane."

"I'll meet you there." Dare ended the call, then shoved the phone in his pocket as he stood and turned toward Ainsley. "That was Reed. We just got a report of another missing woman."

"Oh, my God." Ainsley blinked the confusion from her eyes and immediately pushed to a sitting position. "I hope everything's okay."

Dare offered a small smile despite the unease churning in his gut. "I need to go help."

"Of course. I'll stay here while you're gone."

"No." He shook his head. "We haven't ruled Joel out completely, and I don't want you alone, just in case. You can go to Marley and Troy's."

"That's okay, I don't want to be a bother." Ainsley shook her head as she slid from the bed. "I'll give Kinley a call. I'm sure she won't mind if I hang out for a bit."

Relief rushed through him. "That's perfect."

They quickly changed, then headed downstairs.

Ainsley fell into step next to him as Dare led Sarge outside, then loaded him into the back of the cruiser. "Keep your phone on you. I'll call as soon as I'm done."

"I will. Be careful." She popped up on her toes for a quick kiss. "Love you."

She flashed a tiny, insecure smile like she was embarrassed she'd let that slip out, then started to climb into the car. Wrapping one arm around her bicep, he halted her movement and gently tugged her back to him. "Say that again."

Her cheeks flared bright pink. "What?"

Threading his free hand into her hair, he caught her gaze and held it for several seconds. "Did you mean it?"

She swallowed nervously, then nodded. Something like relief flooded his chest. "Tell me again."

Her teeth cut into her lower lip before she responded. "I love you."

He cupped her face, thumbs tenderly sweeping over her cheeks. "Love you, too."

She melted into him, her eyes going soft. He dipped his head and brushed his lips over hers in a sweet, lingering kiss before finally releasing her. "I'll be as quick as I can. Be safe."

"I will."

The drive was tense, every second stretching into an eternity. When Dare arrived, he pulled to a stop behind the cruiser parked at the curb and glanced up at the house in question. The front door was slightly ajar, a disturbing sign that something was very wrong.

Sawyer met up with him on the sidewalk, concern etched deep in his expression. "Name is Lindsey Gill. The neighbor saw the door standing wide open when she came out to get her mail." He continued to speak as they made their way up the pathway toward the house. "She thought maybe Lindsey had forgotten to close it, so she came over to investigate."

Dare stopped just shy of the threshold and pointed toward the interior. "Did she go in?"

Sawyer shook his head. "She said she called for Lindsey, but when she didn't respond, she called us."

Dare nodded grimly as approached the house. He pushed the door the rest of the way open and called out, "Ms. Gill?"

The unsettling silence spoke volumes. From his spot on the porch, Dare quickly scanned the room, noting several small details. A purse sat on the counter, keys next to it, as if she'd been prepared to walk out the door. A half-empty coffee cup sat on the table just inside the doorway as if she'd been interrupted and had set it down to answer the door.

Dare grimaced. By all accounts, it appeared as though Lindsey had been caught off guard and abducted before she could react.

"Let's clear the house, then you can start working the scene. Once the others get here, I'll take Sarge out."

Sawyer dipped his chin. "On it."

They quickly checked the house to make sure no one was inside, careful not to disturb anything. Once it had been cleared, Dare stepped back outside, scanning the neighborhood, while Sawyer gathered his things.

People were starting to gather, curious and concerned

by their presence. A woman cautiously approached, her face twisted into an expression of worry. "Sheriff?"

"Yes?" Dare dipped his chin her way.

"I'm Martha Sutton. Lindsey's neighbor." She pointed across the street. "I was just wondering... Have you found anything yet?"

"Not yet. I'm sorry." Dare shook his head. "You spoke with Detective Reed earlier, is that correct?"

She nodded and reiterated the story she'd told Sawyer. "Her door was wide open and, well... That's not like her." Her mouth pressed into a firm line. "I wish I'd noticed something sooner."

Dare settled one hand on her shoulder. "We'll do our best to find out what happened and bring her home."

"Thank you."

He nodded, then excused himself just as another cruiser arrived on scene. Dare tipped his head toward Brad Forester and Evan Landry as they climbed from the car.

"Sheriff." Landry glanced around, taking in the scene. "Anything yet?"

"Nothing." He quickly briefed them on the situation. "I'm going to see if Sarge can pick up her scent. Reed's working the scene. I need you to question everyone, see if they saw or heard anything."

"Sure thing, boss."

The two disappeared, and Dare strode toward the cruiser to release Sarge. Dare guided him to the house where Sawyer passed him a shirt that belonged to Lindsey. Sarge immediately lowered his nose to the ground, sniffing the area with intense focus. He moved swiftly, following a scent trail from the front door through the yard. Dare followed closely behind, his eyes scanning the ground for any additional clues.

Sarge's ears perked up, his pace quickening as he picked up a stronger scent. Suddenly, at the edge of the road, Sarge stopped, lifting his head and sniffing the air. He whined softly, turning in circles as if confused.

Goddamn it. He'd lost the scent. Dare tried again, holding the fabric out for Sarge to smell. The dog darted toward the mailbox, then back again, and Dare fought the urge to swear. If Sarge wasn't able to pick up the trail, he could only presume that Lindsey had been taken away by vehicle.

He patted the dog, then loaded him back into the cruiser and went in search of Sawyer. The detective was crouched near the front door of the house, carefully lifting prints, when Dare drew even with him. "Find anything?"

Dare repressed a growl. "Lost the trail almost immediately."

Sawyer grimaced and pushed to his feet. "Aside from the door standing wide open, there's no sign of a struggle. You think she knew him?"

Dare's eyes scanned the room once more, noting that everything seemed to be perfectly in place. "Possibly. We need to find something, anything that tells us where she might be. I'm going to head back to the station, get a search party organized. If you find anything, let me know."

"Will do."

Dare head back to the cruiser at a fast clip. They already had one victim waiting on justice. He wouldn't let Lindsey end up the same way.

CHAPTER
FORTY-ONE

Ainsley watched as Dare climbed behind the wheel, then steered the SUV down the driveway. A tiny pang of anxiety ricocheted through her chest as he disappeared from sight, and she rubbed one hand over the spot.

This was his job; he was used to the danger. But it was new to her. She couldn't stop herself from worrying about him, and she knew the feeling wouldn't subside until he was home once more.

Ainsley let out a little sigh as she dug through her purse and pulled out her phone to call Kinley.

Pulling up her contact list, she tapped her sister's number and waited for the call to connect. Three short rings later, Kinley's voice filled the line. "Hey, Ains. What's going on?"

"I was wondering if I could come over. Dare just left to work a case, and I really didn't want to be all alone."

"Of course. Cam just got called out, too." Her voice was filled with worry. "I hope everything's okay."

Ainsley hesitated, debating whether to offer false

platitudes or not. While she wasn't privy to all the details of the ongoing investigation, she knew it wasn't good. And this most recent woman going missing was looking worse by the minute. "I'm not sure," she finally said. "But I figure it's better to stick together for the time being."

"Definitely. I was thinking of heading over to mom and dad's, but if you want to come over here instead..."

Ainsley bit her lip. She wasn't sure she was ready to tell her parents about everything going on just yet. "Maybe we'll just hang out at your place today."

"No problem. See you when you get here."

Ainsley hung up and turned her attention to the road, her thoughts drifting back to Dare as they always did.

She turned into Kinley's driveway less than ten minutes later, and her sister greeted her with a wave from the small front porch. Ainsley climbed from the car and shot her sister a smile. "Sorry to just drop in like this."

"No problem at all. I was actually just going to make some cookies."

Kinley baked when she was stressed, and sympathy tugged at Ainsley's heart. More than likely her sister was worried about Cam, just as Ainsley worried about Dare each time he was called out for an emergency. "Cookies sound good to me."

She followed Kinley inside and laughed when she saw the counter cluttered with ingredients. "You weren't kidding."

Kinley made a face. "Yeah. I couldn't decide what to choose, so... "

Ainsley laughed. "Well, we better get to it."

Once they had the first batch of peanut butter cookies

in the oven, Kinley slid a look at Ainsley. "So. How are things going?"

"What do you mean?" Ainsley affected an innocent expression as she dropped onto a stool.

One sleek blonde eyebrow arched upward. "I haven't talked to you for a couple weeks, but I can tell something is different."

A smile tugged at the corners of Ainsley's mouth. What hadn't changed?

Kinley's eyes narrowed. "You're sleeping with him, aren't you?"

Heat swept up Ainsley's cheeks, but she could no longer fight the smile that overtook her face. "I don't know what you're talking about."

"You are!" Kinley clapped her hands together excitedly. "I knew it."

Ainsley ducked her head and fiddled with the package of chocolate chips.

"How are things?"

She added a healthy portion of chips into the dough. "It's good. Really good."

Kinley's head tipped slightly to one side as she inspected her sister, and Ainsley fought the urge to shift nervously.

"You look... happy," she finally said.

"I am. I really am."

The doorbell rang, and Ainsley glanced up at her sister. "Are you expecting someone?"

Kinley's brows drew together. "I don't think so. You stay here for a second, and I'll go see who it is."

Ainsley gave a little nod, then plunged her hands back

into the bowl of cookie dough. The sound of the front door opening reached her ears just as she placed a perfectly round ball on the baking sheet.

"Can I help you?" Kinley asked.

"Hello, ma'am," came a thick Southern drawl. "Sorry to bother you, but I'm collecting…"

The rest of his words were drowned out by the beep of the oven. Ainsley scowled at it, staining her ears toward the front door.

"Hold on just a second," Kinley replied.

Ainsley removed the tray of cookies and set them aside to cool, then glanced over at her sister as she trotted back into the kitchen. "Who is it?"

"Someone collecting donations for wounded soldiers." Kinley grabbed her purse off the chair and dug through it for her wallet.

"I thought they did most of those things online now," Ainsley said.

"Maybe." Kinley pulled out a $20 bill, then shrugged. "It's probably easier for them to guilt people into giving the money if they ask face-to-face."

Ainsley made a little sound in the back of her throat. "I'm sure it's for a good cause."

"Of course it is," Kinley replied. "I'm just kidding. Let me run this out to him and I'll be right back."

Ainsley shaped the last of the dough, still listening intently. Metal slid against metal as Kinley unhooked the deadbolt, then opened the door. "Here you go."

"Thank you so much, ma'am," came the man's reply. "Would you mind filling one of these out so we can acknowledge your gracious donation?"

A smile tugged at Ainsley's lips. The man selling it just a touch, though he did sound grateful. Tuning out the rest of the conversation, she washed her hands, scrubbing at the sticky dough. She reached for the second tray just as a soft noise from the living room drew her attention.

Ainsley tapped the button to turn off the oven and listened hard, ears straining to pick up any sounds beyond the kitchen. Several moments passed, but the house remained eerily silent. "Kin?" she called out. "Is everything okay?"

Two seconds passed with no response, then three. The hair on the back of her neck stood on end, and ice water streamed through her veins. Where had Kinley gone? Did she go outside for something, or had the man lured her away?

Her heart beat hard in her chest as she glanced around the kitchen. She heard no movement from the outer room, and every cell of her body went on high alert. Something wasn't right. Had Joel finally found her?

Her gaze immediately darted to the door that led to the back yard. She might be able to escape, but she would have to cross in front of the living room to do so. And what about Kinley? She couldn't just leave her here.

Her gaze swept the room, locking on her purse sitting on the kitchen table, her cell phone next to it. If she could reach her phone, she could call the police. She darted a look toward the doorway to the living room.

She still hadn't heard anything from that direction, and her pulse kicked up. Someone was there, just waiting for her.

The knife block appeared in her peripheral vision, and

she inched toward it. Better to be prepared. Wrapping her hand around the hilt of the chef's knife, she quietly drew the long blade from its slot. It scraped the wood softly as it came free, and Ainsley winced, hoping the sound hadn't carried.

She adjusted her grip on the knife and, quietly as possible, tiptoed toward the doorway that separated the living room from the kitchen. She paused several feet away, cocking her ears and straining to hear anything from the other side. It was deathly silent.

Ainsley bent her knees and crouched low, then sidled closer. Her breath caught in her throat as she risked a peek around the doorway and saw a body on the floor, legs sprawled lifelessly. She slapped a hand over her mouth, barely managing to stifle her cry of horror as she recognized the shoes Kinley had been wearing just a few moments ago.

CHAPTER
FORTY-TWO

Dare heaved a sigh. The first forty-eight hours were crucial in missing persons cases. If this was the same person who'd abducted and killed Jayla Simms, they were going to need all the help they could get.

As the volunteers gathered in the town square, Dare addressed them with a steady, commanding voice. "Thank you all for coming. We need every able hand to search the surrounding areas. Lindsey was last seen at her home, but she could be anywhere. Pair up and cover as much ground as possible. Report back here by sundown, and keep an eye out for anything unusual. Every detail matters."

He assigned groups to different sections of the neighborhood, hoping to find any clue that could lead them to Lindsey. Every minute that passed without finding her felt like a weight on Dare's chest.

The crowd dispersed, determined and focused, and Dare watched them go, the weight of responsibility resting heavily on his shoulders. He cut across the town square and was intercepted by Cam the moment he stepped inside the station. "Boss, we got the lab results back from the evidence we found at the car. You need to see this."

He grabbed the report from Cam's outstretched hand, his gaze already skimming the information. They needed a break in this case, and he hoped this was it.

As they'd suspected, no prints had been found in or around the car. His heart slammed against his ribs as his gaze moved lower, and he froze, a cold wave of fear rolling through him. The cigarette butt found near the road had a positive DNA match.

"Wade Cottrell."

Cam nodded, his expression grim. "Joel had an alibi for the shooting, but this... It potentially puts Wade at the scene."

Dare struggled to steady his breathing, the implications of this discovery rattling him to his core. Wade had held a grudge for the past several years, blaming Dare for his brother's death. Had he been wrong all along? Maybe Wade had been aiming at him that day in the parking lot. Or maybe he had seen Ainsley with Dare, and assumed they were together...

Dare's lungs constricted. "We need to talk to Wade."

Cam dipped his chin. "Let's go."

The drive to Wade's house was tense, the silence thick and heavy. They pulled up to the small, rundown house on the outskirts of town, the lawn overgrown and the paint peeling.

Dare knocked on the door, the sound echoing hollowly in the stillness. No answer. He knocked again, louder this time. "Wade, it's Sheriff Jensen. We need to talk."

Still nothing. He exchanged a glance with Cam, who nodded. They circled the house, peering through windows and checking for any signs of life. The house appeared empty.

Fear welled up, causing Dare's chest to constrict. They needed to find Wade—before he found Ainsley.

CHAPTER
FORTY-THREE

"I know you're there."

Chills raced down her arms as Joel's voice, no longer disguised, floated toward her.

Her heart stuttered in her chest as his face came into view. "Joel. What are you doing here?"

"I came for you, of course." His head tipped slightly to one side as he studied her, and a smirk lifted the corner of his lips. "Did you really think I was just going to let you go?"

No, she didn't. Tess had paid the price for that, and now...

Ainsley swallowed hard. "What did you do to my sister?"

His gaze dropped to the knife still clutched in her fist, and one eyebrow shot upward. "I think the better question is—what do you think you're going to do with that?"

"Stay away." She brandished the knife in his direction. "Don't come any closer."

Joel laughed, the sound grating on her frayed nerves. "You know you won't hurt me. You don't have it in you."

"I'm warning you." She sliced the knife through the air. "Stay back."

Her brain was a maelstrom of emotion, but she forced herself to focus. The backdoor was behind her to the left. To get there, she would need to cross the doorway, then get around the table. She slowly stepped in that direction, keeping as much distance between them as possible.

"Put the knife down."

She flinched at his commanding tone but stood her ground. "No."

His gaze narrowed. "You're starting to piss me off. I said, put the knife down."

Her hand shook as she frantically searched her mind for a way out of this mess. She didn't have time to analyze her options. Instinct kicked in as he took another menacing step toward her, and she took off at a panicked run toward the back door.

An agonized scream tore from her throat as Joel caught a handful of hair in his fist and yanked her back. She swiped at him with the knife and was rewarded when he let out a howl of pain.

Suddenly the hand in her hair loosened and she pitched forward, hitting the tile floor hard on her hands and knees. She watched with dismay as the knife went skittering under the kitchen table.

"No!" She clawed at the ground and scrambled after the knife, but he grabbed one ankle and pulled her roughly down again. Her chin bounced off the hard floor, and she let out a mewl of pain as it sent a shockwave through her jaw.

A blood-curdling shriek tore from her throat and she fought him in earnest, arms and legs flying. "I hate you! You won't get away with this!"

Ainsley's vision went black for a moment and pain lanced through her as Joel's fist slammed into her temple. Wincing, she fought against him with all her might, funneling her anger and rage into her blows as she struck out at him.

They rolled across the floor, each trying to overpower the other. Joel let out a grunt as one of her knees connected with his groin, but her satisfaction was cut short when he rolled her back under him.

Joel rolled her over and pinned her arms above her head. "Damn it, Ainsley. Look what you did. You wouldn't have gotten hurt if you'd just listened to me. Why don't you *listen*?" He shook his head at her, his pitch rising with every word.

Her eyes darted wildly around the room, searching for anything that she could to fend him off. She felt Joel's weight hovering above her as she twisted and writhed, trying to escape his grasp. She struggled against him, slowly inching toward the table.

She was so close. If she could just get to the knife... Her feet slipped on the cool tile, and a scream of frustration broke free.

Suddenly, one of her hands was free as Joel released her, and hope bloomed in Ainsley's chest. The fleeting emotion was doused seconds later when his palm cracked against her face, snapping her head to the side.

"Shut your mouth, you're going to draw attention."

She opened her mouth to scream again and his hand wrapped around her throat, pressing against her delicate trachea, effectively silencing her. Her eyes widened in fear and she stared helplessly up at him.

Panic surged through her veins as she fought for breath, the world around her fading into a blur of pain. She clawed at Joel's arms, her nails digging into his flesh as she struggled to break free, but his hold only tightened, his fingers crushing the life from her with every passing moment.

Black slowly crept in around the edges of Ainsley's vision and she struggled harder against his grasp. The pressure on her throat receded and pain exploded up the side of her face as a second blow landed hard on her cheek. Tears burned the backs of her eyes as the metallic tang of blood filled her mouth.

"Please..." She managed to gasp out the word.

His weight lifted off of her and she sucked in a shaky breath. The sound of blood rushing through her veins filled her ears, and she could feel every beat of her heart as it threatened to beat from her chest. She could still escape, outwit him, if only...

Stars exploded before her eyes as her skull collided with the ground. "You don't get to tell me what to do, Ainsley," he spat, his words like venom as his hands tightened around her throat in a vice-like grip.

And then, just as she felt herself slipping away, a new voice cut through the air. "As much as I'm enjoying the show, it's my turn."

Ainsley sucked in a breath as Joel's head jerked

upward, his attention firmly fixed on the man standing just a few feet away. "Who the hell are you?"

"Name's Wade. And the girl is mine now."

The man lifted the pistol he'd had concealed at his side, pointed it at Joel and fired.

CHAPTER
FORTY-FOUR

The gnawing feeling in Dare's gut told him something was terribly wrong. He glanced at Cam as they strode away from Wade's house.

"Have you heard from Kinley recently?"

Cam checked his phone. "Not recently. Why?"

Dare shook his head, his worry mounting. "I need to check on Ainsley. I have a bad feeling about this."

They climbed into Dare's SUV and he cranked the engine. As soon as it caught, he threw the transmission into gear, then slammed the accelerator to the floor. The engine roared to life, and they sped back toward Brookhaven.

"When I left the house, she was supposed to go over there until I got back." As he spoke, Dare tapped the button on the dash to call Ainsley. The sound of the phone ringing filled the cab, and Dare's anxiety ratcheted upward with each passing second.

One ring rolled into two, then three. His pulse accelerated with each harsh ring until an automated message picked up. A spike of fear shot through him, cold and sharp. He tried again, but still no answer. "Call Kinley. Make sure everything's okay."

Cam nodded, quickly dialing Kinley's number. He waited, frowning as the phone continued to ring. He shook his head, concern etching deeper lines into his face. "No answer."

"Damn it." Dare's stomach twisted into a tight knot, a cold sweat breaking out on his forehead. Fear clutched at his throat, making it hard to breathe. The thought of Wade getting to Ainsley and Kinley was unbearable. "We need to get to Kinley's house now."

Dare tried to call Ainsley again, his hands gripping the wheel so tightly his knuckles turned white. The phone rang and rang, then went to voicemail again. "Ainsley, it's Dare. I'm on my way to Kinley's. Call me back as soon as you get this. I need to know you're okay," he said, his voice cracking with worry before hanging up.

Cam's hand tightened on the handle over the door, his face looking as worried as Dare felt. "We'll find them, Dare. We'll make sure they're safe."

Dare nodded, though his heart pounded erratically. Wade was dangerous. If he'd gotten to them...

He shook the thought away, the fear too overwhelming. They were going to be okay. They had to be.

CHAPTER
FORTY-FIVE

Ainsley stared in stunned horror at the man in the doorway, then back to Joel who lay on the ground, unmoving. A dark pool of blood had begun to gather around his torso, and Ainsley's stomach flipped violently. She swallowed hard and ripped her gaze away, turning back to the man who'd saved her.

Ainsley tried to scramble to her feet, but Wade leveled the gun at her, stealing her words. "Where do you think you're going, missy?"

She froze, trapped between the table and chairs behind her. Automatically, she raised her hands in front of her. "P-please. I—"

"Huh uh." He shook his head. "Not done with you yet."

Ainsley's heart rate kicked up as Wade loomed over her, his eyes gleaming with a malevolence that sent a chill down her spine. For a fleeting moment, hope had sparked within her when he first entered, believing he was there to rescue her. But that hope was quickly extinguished as his words sunk in.

Ainsley shrank back as Wade lifted the pistol in her direction. He chuckled, the ugly sound washing over her. He stroked the barrel of the gun over her face, tracing a cold, hard line along her jaw, along her throat, and down her sternum.

Tears pricked her eyes as he grasped his belt buckle and released it with a soft metallic click. She clenched her eyes closed, the sound of leather sliding through the belt loops barely penetrating the sound of blood rushing in her ears.

"Look at me!"

She forced herself to meet his gaze as his fingers dug into her cheeks and turned her face to his. The man glared down at her. "Do you know who I am?"

Stricken with fear, unable to speak, she shook her head.

"I know who you are." She tried to jerk away as he trailed a finger over her jaw, but he pressed the gun harder into her chest, making her blood freeze in her veins.

"What... what do you want?"

His eyes were wild, filled with a mixture of rage and twisted pleasure. "He killed my brother," Wade snarled. "Did you know that? How does it feel to sleep with a killer?"

Ainsley recalled Dare's story about Wade's brother, Cy. "He didn't mean to, he—"

Her head whipped to the side as his hand connected with her cheek. "Shut up!"

Tears pricked her eyes as pain radiated across her face. Wade didn't want help. He wanted revenge. He wanted blood. And he wanted her to suffer before she died.

"That bastard took my brother away." She flinched as spittle flew from his mouth and spattered her face. "He ever tell you about that gunshot wound? Courtesy of my brother, before that asshole killed him in cold blood."

"Please, I—"

"I dreamed of killing that bastard," Wade said. "Then, all of a sudden... you came along." Wade pointed the gun at her face. "I see the way he looks at you. He loves you, doesn't he?"

Ainsley couldn't form words through the haze of fear surrounding her. She flinched away from him as he tapped her forehead with the pistol, her back bumping the leg of the table. "I asked you a question. Does he love you?"

"Y-yes." Her voice shook, her body trembling fiercely.

"I loved my brother, too. He was the only family I had left, and that motherfucker took him away," he seethed. "Now I'm going to show him how it feels."

Her heart skipped a beat as she stared into his eyes, feverish with retribution. "Take your shirt off," he commanded, his voice dripping with sadistic anticipation. "I want to see what the sheriff's been sampling."

Oh, God.

Every cell of her body froze. She'd expected him to kill her, but this... Her stomach churned, bile creeping up her throat.

"What?" His gaze darkened. "You're good enough for him, but not for me?"

Ainsley's breath came in shallow gasps. She felt the room closing in on her, the acrid smell of unwashed flesh mingling with the tang of blood pooling on the floor beneath her. Joel's lifeless eyes stared at her, taunting her.

Unless she came up with something, and quick, she was going to end up just like him.

"Do it!"

Trembling, Ainsley reached for the hem of her shirt. Her hands were slick with blood, the metallic scent filling her nostrils. Her mind raced, desperately seeking a way out. She couldn't fight him off—he was too heavy, too strong. But she couldn't just give in. As she lifted her shirt, Wade's eyes darkened with approval. Fisting his hands in her shirt he ripped the fabric away, exposing her skin to the cool air.

Wade's touch was like fire, scorching her skin as his filthy hands traced the contours of her body. Her mind screamed for escape, but her muscles were paralyzed with fear. He roughly grasped her breast, plumping the flesh. He grinned lasciviously as he worked the cup of her bra down until her nipple was bared to his view.

Her stomach pitched violently and she turned her face away, unable to look at him. She needed a plan, needed—

From beneath the table, a subtle glint of silver caught her attention and her heart leaped. The knife was still there, hidden just out of Wade's sight. If she could get to it...

Wade's hands roamed her body, his touch growing more aggressive. She had to act fast. Summoning every ounce of strength and willpower, Ainsley shifted slightly, inching closer to the knife.

Suddenly his hands left her body. "Take off your pants."

Ainsley froze, her fingers just inches from the knife. Wade watched her intently, eyes blazing. Her muscles trembled as she reached for the snap on her jeans, her fingers clumsily fumbling with it before finally managing to push the button free of its hole.

She pushed the fabric down her thighs, until she reached the spot where he was suspended over her legs. He shifted his weight so he hovered slightly above her then grabbed her jeans. He gave a hard tug, yanking them down her legs and pulling her with them. A soft cry escaped as she fell to her back, and the back of her head smacked against the chair.

Wade yanked on the fabric again and hope leaped in her chest. Ainsley used the motion to push herself backward, fingers searching for the knife. Her heart slammed against her rib cage. She had to find it. Where the hell was it?

Wade grinned as one foot pulled free of the fabric, then the other, just as her fingers brushed the hilt of the knife. Relief exploded through her chest as she wrapped her fingers around the polished wood handle.

She had one chance. One shot at survival.

The floor was slick with blood, and she slid through the sticky liquid as he pulled her closer. His eyes were bright as he stared down at her. Rage simmered in her blood, spiraling outward to the tips of her fingers. She pulled the knife from its place under the table and Wade's eyes widened as his gaze landed on the weapon.

"Wh—"

The rest of the word was cut off as she lunged forward, her hand cutting a swift arc through the air. He jerked backward, but he wasn't fast enough. The blade slashed through the soft flesh of his neck, sending a spray of blood spattering across the wall and floor.

CHAPTER
FORTY-SIX

Cam's heart pounded as Dare's SUV screeched to a halt in front of Kinley's house. Dare jumped out, his hand hovering near his gun. "I've got the back."

With that, Dare took off around the side of the house. Cam sprinted up the front porch steps, the wooden boards creaking under his weight. He hesitated for a brief second before peering through the window, his breath catching in his throat at the sight that greeted him. Kinley lay motionless on the floor, surrounded by a pool of blood.

Oh, God, no. Not Kinley.

His heart flipped over in his chest as he pushed the door open and rushed inside, skidding to his knees beside her. His hands trembled as his fingers pressed against her neck, searching for a pulse. There it was—faint and thready, but it gave him a small measure of relief.

"Stay with me, sweetheart," he whispered, his voice cracking on the words. He loved her so much, and the thought of losing her, never getting to tell her how he truly felt, was unbearable.

A gash in her forehead oozed blood, and it pooled on the floor around her. Grabbing up a blanket from the nearby couch, he pressed it against the wound, doing his best to staunch the bleeding. He needed to call for medical help, but first he had to make sure Ainsley was safe. He tore himself away from Kinley, fury turning his blood to fire as he stumbled to his feet and stalked through the house.

He was going to find whoever had done this, and there was going to be hell to pay...

CHAPTER
FORTY-SEVEN

In the blink of an eye, Dare surveyed the scene before him. A man—Joel, he presumed—lay sprawled on the floor in a pool of dark blood. A few feet away, Ainsley lay on the floor next to the kitchen table, a second man suspended over her.

Wade.

Blood covered his torso, and fear stilled Dare's heart as the man reached for her. Dare didn't think twice. He leveled the pistol at the man and fired twice. His body jerked and his eyes flew wide with surprise as the rounds pierced his torso. His mouth opened, but nothing came out. For an interminable moment, he wavered in the air before slumping forward.

Ainsley shrieked as the man landed heavily on top of her, and Dare leaped around the table, reaching them in two long strides. Cam got there first, and he yanked Wade off her, dragging him to the side to check his pulse.

Dare pulled her into his arms, and she cried out as she struggled against him, her mind still processing whatever had happened. He relaxed his hold, using words instead to cut through her fear.

"Ainsley. Ainsley! It's just me, honey. It's Dare." He knelt beside her and coaxed her closer. "Everything's going to be okay. We're going to get you out of here."

He met Cam's gaze over her head, and the man gave a quick shake of his head before sprinting back toward the living room. Dare heard the radio crackle to life as Cam called in the incident, and he turned his focus back to Ainsley.

Her pants lay discarded on the floor, and her entire body was smeared with blood. What remained of her shirt was torn and bloody, leaving her torso completely exposed. He pulled the edges together and eased her into his arms, then carried her outside, away from the two dead men. She remained rigid in his arms, her face pale, her pulse beating rapidly under his touch. Her eyes were still wide and he gently rested her against the side of the house, recognizing the first signs of shock.

He spoke quietly as his hands skimmed over her, searching for the source of the blood. "Are you hurt, sweetheart?"

She shook her head, a note of hysteria tinging her voice. "Where's Kinley? I need—"

Cam hadn't reappeared yet, which didn't bode well. He hoped to hell Kinley was okay, but Ainsley had been through enough already. He didn't want to worry her even more. "Cam is with her," he said quietly. "He needs to be with her right now."

She nodded a little and another shudder racked her

body. Dare kissed the top of her head. "Stay here. I'm going to get something to cover you up."

Dare swiftly moved into the kitchen, skirting the men's bodies. His gaze dropped to a knife lying on the floor, the blade covered in dark blood. He glanced over at Wade, his eyes wide and vacant as he stared sightlessly at the ceiling.

From this angle, Dare could see the vicious slash at the base of the man's neck. His jaw clenched as his glare skated over Joel's prone form. God, how he wanted to make him suffer for everything he'd put Ainsley through. He'd tried to hurt her and had paid the ultimate price. Dare couldn't even bring himself to be upset about it.

He moved into the living room, his gaze sweeping over Cam who knelt next to Kinley, one hand wrapped around hers, the other holding a blanket to her head.

"How is she?"

Cam barely glanced up at him. "Not good."

Dare didn't press for more. He grabbed another blanket and made his way back to Ainsley, whose eyes were closed, her head tilted to the side. He scooped her up, wrapping the blanket around her and settling her in his lap.

Ainsley lay against him, limp and exhausted, silent except for her shallow breathing, and he could practically feel the energy drain from her body. He knew the feeling, coming down from an adrenaline rush like that, but the sound of approaching sirens meant their ordeal was far from over.

He briefly closed his eyes, thanking every deity known to man that Ainsley was okay. Dipping his head, he spoke softly in her ear. "You still with me, honey?"

Her head bobbed in an infinitesimal nod and he kissed her temple. "The ambulance is here. They're going to take you to the hospital."

Her eyes popped open at his words and she clutched his arm. "No! I don't want to go. Don't let them take me."

His heart broke at her desperate plea and he hugged her tight. "No one will ever take you away from me. I'll never let that happen." He pulled back just enough to meet her gaze. "Never. You get me?"

After what felt like forever, she finally nodded.

He took her hand in his, lacing their fingers together. "You need to go to the hospital, sweetheart. But I'll be right beside you, I promise."

Dare mentally tracked the EMTs as they stepped inside and assessed the situation. Antonio appeared in the doorway a moment later, his gaze zeroing in on Ainsley where she was curled in Dare's lap.

He cautiously squatted next to her and offered a small smile. "We need to stop meeting like this."

Ainsley tried for a smile, but it fell flat. Antonio's gaze swept over her from head to toe. "Any injuries?"

She shook her head. "I'll be fine. How's my sister?"

"My partners are getting her loaded up right now so we can get her to the hospital and check her out."

He flicked a glance at Dare, imparting what he didn't want to say in front of Ainsley. Kinley was in much worse shape than Ainsley, so they were taking care of her first.

He turned another soft smile on Ainsley. "While they get her taken care of, I'm going to take your vitals, okay?"

Dare reluctantly turned Ainsley over to him, staying

close to keep her calm. Antonio spoke as he worked, his movements quick and efficient.

The deputies not working with Lindsey Gills's search party showed up and began to secure the scene. Dare extricated himself from Ainsley long enough to speak with Forester. "I'm going to ride with her to the hospital, but I'll be back as soon as I can."

The deputy dipped his chin in acknowledgment. "Take your time, boss. You should be with her right now."

The next hour was a whirlwind of activity as they sped to the local hospital and both Ainsley and Kinley were admitted to the ER. Dare called Sawyer and Yvonne to fill them in on what had happened and let them know that he and Cam would be tied up at the hospital for a while.

Dare took a seat in the waiting room, his leg bouncing nervously, eyes darting every few seconds to the large grey double doors that opened into the emergency room. Next to him, Cam sat with his head in his hands.

Dare settled a hand on his shoulder. "She's going to be okay."

Cam shook his head, then leaned back and stared at the wall across from them. "It's bad," he whispered. "There was so much blood..."

Dare strove for confidence. "Head wounds always bleed like a bitch. They'll make sure she gets the best care."

"What if...?" Cam trailed off and glanced away.

Dare didn't have the answer to that. All he could do was hope for the best.

Ainsley's parents arrived, looking haggard but hopeful, and Dare quickly explained what happened. Charlene took a seat next to Cam and Dare watched as she wrapped an arm around his shoulders, pulling him in for a hug. His chest tightened at the sight. He knew Cam was closer to Kinley than his own family, and if something happened to her... It would kill him.

Garrett Layne held a hand out to Dare, his expression a mixture of worry and gratitude. "Thank you for helping my girls."

Dare slipped his palm into the other man's for a firm shake. "My pleasure, sir."

A striking blonde strolled in next, and Dare immediately recognized the youngest daughter, Brynlee. He'd only seen her a couple of times, but there was no denying she was part of the Layne family with her golden hair and cerulean eyes.

Worry pinched her features as she moved toward them and dropped into the seat next to her mother. "How are they?"

"We're still waiting," Charlene replied. "Hopefully it won't be long now."

Every time the door opened and a nurse called someone's name, his patience frayed a little more. He was almost down to his last nerve.

Restless, needing to move, he paced the length of the room. Waiting was excruciating, and he knew he wouldn't be able to relax until he could see Ainsley again for himself, and he knew Cam was ready to break down the doors to get to Kinley.

A quick glance down at his uniform smeared with Ainsley's blood sent a mixture of fury and concern billowing through him. He ran a hand over the dark brown stains, his anxiety ratcheting tenfold. He needed to see her, just for a second, just to make sure she really was okay.

He glanced at his watch and grimaced. Goddamn it. He needed to get back to Kinley's house and relieve the others.

"You holding up okay?"

Dare glanced over at Garrett Layne. "I was hoping to see her by now."

Mr. Layne nodded. "If you need to go, we'll understand."

He was torn. He hated to leave Ainsley here alone, but she had her family to wait with her until he got back.

"If it weren't absolutely necessary..."

"I understand." Mr. Layne dipped his head. "I'll call you as soon as I hear something."

Relief rushed through him. "Thank you, sir."

"No need to thank me." Garrett placed a hand on his shoulder. "Just get back to her when you can."

"Yes, sir." Dare excused himself then made his way over to Cam. He crouched next to him and spoke quietly. "I'm headed back to Kinley's house. You can wait here, but if you need something to do..."

Cam jumped to his feet, eager to do something to keep his mind off the woman in the other room. "Let's go."

Dare nodded to Mr. Layne once more, then left the hospital, Cam at his side. They had a few loose ends to tie up, and he wanted to get it over with sooner rather than later so he could get back to the woman he loved.

CHAPTER
FORTY-EIGHT

Emotion slammed into him the moment he pulled to a stop in front of Kinley's house, the area cordoned off with yellow police tape. Dare had always prided himself on being able to separate work from his personal life, but now it hit him full force. He'd never been so deeply affected before. Then again, he'd never cared so much for any of the victims he'd helped.

He swallowed hard as he stared at the house, memories from this afternoon washing over him. In the passenger seat, Cam was deathly silent, his knee jumping nervously as his fingers drummed a nervous tattoo against the console.

Ainsley and Kinley deserved answers, and it was up to him and Cam to provide them. He reached for the door handle. "Ready?"

Cam didn't say a word as he slipped from the cruiser, then ducked under the tape and made his way up to the front porch. He paused at the threshold, and Dare settled a hand on his shoulder. "Work it just like it's a regular scene. You're one of the best cops I know. You can do this."

Cam expelled a harsh breath, then nodded.

Duke Turner met them at the doorway, and Dare nodded at the deputy. "Thanks for holding down the fort. What do we know so far?"

Turner pointed at the front door. "No sign of forced entry, so I'm guessing whoever came in the front door probably talked his way in."

"Parsons," Cam muttered as he inspected the door knob. "The asshole is smooth enough."

Dare agreed with his assessment. Not to mention, Wade wasn't exactly the kind of person Kinley would have invited into her home.

Cam pointed to a discarded clipboard that lay just a few feet away. "What's that?"

"Appears to be a donation form. Probably how he gained entrance," Turner replied.

Dare's gaze moved to the large blood stain saturating the carpet near the front door. The sight made his blood boil, and he clenched his fists, pushing down the rage that threatened to consume him. If they'd just been a little quicker...

He shook the thought away and focused on Turner's words. "Hines found Parsons's car parked a few blocks away."

"Both men must have had eyes on the women to show up here at almost exactly the same time," Hines said from the doorway that opened into the kitchen. "There's no sign of forced entry back here, either, but I'm guessing he caught them off guard."

Markers had been set up next to the evidence, and they

carefully skirted them as they moved to the back of the house. As Dare stepped into the room, the memory of walking in on Wade hovering over Ainsley slapped at him, and a chill slithered down his spine.

The bodies had been removed, leaving behind streaks of blood that stood out against the pristine white tile.

He cleared his throat. "Parsons was dead when I got here," he said, recounting the details of the scene he'd walked in on earlier. "So, we can assume Joel arrived first, incapacitated Kinley, then went after Ainsley."

Hines nodded. "My guess is Wade came in through the back, shot Parsons, then went after her himself."

"We found impressions of a footprint outside," Turner cut in. "We'll compare it to both men's shoes to be sure, but I'm guessing from the tread that it was a work boot. Parsons had on dress shoes."

Dare struggled against the tightness constricting his chest. They would need to get an official statement from the women later to verify, but it sounded feasible enough. "Great job. Let's get everything wrapped up."

He would need to hire someone to clean the house while Kinley was in the hospital. The last thing he wanted was for her to come home and have to relive it all over again.

His phone rang, snapping him out of his thoughts. He dug it out of his pocket, his brows pulling together at the sight of the unfamiliar number. He swiped the screen and lifted it to his ear. "Jensen."

"Dare, this is Garrett Layne. I wanted to let you know that Ainsley's been cleared for visitors," the older man said.

Relief coursed through him, and Dare felt a weight lift from his shoulders. "That's great news. What about Kinley?"

"She's been scheduled for a CT scan, but Charlene got to see her for a few minutes. Said she woke up briefly, was confused and in some pain."

"Thanks, Mr. Layne. We're on our way."

"What's wrong with Kinley?"

He hung up and turned to meet Cam's concerned gaze. "She's going back for a CT scan shortly, but she was awake a little while ago."

Cam's brows dipped into a severe V-shape. "But she's okay?"

Head injuries were tricky, they both knew that. Dare wanted to stay positive, but he wasn't going to lie to him, either.

"I don't know for sure," Dare replied quietly. "We'll have to wait for the results to come back."

Cam nodded. "Let's go."

The drive to the hospital felt interminable, each second stretching longer than the last. When they finally arrived, Dare practically ran through the halls, his heart pounding in his chest.

His gaze swept the waiting room and landed immediately on Brynlee. "Where are they?"

"Mom is with Kinley, and Dad is with Ainsley. I told them I'd wait for you." She rattled off the room numbers. "Kinley just got back, but she's exhausted."

Cam was already gone, striding down the hallway toward Kinley's room. Dare let out a pent-up breath as he dropped into a chair. He was champing at the bit to see her, but he would give Ainsley's family time to see her first.

"You love her."

Dare lifted his gaze to Brynlee. "Yeah. I do."

"Good." She smiled. "I was hoping it would work out that way."

Dare cocked his head in question. "What do you mean?"

She lifted one shoulder. "I had a feeling something was going on. She'd changed so much over the last couple years. She was so closed off... Never smiled anymore."

Dare's chest tightened. That smile was one of his favorite things about her, and he hated that it had ever been taken away from her, even for a moment.

Her sister continued, "I just never dreamed this would have happened."

His stomach twisted violently. "I should have been there for her. I should have known—"

Brynlee shook her head, cutting Dare off. "That's not what I'm saying at all. I'm saying she was lucky you were there for her. Joel isn't—wasn't—healthy. What he did was completely out of your control."

Dare stared at her for a moment. "You're not upset with me?"

"You saved my sisters," she said bluntly. "Of course I'm not upset with you." She leaned forward. "Besides, I was the one who sent Ainsley your way."

Dare blinked. "Why?"

Brynlee laughed. "Because I had a feeling about the two of you. When I saw your ad..." She shrugged. "Mama's wanted Ainsley to move home forever. I told her that renting your suite would be perfect."

Dare let out a little laugh. "Matchmakers, the lot of you."

Brynlee sat back in her chair with a grin. "You're not complaining, are you?"

He shook his head. "Not one damn bit."

CHAPTER
FORTY-NINE

Cam braced himself as he paused in the doorway of Kinley's room. It felt as if his pulse hadn't slowed since the moment he'd seen her lying on the floor in a dark puddle of blood.

Bile rose up his throat, and he forced it down. From this moment on, he would never leave her side.

He stepped into the room, his gaze scanning the small space. His heart almost stuttered to a stop at the sight of her. She looked so tiny and frail, dwarfed by the large hospital bed, a white sheet pulled up to her chest. Her eyes were closed, her face tipped slightly to the side, and he wondered if she'd gone back to sleep. It wouldn't matter if she had, he just needed to be with her.

From her spot next to the bed, Charlene caught his gaze and offered a small smile. "Come in."

Cam ventured closer, throat tight with fear and worry. "How is she?"

"Tired." Charlene turned her attention back to Kinley. "She woke up for a few minutes before they took her back for the CT scan. She was a little confused, but that's to be expected."

His hands shook, and he clamped his fingers around the opposite wrist to keep from reaching for her and dragging her into his arms. "Did the doctor say when she would wake up?"

She shook her head. "They didn't see anything abnormal, so that's good. Her body just needs some time to recover."

Cam nodded. "Do you mind if I...?"

An understanding smile curled her lips. "She'd be happy knowing you're here."

Charlene gave his arm a little squeeze then disappeared from the room. Cam quietly pulled the chair in the corner closer to the bed, then sank into it and propped his elbows on the mattress. His eyes slid over the parts of her body not covered with the sheet.

A bandage had been wrapped around her head, obscuring the stitches he knew she'd received. A few small cuts and bruises marred her skin but, for the most part, she looked healthy. Unfortunately, he knew that most of the damage had been done below the surface.

He watched her quietly for a few moments, absorbing every detail of her beautiful face. Her hands lay still by her sides, and he gently took her hand in his, feeling the coolness of her skin and the faint, reassuring pulse beneath his fingers. "I'm so sorry, sweetheart," he whispered.

A profound sense of guilt gnawed at him. He wished he had been there to protect her, to prevent her being hurt. He wished he could take her pain away, bear it himself. He would never let her down again.

He lifted her hand to his lips and pressed a kiss to her knuckles. "I won't let anything happen to you ever again. I promise."

The rhythmic beeping of the monitors and the hushed whispers of the hospital staff faded into the background as Cam stared down at her.

Leaning closer, he whispered, "I'm here, Kinley. I'm not going anywhere. I'll be right here when you wake up, and every day after that."

When she finally opened her eyes, he wanted to be the first person she saw. "Wake up so I can tell you how much I love you," he whispered. "How much I've always loved you."

CHAPTER
FIFTY

"You can go ahead now." Dare jerked his head up at the sound of Charlene's voice as she entered the waiting room, Garrett by her side.

He stood and flicked a look at Brynlee, who shot him a soft smile. "I'll be quick."

He nodded, and Brynlee disappeared from the room. Dare moved toward Charlene, his heart hammering in his chest. "How are they?"

"Kinley needed a couple dozen stitches, but... I'm hopeful she'll be okay." She offered a tight smile, worry for her daughter pulling at the corners of her eyes. "Right now she's resting. We can only hope for the best."

"And Ainsley?"

His fear must have shown in his face, because she offered a sympathetic smile. "She's a tough one. She'll bounce back."

Dare exhaled. "She's been through so much already. I hate that she was hurt."

"She's lucky you were there." Charlene caught his arm

and searched his eyes. "Honestly, Sheriff. Thank you for taking care of her."

He pulled her into a tight hug. "She means everything to me."

Mrs. Layne squeezed him once more before releasing him, and Garrett held out a hand. Dare shook it and was pulled into a one-armed hug. "Thank you."

Dare shook his head. "I should be the ones thanking you. Ainsley is amazing. I don't know what I'd do without her."

Charlene's eyes misted over even as she graced him with a smile. "I'm glad to hear that."

Dare strode down the hallway toward Ainsley's room, anxious to see her. Soft feminine voices lilted on the air, and his chest constricted as he paused just outside the doorway.

He peeked around the frame, and Ainsley's attentive gaze immediately locked on his. A small smile lifted her lips, reaching straight into his chest and wrapping around his heart. "Dare. You're here."

"Couldn't keep me away."

Brynlee smiled as he stepped into the room and moved closer to Ainsley's side. "I'm going to go check on Kinley. I'm glad you're feeling better."

With one last hug, Brynlee left the room. Dare turned his attention back to Ainsley, who peered up at him with those big blue eyes he adored so much. Unable to put into words how he was feeling, he wrapped one hand around the back of her neck, then kissed her long and slow.

At the feel of her skin beneath his, the tension he'd been carrying around finally began to lift. He broke the kiss and pressed his forehead against hers. "You scared the hell out of me."

Her eyes closed briefly and nodded. "I'm okay. Bryn says that Kinley needed stitches. Have you seen her yet?"

"Not yet, but Cam is with her right now."

"That's good."

Dare picked up her hand, lacing his fingers with hers. "How are you feeling?"

She lifted one shoulder. "My head hurts. The nurse says I have a mild concussion."

He propped a hip on the bed next to her and looped his free arm around her shoulders, pulling her close. "I'm sorry, honey."

"It's not your fault." She leaned her head on his chest, and he kissed the top of her head.

"I knew you would come for me. I..." She let out a ragged breath. "I was so scared when Joel showed up. He was so angry, completely irrational. And when that other man showed up..."

She broke off and swallowed hard. "He killed Joel. I... At first I thought he was there to help, but then..."

A shudder racked her body, and he pulled her into his arms, holding her as tightly as he dared. "I'm so sorry, honey. I can't imagine what you went through."

She bit her lip. "The man. Wade. Is he...?"

Dare shook his head and took her hand, softly stroking the back with his thumb. "He's gone, sweetheart. You don't have to worry about him anymore."

She sucked in a breath. "I... killed him?"

"No," he lied. He'd shot Wade just moments after

Ainsley had slid the knife up into his throat, but the only clear target he'd had was the man's shoulder.

On the way back to the hospital he'd spoken with the medical examiner, who had confirmed what he already knew. But he would never tell her that. Killing someone was a hard thing to live with, and he was glad for her sake that it wouldn't be a burden to her conscience.

Her eyes were still moist with tears and he stroked a finger over her cheek. She tipped her head up and he brushed his nose against hers before catching her lips in a gentle kiss.

"It doesn't seem real." She shuddered, and Dare slid his arms around her, holding her tight.

"I know, sweetheart." He kissed her temple. "I wish I'd gotten there sooner."

He studied her face for a moment. She looked calm and serene on the outside, but he knew she had to be a bundle of nerves inside. "How are you holding up?"

"I'm..." She blew out a harsh breath. "I'll be okay. I'm so glad you showed up when you did. Thank you."

Dare took her hand again and shook his head. "I'm so sorry you had to go through that. I should have been there for you. I—"

He was interrupted by a familiar voice. "Mind if I come in?"

Ainsley glanced up at the doorway and a smile lit her face when she saw Marley standing there, a bright bouquet in hand. "Of course not. Come on in."

Though Dare would much rather have had more time alone with Ainsley, he pushed to his feet and welcomed Marley with a hug. "Hey, sis."

Troy was just a few steps behind, and Dare held out his hand for a quick shake. "Ainsley, this is Marley's husband, Troy."

"Nice to meet you." Ainsley smiled. "The flowers are beautiful. Thank you."

Dare extracted the flowers from Marley, then set them aside as Marley moved to her bedside. "How are you feeling?"

She glanced up at Dare as he laced his fingers through hers, a silent show of support. "I'm feeling better already."

Marley smiled. "I'm glad to hear that."

They visited for a few minutes before making their excuses and heading home with the promise to check back in tomorrow. Once they were gone, Dare turned back to Ainsley. "You should probably get some rest."

"Not yet." She reached for him, and he obliged, sliding onto the bed next to her. "Stay with me for a while?"

"Of course."

He stretched out next to her and pulled her against him so her head rested on his chest. She was finally back where she belonged. He'd never let her go as long as he lived.

CHAPTER
FIFTY-ONE

Ainsley was still exhausted when she woke up the next morning. Sleep had been elusive, broken constantly by the hum of hospital machinery and the routine checks by the nurses. Every sound, every creak in the hallway, kept her on edge, unable to relax.

The nurses had been vigilant, ensuring there were no symptoms of concussion, but the restless night left her feeling drained.

A soft knock from the doorway drew her attention to the nurse who'd taken over during shift change early this morning. "How are you feeling?" she asked.

"Good so far," Ainsley replied, her voice raspy with exhaustion. "I was wondering if I could go see Kinley."

The nurse nodded. "Shouldn't be a problem. Let's take a quick look at you, then we can get you over to see your sister."

After a few moments of checking her blood pressure, pulse, and other vitals, the nurse smiled. "Everything looks good. I'll take you to Kinley's room."

Ainsley followed the nurse down the sterile hallway, her heart pounding as fear and worry mingled in her chest. Peeking her head around the doorway, she saw Kinley lying in the stark white hospital bed, Cam in a chair by her side.

"Take your time," the nurse whispered, "and let me know if you need anything."

Ainsley smiled her thanks, then turned to Cam. "Hey," she said, pitching her voice low so they wouldn't wake Kinley.

"Hey." He turned a tired smile her way. "How are you feeling?"

"A little sore, but otherwise I'm fine."

Climbing to his feet, he pulled her into a hug. "I'm glad to hear that."

Ainsley studied his face, lined with exhaustion, and shock momentarily rooted her feet to the floor. "Have you been here all night?"

"Yeah." He offered a small smile that didn't reach his eyes. "I didn't want her to be alone when she woke up."

Ainsley turned worried eyes on her sister. Kinley was asleep in the hospital bed, a bandage covering the stitches on her forehead. "I thought Mom said she was awake last night."

"Only for a few minutes." He gestured to the empty chair, and Ainsley dropped into the seat as he continued, "She woke up briefly a few hours ago but crashed right back out."

She bit her lip and glanced at Kinley before returning her gaze back to him. "What did the doctor say?"

"Her brain scan showed normal activity, so she's hopeful there won't be any permanent damage. She'll be weak for a bit, but she should be out of here in a couple days."

"Well that's good news at least."

Kinley shifted on the bed and her eyes fluttered open. A small smile crossed her face when she saw the two of them at her bedside. "Hey."

"Hey, yourself." Ainsley stood and leaned over the bed to pull her into a gentle embrace. "How are you feeling?"

Kinley lifted a hand to her head and laughed low in her throat. "Like I got hit by a train."

Cam made a face, and Ainsley quickly spoke up. "Do you remember what happened?"

"Bits and pieces." Kinley's gaze sharpened by increments as she came awake. "I remember talking with that salesman, but it's a little fuzzy after that."

Ainsley grimaced. "That was Joel. He must have been watching the house. I'm so sorry."

Cam cleared his throat. "I should get going. I'll let you two catch up." He squeezed Kinsey's hand. "Call me if you need anything."

"I will." She tossed him a soft smile, and he disappeared a moment later.

"How are you?" Kinley turned back to Ainsley. "I was so worried."

Ainsley forced a smile. "I'm okay. Just a few bumps and bruises."

"I was so scared." Kinley's eyes glazed with tears. "When I woke up, I asked Mom what happened, but she didn't tell me much."

Ainsley took a deep breath and shook her head. "Honestly, I don't even know where to start."

Kinley already knew how Joel had sweet-talked his way into the house. Ainsley started from the very beginning, telling her about Joel's controlling tendencies, how she'd left him after years of abuse. She explained about Tess's murder and how, after Joel had knocked Kinley unconscious, he'd come after Ainsley.

Kinley's eyes widened in shock, a mix of relief and horror crossing her face as Ainsley continued, "Do you know Wade Cottrell?"

When Kinley shook her head, Ainsley explained the bad blood between Dare and the youngest Cottrell brother. "Wade broke in and killed Joel. His plan was to kill me to make Dare suffer. I cut him with the knife, but then... then Dare showed up. It all happened so fast."

Kinley let out a shaky breath, her body relaxing into the bed. "That's... crazy. Why didn't you say anything? We would have helped you."

Ainsley toyed with the sheet covering the bed. "I was ashamed."

Kinley opened her mouth to speak, then snapped it shut again. She gave a little nod. "I'm sorry about everything you went through."

"It doesn't matter now. It's finally over." Ainsley forced a smile.

Kinley shook her head. "I still can't believe he went off the deep end like that. Thank God Cam and Dare showed up."

Ainsley nodded, her thoughts drifting to Dare as they often did. "I owe him so much."

"What are you going to do now?"

Emotion clogged Ainsley's throat. It still didn't feel

real. She swore she could still feel his eyes on her, like if she glanced over her shoulder she would find him there, watching her.

But Joel was gone. She'd watched him die, watched the life drain from his eyes as the blood pooled around him. She'd spent so long fearing him, loathing him, that his death brought an unexpected wave of emotions.

She was free to do anything she wanted. She should feel ecstatic. Instead, a maelstrom of emotion swirled within her. Disbelief. Relief. Guilt.

She felt as if she was standing on the edge of a precipice, completely unsure how to proceed. And Dare— would he still want to be with her?

She blew out a breath. "I'm honestly not sure. I—"

"There you are."

Ainsley glanced up to see Dare standing in the doorway, relief flooding his features as he moved toward her. "I was worried when I didn't find you in your room."

"I'm sorry. I wanted to see Kinley," Ainsley replied, standing up to greet him. "I didn't mean to worry you."

Dare shook his head and wrapped an arm around her waist. "I'm just glad you're here."

He turned toward Kinley. "How are you feeling?"

"I'm okay, thanks for asking." She tossed him a small smile. "I'm glad you guys showed up when you did."

"Me, too." Dare's arm tightened around Ainsley's waist, and she leaned into him.

Familiar voices drifted their direction, and a moment later, Mr. and Mrs. Layne entered the room. They exchanged small talk for a while until Kinley began to tire again.

The nurse came by to check on her once more and smiled when she saw Ainsley. "The doctor should be making her rounds in just a bit. She'd like to take one more look at you, then you should be good to go."

"Great." Ainsley smiled, but it quickly fell away, her relief overshadowed by nervousness as Dare guided her out of Kinley's room and into her own.

Inside, Dare turned her to face him. He studied her for a moment before speaking. "How are you?"

She lifted one shoulder. "I'm okay."

"The truth."

He gave her a little squeeze, and she sighed. "It's just been a long couple of days."

"I know." He eased her closer and kissed her temple. "We'll be home soon enough, then you can take all the time you need."

That sounded damn good to her.

CHAPTER
FIFTY-TWO

Dare guided Ainsley carefully up the porch steps, his arm curled around her waist for support. The hospital discharge had gone smoothly, but he couldn't shake the anxiety that lingered.

"Finally home," he said quietly as he opened the door and led her inside.

Sarge was immediately there, brushing against Ainsley's legs, sniffing every inch of her he could reach, whining happily. Dare grinned. "Someone's been eager to see you."

Ainsley leaned down and petted the dog, scratching behind his ears until he gave a happy sigh, then loped off. Dare took her hand and guided her to the couch, then helped her settle down. He sat next to her, his gaze sweeping over her from head to toe. She hadn't said much on the ride here, so he was at a loss as to how to proceed.

He wanted to ask her how she was feeling, but it was a stupid question. She'd been through so much over the past couple of months; her emotions were probably still all over the place.

The last couple of days had been a whirlwind of activity. Ballistics had confirmed that the gun Wade Cottrell used to kill Joel Parsons had also fired the bullet found after the drive-by shooting at the plaza. Accordingly, the partial footprint found in Ainsley's flower bed matched the shoes Wade was wearing at the time of his death.

The case had wrapped up pretty quickly after that, and Dare felt like a weight had been lifted off his chest. There were just a few last details to iron out—and all of them revolved around the woman sitting next to him.

Ainsley let out a deep breath and leaned back, her body visibly relaxing into the thick cushions. "It feels good to be here," she admitted.

He settled in next to her then took her hand, their fingers intertwining naturally. For several moments they just sat there, the thick silence pressing in on them. Finally he could stand it no longer.

He cleared his throat, gaze pinned to the wall across from them. "I know that with Joel gone, you have a lot of freedom now. You can do whatever you want, go wherever you want."

Silence met his statement, and he turned to look at Ainsley who had gone pale. "Ains?"

She glanced up at him and pasted an overly bright smile on her lips. "That's true. You don't have to keep watch over me anymore," she said, a false lightness tinging her voice. "Now you can rent the suite to someone who actually needs it."

Dare shook his head. "I never did it for the money, Ainsley. I wanted you here. I still do."

She shifted uncomfortably, avoiding his gaze. Dare could sense the turmoil plaguing her and wisely kept quiet, allowing her time and space to work through her jumbled thoughts. The last thing he wanted was for her to feel like he was trying to make decisions for her.

After a few moments, she mustered the courage to look up at him. "You want me here?"

He tipped his head her way. "Of course."

"You mean, like... You want me to move in?" Her voice wavered with uncertainty even as she shook her head. "You don't have to offer if it's not what you really want."

"What if it's exactly what I want?" he countered, leaning closer. "Is it what you want?"

Ainsley drew in a deep breath, teeth cutting into her bottom lip. Her gaze flicked away before meeting his again. "Yes," she said on a soft exhale, her voice barely audible.

"Good," he said. "Then this is definitely not me asking you to stay with me."

"That would be crazy, wouldn't it?" Ainsley said, a hesitant smile tugging at her lips.

"Maybe." He grinned back at her. "But it would make the next step easier."

Her head tipped to the side in question. "And what's that?"

"Rings. Picket fence. Couple rug rats." A smile tugged at the corners of his lips.

Her eyes widened, and her mouth dropped open a fraction in shock. "You want... to get married?"

"Eventually. When you're ready." He lightly ran a

finger over her cheekbone. "Do you think that's something you want?"

Ainsley nodded mutely, still staring at him like she couldn't quite comprehend the events of the past couple of minutes.

He nodded decisively. "Okay."

She stared at him for nearly a minute. Her mouth opened and closed several times, but nothing came out. Finally, she swallowed hard. "Are you..." Her cheeks flared bright red. "I mean..."

He bit back a smile as her skin grew pinker and she pressed one hand to her cheek, clearly flustered. Deciding to take pity on her, he curved a hand around the back of her neck and pulled her close. "I just want you Ainsley. We can take things as slow as you like, but... I want you to choose me. Not because it's safe or because you feel obligated—but because you want to."

She met his gaze and swallowed hard. "There's nowhere I'd rather be."

"Me either." He shifted to his back, pulling her with him until she was draped over him, her mouth moving slowly over his in long, lingering kisses.

A few moments later, she lifted away from him and met his gaze. "Maybe you should ask."

Dare grinned. "Maybe I will."

CHAPTER
FIFTY-THREE

Lindsey Gill's eyes fluttered open, and she immediately winced against the glaring light overhead. She closed her eyes again and drew in a deep breath as she willed herself to shake off the vestiges of drowsiness.

She felt exhausted, like she could go back to sleep for the rest of the week and it still wouldn't be enough. Her head pounded and her mouth felt as dry as sandpaper. She lay on her side, the threadbare sheet scratching against her cheek as she shifted slightly. She stretched her legs out, trying to alleviate the soreness in her body.

A sharp pins-and-needles sensation exploded over her nerve endings, and she bit back a cry. Her muscles were tight and cramped, the same tingly sensation that she felt when her foot fell asleep. She tried to sit up but was brought to an abrupt halt when her hands refused to move. Her eyes popped open and her heart rate kicked up as she yanked at her arms again, to no avail.

"What the hell?"

It took her hazy mind a moment to realize her hands

were bound behind her back. She rolled her shoulders, struggling frantically against the bonds. The rope only tightened, biting into her wrists, hard and unforgiving.

Oh, God.

She struggled helplessly, rolling first to her stomach before wiggling her knees underneath her. She was panting heavily by the time she managed to lever to a sitting position. For a long moment she sat there, blinking owlishly at her surroundings.

Where the hell was she?

She knelt on a filthy mattress, springs poking through the thin, sweat-stained fabric, a sheet haphazardly tossed over the surface. The air was thick with damp and decay, assaulting her senses with its rank stench. A single bulb dangled from the ceiling overhead, and she squinted past it.

Concrete block walls surrounded her, their surfaces cold and unyielding. The floor was gritty under her, covered with years of dust and debris. Panic began to rise in her chest, but she forced it down. If there was even a slim possibility that she might escape, she needed to get her hands in front of her. She twisted her wrists, a soft cry escaping as the rough rope abraded her skin.

Damn, that hurt!

She bit down on her lip to stifle her cry of pain, and the tangy taste of blood filled her mouth. The ropes cut deeply into her flesh, and she could feel the slick liquid coating her skin as blood and fluid welled from the wounds, easing the slide of the ropes as she worked them loose. Tears burned her eyes and she blinked them away. She would get free— she had to.

She dipped one shoulder and yanked on the ties as hard as she could, trying to pull them as far as they would go. Her muscles ached as they stretched farther than they were designed to, all the while trying to maneuver them low enough to clear her hips. Her heart lurched as the material finally gave enough to the point that she could wiggle them under her bottom.

Fierce satisfaction flowed through her as, inch by inch, she got closer to being free. She contorted her body, angling her knees through the odd-shaped space created by her arms and torso. She held her hands up in front of her, relief flooding through her.

Unfortunately, the feeling was short-lived as she assessed her situation. Her wrists were bloody and raw, fibers of the rope clinging to the wounds. She grimaced. Infection would set in soon if she didn't get them cleaned and get the hell out of here.

Shielding her eyes against the light overhead, she glanced around. Her heart fell. Aside from a small bucket in the corner—she could guess what that was for—the basement appeared to be lacking anything useful that she could use as a weapon or as a tool. She was certain that was by design. She glanced down at the mattress. Maybe if—

A soft whimper jerked her attention to the opposite side of the basement. "Hello?"

For a moment there was only silence. Goosebumps sprouted over Lindsey's skin. "Is someone there?"

A moment later, a thready voice called back, "I... I'm here."

Lindsey practically vaulted off the mattress, stumbling as she forced her uncooperative muscles to move. No longer in the circle of bright light, she maneuvered through the darkened space, feeling her way along the rough walls.

She rounded a corner, and the dim glow of light up ahead illuminated her path. Watching her footing, she rounded a large storage shelf stocked with canned food. The sight in front of her stopped her dead in her tracks.

In the corner of the basement, curtains hung from the ceiling to mark off the makeshift room. Within, a mattress, much like the one Lindsey had woken up on, took up most of the small space. A woman lay in the middle of the bed, her stomach swollen and round.

Bile rose up Lindsey's throat, threatening to choke her, and she swallowed it down. She pasted a soft smile on her trembling lips and crawled over to the woman, her knees scraping against the cold, harsh floor. "Hey. I'm Lindsey. What's your name?"

The woman swallowed hard, and took a deep breath. Her lips were cracked and dry, and perspiration and filthy marred her skin. "H-Hilary."

Lindsey lightly rested her hand on the woman's arm. "Are you okay?"

Hilary nodded, and Lindsey's gaze strayed to the filthy nightgown stretched over the woman's taut, round belly. "And the baby?"

"G-good, I think," she responded.

Lindsey nodded slowly. "How far along are you?"

Hilary shook her head. "I... I'm not sure."

Lindsey forced a smile despite the mixture of panic and fear that raced through her. How long had the woman been here? "I'm going to help you," she whispered. "Do you know who did this?"

The woman shook her head. "I never saw him before..." She licked her lips as she trailed off.

Lindsey nodded. "It's okay. Just rest."

Her stomach flipped as she took in the thick leather cuff encircling the woman's neck, like a collar. Her gaze followed it to a cable suspended from the ceiling. The cable attached to her collar was looped through a second cable that stretched overhead, allowing the woman to move around the space without straying too far.

She grasped the cable attached to the woman's collar and inspected it. The metal cable was coated with a thick plastic and had been looped through a link on the collar. Standing, she ran her fingers upward as high as she could reach. She gave a gentle tug to the cable, making the secondary cable overhead dance and sway. She followed one end to the wooden beam overhead, and her heart sank when she saw the heavy duty bolt protruding from the wood. The fixture had been reinforced with a wide piece of steel, ensuring it wouldn't come loose.

Lindsey dropped back to her knees beside Hilary. "The cables are bolted in. I can't get you free."

Tears glistened in the woman's eyes, and Lindsey grasped her hand, giving her a gentle squeeze. "I'm going to go get help. I promise I'll come back for you."

The woman nodded, her eyes dull and hopeless. "I promise," Lindsey reiterated. "I won't let anything happen to you."

Hilary stared at her for a long moment before offering a wan smile. "Thank you."

With one last squeeze, Lindsey released Hilary and pushed to her feet. High to her right, a small, grimy window let in a sliver of weak light. She counted the cinder blocks from the floor to the bottom of the window, mentally calculating the height. It was a good foot above her head and very likely too narrow to offer any hope of escape.

She stared wistfully at it for a moment before shaking her head. The window wasn't going to be an option. Even using the bucket, she wouldn't be able to get up high enough to crawl through the opening.

She cautiously skirted the storage unit and moved toward a flight of wooden stairs tucked away next to the furnace. She placed one foot on the bottom step, the old wood creaking under her weight. The sound echoed ominously in the confined space as she shifted her weight and continued to climb, making her way toward the wooden door at the top.

Her heart pounded as she reached the door, fearing it might be locked. To her relief, the handle turned with a soft click. She pushed it open slowly and peered through the crack. The house beyond was quiet—eerily so. She crept up the last few stairs, muscles tensed, heart pounding against her ribcage.

Her breath came in shallow gasps, adrenaline propelling her forward as she inched the door open. Bright moonlight streamed through a window across from her, and the sight filled her with elation. She tossed one more quick glance around the room, but everything was quiet. She was alone.

Giddiness bubbled up, and she strode forward, toward

freedom. Just as she reached the window, a strong hand grabbed her from behind, yanking her back with brutal force.

"Where do you think you're going?"

Don't miss the next book in the Secrets of Brookhaven Series! When a boater discovers the skeletal remains of a young woman, Campbell McCoy unveils a sinister ploy that spans decades, weaving past and present in a tangled web of lies, deceit, and betrayal...

Keep reading for a sneak peek of Out of Breath!

OUT OF BREATH

CHAPTER ONE

The sun glistened off the calm surface of the lake, casting a shimmering path that stretched out before the sleek speedboat. Jared revved the engine, causing the boat to leap forward. Gabby clutched the side, her knuckles white as they sped across the water, much too close to the shore for her comfort.

"Jared, slow down!" Gabby shouted, her voice nearly drowned out by the roar of the motor.

Jared just laughed, the wind whipping through his hair. "Relax, Gabs! We're fine!"

But Gabby wasn't convinced. "Seriously, Jared, stop it!"

Jared grinned and whipped the wheel hard. Gabby screamed as waves slapped against the side of the boat, making it lurch frantically from side to side. Gabby grabbed the edge of the seat, clinging to the fabric with all her might. "Jared! You better stop before you get caught!"

They were already deep into the no-wake zone, and the waves crashed against the shore with violent force, frothy and white.

Jared rolled his eyes. "We're not going to get caught. There's no one out here."

"The people who live here will be pissed," she said, gesturing toward the homes tucked within the canopy of trees along the shoreline. "They're going to call the cops on you."

"Fine." He turned the wheel again and pushed the throttle, sending them back out toward the middle of the lake.

The boat shot forward, and a scream caught in her throat as Gabby was jolted off the seat. A sickening screech filled the air as the bottom scraped against something below the surface.

"Shit!" Jared eased off the throttle, and the boat slowed to a stop.

"I told you," Gabby shot back. "There's all kinds of stuff this close to shore. You better hope you didn't ruin your dad's boat. He'll be pissed."

Gabby peered over the side of the boat, straining to see into the depths. A dozen feet away, a patch of blue bobbed in the water.

She pointed at the object. "What's that?"

Jared squinted, then shrugged. "Probably just some trash. Grab it before it gets caught in the propeller."

Gabby dug out an oar then leaned over the side, using the paddle to slap at the water, dragging the object closer. It drifted toward her, trapped air lifting it to the surface. From here she could make out what appeared to be fabric, once bright blue but now faded with age and stained from the lake.

Gabby angled the oar downward, trying to pin the fabric and drag it toward her. It was heavier than she expected, and she struggled to pull it in. "It's stuck on something," she muttered, giving it a harder tug. "You probably hit a log or something down there."

She tossed a look over her shoulder at Jared, who shrugged sheepishly. "My bad."

Rolling her eyes, Gabby turned her attention back to the task at hand. *Nice of him to help*, she thought to herself as she dragged the fabric closer, aided by the gentle rolling of the water.

"Almost got it…"

She bit her lip and strained her muscles, reaching just a bit farther. She dragged the oar over the rippling water, the fabric trailing in its wake. The surge of satisfaction that shot through her quickly turned to dread as the fabric rolled under the pressure of the oar and something began to take shape.

"What the…?" Her brows drew together as the object dipped below the surface, then reappeared.

The fabric slipped free of the oar and as it did, something dark began to rise from the depths. Terror slid through her as Gabby found herself staring into the empty sockets of a human skull, its mouth agape in a silent scream.

. . .

Don't miss Out of Breath, available now!

ALSO BY MORGAN JAMES

Thrillers and Mysteries

SECRETS OF BROOKHAVEN

Out of Sight

Out of Breath

Out of Time

———

Romantic Suspense

QUENTIN SECURITY SERIES

Twisted Devil – Jason and Chloe

The Devil You Know – Blake and Victoria

Devil in the Details – Xander and Lydia

Devil in Disguise – Gavin and Kate

Heart of a Devil – Vince and Jana

Tempting the Devil – Clay and Abby

Devilish Intent – Con and Grace

Quentin Security Box Set One (Books 1-3)

Quentin Security Box Set Two (Books 4-6)

*Each book is a standalone within the series

RESCUE & REDEMPTION SERIES

FRIENDLY FIRE – GRAYSON AND CLAIRE

CRUEL VENDETTA – DREW AND EMERY

SILENT TREATMENT – FINN AND HARPER

RECKLESS PURSUIT – AIDEN AND IZZY

DANGEROUS DESIRES – VAUGHN AND SIENNA

COLD JUSTICE – NICK AND EDEN

RESCUE & REDEMPTION BOX SET ONE (BOOKS 1-3)

RETRIBUTION SERIES

UNREQUITED LOVE – JACK AND MIA, BOOK ONE

UNDENIABLE LOVE – JACK AND MIA, BOOK TWO

UNBREAKABLE LOVE – JACK AND MIA, BOOK THREE

PRETTY LITTLE LIES – ERIC AND JULES, BOOK ONE

BEAUTIFUL DECEPTION – ERIC AND JULES, BOOK TWO

HIDDEN TRUTH – JOHN AND JOSI

SINFUL ILLUSIONS – FOX AND EVA, BOOK ONE

SINFUL SACRAMENT – FOX AND EVA, BOOK TWO

RETRIBUTION SERIES BOX SET 1

RETRIBUTION SERIES BOX SET 2

RETRIBUTION SERIES BOX SET 3

THE COMPLETE RETRIBUTION SERIES

ABOUT THE AUTHOR

Morgan James is a USA Today bestselling author of thrillers and romantic suspense novels. She spent most of her childhood with her nose buried in a book, though she now loves to weave stories of her own. When she's not writing, Morgan can be typically be found experimenting in the kitchen (making a mess more often than not). She currently resides in Ohio and is living happily ever after with her husband and their two kids.

Keep up with Morgan and stay up to date on sales, giveaways, and new releases at AuthorMorganJames.com

Shop her books at MorganJamesBookShop.com